MORGAN'S M
LOVE & DANGER

"What are you running from?" Sabra whispered.

Breathing hard, Craig turned away from her. "That's none of your business."

"Oh, yes, it is. If we're going on this mission together, I have every right to know."

Craig spun around, eyes blazing. "It has nothing to do with this mission."

Sabra stood before him like an avenging angel.

And the look in her eyes—lustrous with the need to understand him—was nearly his undoing. Her compassion was genuine. She was concerned about him. About his ghosts.

And something deep inside him moved, cried out.

But bitterness coated his throat and mouth. And Craig squelched the sudden desire to tell this strong, beautiful woman exactly what hideous inner demons he was running from.

"Believe me," he rasped. "You don't want to know...."

Dear Reader,

Book #1000?! In February, 1982, when Silhouette Special Edition was first published, that seemed a far distant goal. And now, almost fourteen years later, here we are!

We're opening CELEBRATION 1000 with a terrific book from the beloved Diana Palmer—*Maggie's Dad*. Diana was one of the first authors to contribute to Special Edition, and now she's returned with this tender tale of love reborn.

Lindsay McKenna continues her action-packed new series, MORGAN'S MERCENARIES: LOVE AND DANGER. The party goes on with *Logan's Bride* by Christine Flynn— the first HOLIDAY ELOPEMENTS, three tales of love and weddings over the holiday season. And join the festivities with wonderful stories by Jennifer Mikels, Celeste Hamilton and Brittany Young.

We have so many people to thank for helping us to reach this milestone. Silhouette Special Edition would not be what it is today without our marvelous writers. I want to take a moment, though, to mention one author—Sondra Stanford. She gave us Book #7, *Silver Mist*, and many other wonderful stories. We lost her in October 1991 after a valiant struggle against cancer. We miss her; she brought a great deal of happiness to all who knew her.

And our very special thanks to our readers. Your imaginations and brave hearts allow books to take flight— and all of us can never thank you enough for that!

The celebration continues in December and January—with books by Nora Roberts, Debbie Macomber, Sherryl Woods and many more of your favorite writers! Happy Book 1000—to each and every romantic!

Sincerely,

Tara Gavin, Senior Editor

Please address questions and book requests to:
Silhouette Reader Service
U.S.: 3010 Walden Ave., P.O. Box 1325, Buffalo, NY 14269
Canadian: P.O. Box 609, Fort Erie, Ont. L2A 5X3

LINDSAY McKENNA

MORGAN'S SON

Silhouette®

SPECIAL EDITION®

Published by Silhouette Books
America's Publisher of Contemporary Romance

To my brother Brent Gent and his family: Jeanne Gent, Erin Gent
and Lauren Gent; my brother Gary Gent and his family: Debbie Gent,
Kimberly Gent and Brian Gent; to my sister Nancy Gray, and her son
Corbette Gray; and to the two Scorpios in my life: David Nauman,
my husband of twenty-two years, and my mother, Ruth M. Gent,
seventy-eight years young and going strong! What fun a Gemini has
keeping you two on your collective toes! Ain't life great? And to my
grandmother, Inez Cramer, ninety-eight years old and young at heart!

SILHOUETTE BOOKS

ISBN 0-373-09992-4

MORGAN'S SON

Books by Lindsay McKenna

LINDSAY McKENNA

spent three years serving her country as a meteorologist in the U.S. Navy, so much of her knowledge comes from direct experience. In addition, she spends a great deal of time researching each book, whether it be at the Pentagon or at military bases, extensively interviewing key personnel.

Lindsay is also a pilot. She and her husband of twenty-two years, both avid "rock hounds" and hikers, live in Arizona.

Dear Reader,

In 1983, when I first published *Captive of Fate* with Silhouette Special Edition, I had no idea I'd continue to write a total of thirty-three novels for Silhouette Books. Now, Special Edition has hit 1000 great romance novels, and I'm thrilled to be part of a wonderful, continuing tradition.

I have always loved the freedom to write what inspires me. At Silhouette, my interest in the military has been nurtured and supported enthusiastically. With Silhouette's support, I helped to create the subgenre of military romance novels. It has met with resounding success—thanks to you!

That is why MORGAN'S MERCENARIES: LOVE AND DANGER is an achievement not only for Silhouette Special Edition, but for readers who have loved the Trayhern family since LOVE AND GLORY. And everyone, judging from the thousands of letters I've received over the years, fell in love with Morgan Trayhern and Laura Bennett.

Well, after all those years of pleading to see what happened to Morgan, Laura and their family, I have created a four-book series that answers all your questions! This series came about because of *you,* and I hope it gives you as much pleasure reading it as it gave me to write it. So don't think that your heartfelt thoughts and feelings about an author's characters don't count with her and her editors—this is living proof that it does!

I hope you enjoy MORGAN'S MERCENARIES: LOVE AND DANGER.

Warmly,

Lindsay McKenna

Chapter One

"Jake, who do we have to rescue my son?" Laura looked at him steadily, struggling to keep her voice even and low despite her excitement at Jason's being located. To Jake's right and left at the War Room's familiar the oval table sat Wolf Harding and Sean Killian, their faces kind but impassive. Jake's brow furrowed.

"Well," he rumbled hesitantly, flipping through some reports before him, "we've got one member available from each of two different teams that have just come out of the field."

"It isn't a good idea," Wolf said, looking across the table at Laura. "Putting members from two different teams together to create a new, untried team."

Laura felt her throat closing up with tears at Wolf's pronouncement. Since her own release from the hellish prison on Garcia's Caribbean estate, she seemed to burst into tears easily and often unexpectedly. Her therapist, Pallas Downey, assured her that her response was normal for anyone who had been drugged, raped and had her family kidnapped. Holding tightly to a delicate, embroidered hand-kerchief beneath the table, she tried to focus calmly on Wolf's concerns. "Why not?" she asked quietly.

With an apologetic shrug, Wolf said, "Teams are teams, Laura. Team members have adjusted to each other's quirks and foibles, so to speak."

"Team members often know intuitively what their other half is going to do," Jake offered. "If you throw together two people who don't know each other, it can be detrimen-tal to a mission—especially one as complicated as this res-cue attempt for Jason."

As tears clawed their way up her throat, Laura turned to Killian, whose face remained unreadable, as always. His green eyes glittered as she looked into them. "What do you say, Killian?" In spite of his taciturn nature, Laura knew Sean's depth of experience was something they could all count on.

"I say it depends on the individuals concerned."

"Well," Jake said slowly, "that's true."

"Who are they?" Laura asked, trying to blot her eyes as inconspicuously as possible.

"We're lucky," Jake said. "The woman is Sabra Jacobs. She's been with Perseus since Morgan started it. She's got time in grade, she knows the system and she takes only high-risk assignments."

"Sabra?" Laura whispered the name, hope springing to life in her breast. "Why, Jason knows her! Between assign-ments, Sabra lives here, near us. She's baby-sat for us many times. Jason loves her. He calls her 'Auntie S' because he can't quite pronounce her name yet."

Jake held up his hand. "I know it sounds like good news, Laura. But unfortunately, Sabra's partner, Terry Hayes, suffered a heart attack overseas. We can't ask him to climb out of his hospital bed and join us."

"Who's the person on the second team?" Laura de-manded, hope spiraling crazily through her despite Jake's words of caution. Sabra Jacobs was one of the most de-pendable, solid women she'd ever met. If there was anyone who could rescue Jason, it was Sabra.

Jake grimaced. "A merc by the name of Craig Talbot. He's only been with Perseus six months. He's an ex-marine helicopter pilot who came to us after Desert Storm."

"That sounds like a wonderful combination!"

"Laura, I wish I could be as enthused as you are," Jake warned, "but Talbot has been involved only in low- and medium-risk assignments."

"So what?"

"So, he doesn't want any high-risk assignments."

Laura sat there assimilating Jake's words. "But why?" she managed to ask after a moment.

"I don't know." Jake glanced at Wolf. "All we know is that shortly after Desert Storm, Talbot, who was a captain, resigned his commission from the Marine Corps to knock at Perseus's door."

"Do you have Mr. Talbot's personnel file?"

"Yes."

"I want to see it."

"Laura, the first thing we have to do is find out if these players are willing to take this assignment. Sabra no doubt will jump at the chance, because she has a personal stake. She's close to you and your children."

"Is she here?"

"Sabra should be here in about half an hour," Wolf said, looking at his watch.

"And Craig Talbot?"

"He's still in the air," Killian muttered. "We've sent someone to the airport to pick him up. We should be able to talk to him in about an hour and a half, if traffic cooperates."

Laura looked at her watch. It was shortly after noon and she should be hungry, but even the thought of eating these days made her nauseous. Her therapist assured her that, too, was a normal reaction after what she'd experienced. Still, she had to keep up her strength. She would have to force herself to eat.

"I want to be here when you interview them, Jake."

"Of course," he said, picking up his nearly cold cup of coffee and taking a swallow.

"Are they well rested?"

"Sabra is, but Talbot's just coming off an assignment that should have been labeled high risk."

"What happened to his partner?"

"Died in an auto accident. Talbot wasn't with her. He was tailing one of two suspects in Vienna, Austria. Jennifer Langford, his partner, was tailing the other one."

Laura felt her heart squeeze. "Oh, how awful...."

Jake slowly rose. "Laura, I really don't think you should be here, under the circumstances. You're still too raw from your own ordeal, and sitting in on team debriefings won't do you any good. You're white as a sheet."

Shamed, Laura touched her cheek, then stood. "I know you're right, Jake, but I can't help myself. My son, my husband... It's so hard to stay home, to go through the motions of my day...."

Jake came around the table and placed his arm gently across Laura's drooping shoulders. "I know how hard this is on you," he rasped. "We're doing everything humanly possible to locate Morgan."

Laura looked up into his dark, worried features. "I don't know what we'd have done without the three of you," she said solemnly. "You've held Perseus together. I—I'm so grateful." Then the hot tears spilled from her eyes and down her cheeks. Managing an embarrassed, apologetic laugh, she eased away from Jake and wiped at her eyes. Then she took a deep breath and again leveled her gaze on Jake's.

"Please let me stay for the interviews and assignments, Jake. Then, I promise to get out of your hair and leave you to the unpleasant realities. Okay?"

"That's fine, Laura," Jake said gently, his harsh features softening. "Come on, let's all go get something to eat. When we get back, Sabra should be here and, with any luck, Talbot about an hour after that."

"I'm just so glad Sabra is coming," Laura whispered. "So glad."

"She's one of the best," Jake agreed, guiding her toward the heavy oak door.

"And Jason knows her," Laura said, walking with him. "I feel that's so important."

"Yes," he agreed, "it's a lucky break for us."

Laura waited as Jake opened the door. Then, clenching the now-damp handkerchief in her left hand, she walked out into the spacious reception area, where Marie was working at her computer. Laura smiled warmly at Morgan's assistant, who had so ably taken on a much-larger area of responsibility in the wake of the kidnappings. Her mind rushed back to the fact that Killian and the CIA had stumbled on information about Jason's whereabouts. That was the best news yet, she reminded herself as she worked to shore up her broken, scattered emotions—an improvement on the numbness that stalked her lately, between brief periods of euphoria and gut-wrenching fear.

But if anyone should be on this assignment, it was Sabra. Laura was grateful for the woman, for her loyalty not only to Perseus but to the Trayhern family. A trickle of real hope entered her heart. Yes, with Sabra heading up the team, Laura just might actually get her son back—safe and sound.

Sabra entered the Perseus office at exactly 1300, the time she'd promised Jake she'd show up. Marie looked up from her desk and smiled.

"Hi, Sabra."

"Hello. Where is everyone?"

"They went to lunch." Marie looked at her watch. "But they should be back soon." Standing, she said, "May I get you some tea while you wait for them in the War Room?"

"I'd love a cup, thanks."

"Earl Gray, right?"

"You never forget anything, do you?" Sabra smiled and shook her head. She liked Marie immensely. The gray-haired woman was the soul of efficiency.

"Well," Marie said with a worried chuckle as she opened the War Room door for Sabra, "I try not to, but with the way things are now, I'm afraid I sometimes am forgetful."

Sabra lost her partial smile. "What do you mean?"

"It's not for me to say, Sabra. Jake Randolph will want to fill you in himself," the woman replied in a low voice, motioning Sabra to take a seat at the oval table. "Jake is heading up Perseus for now, with Laura's blessing. Wolf Harding and Sean Killian are assisting him."

Raising her eyebrows, Sabra nodded thoughtfully, wondering where Morgan was.

"Do you know any of them?" Marie asked.

"I know Killian, but I've only heard of Harding and Randolph through the grapevine, so to speak." Sabra took a seat, propping her elbows on the table's highly polished surface.

"I'll get your tea," Marie offered. "Have you eaten?"

"Yes, tea will be fine. Thanks." She watched Marie shut the door. The War Room felt comfortable to her after all these years. It was where Morgan had given her and Terry every one of their assignments. The expanse of oak, shining from the obvious care given it, stretched before her. Ten chairs surrounded the table, but the room seemed ominously quiet. Sabra knew the entire room had been shielded with a thin, space-age metal to prevent eavesdropping by any spying country. Reports could be made and assignments given with full confidence here.

Absently, she ran her fingers across the table's smooth surface. Wood had such a warm feel, almost like skin. But then, Sabra wryly reminded herself, she was always close to nature. Was it her Irish heritage through her mother, born to a fishing family on the seacoast? she wondered idly, as she had so often before. Or the French grape-and-wine-country ancestry of her Israeli father, now a general in the Mossad? Both her parents had soil in their souls, and she was glad of it. Sabra frequently used her thirty days of rest between assignments to visit either her mother's parents, who still lived in a thatched hut by the wild Irish Sea, or her own parents, in Jerusalem. In Ireland, she reveled in the endless green carpet of grass. In Israel, she felt the ancient gnarled strength of olive trees that surrounded her parent's desert home.

Sabra placed her small leather purse on the table. Greenery and desert. What a dichotomy. But then, she supposed, so was she. How did one reconcile the richness of Ireland with the arid desert of Israel? A half smile curved her lips, and she absently smoothed the cinnamon-colored silk skirt that draped around her nearly to her ankles. She had inherited her mother's rich black hair shot through with red highlights and her father's large gray eyes, patrician nose and square face. Her lips and tall, fluid build were her mother's again.

At thirty-two, Sabra often felt as if she were a citizen of two entirely different worlds. Part of her was thoroughly Irish, and that wild nature had led her to join the Mossad after getting a degree in biology, despite her mother's protests against the dangerous work. Somehow Sabra seemed to thrive on the terror that became a very real companion in her undercover spy work. Her father had wanted a son, and she had to admit that that knowledge, too, had affected her decision. She'd wanted to prove to her father that even though she was a woman, she could compete and succeed in his world.

A soft sigh escaped Sabra, and she folded her hands in her lap. Her father had tried to curtail her Mossad activities. Her skill had garnered her many high-risk assignments. But with her father a general, influential in case responsibility, Sabra had found herself getting fewer and fewer of those toughest jobs. Luckily for her, she had found Perseus and slipped from beneath her father's huge shadow. At Perseus, she was free to use all of her considerable talents and skills—at her own discretion.

Sabra's thoughts ranged back to her dear friend and partner, Terry. Quite suddenly and without warning, he'd suffered a heart attack, that had prevented them from completing their recent assignment. Terry was only forty-five, and no one had been more shocked by his attack than she. They'd been a team for five years, and they shared the kind of good chemistry that was absolutely essential in their kind of work.

Who would she be teamed with now? Sabra wondered. And what was this unexpectedly urgent assignment? She was glad that Perseus wasn't giving her the usual month of leave between assignments. She felt unfulfilled by the aborted mission with Terry. She wasn't the kind of person not to complete something she started.

The War Room door opened. "Here you are," Marie said pleasantly, placing in front of her a small tray holding a fine china cup and teapot, a spoon and napkin. Cream and sugar waited in gleaming silver receptacles.

"Thank you, Marie." Sabra smiled. "I see you've put my favorite cookies on there, too, just in case..."

"Just in case you were a mite hungry," Marie agreed, smiling back at her.

A small plate of Oreos sat next to the steaming tea on the silver tray. Touched by her thoughtfulness, Sabra picked one up and bit into it. "I hope someday, when I get married, I'll have a husband who will spoil me like this."

Tittering, Marie straightened. "When my husband was alive, he made it his business to know my likes and dislikes. He spoiled me, but I spoiled him, too."

"Marriage is a two-way street," Sabra agreed, enjoying the taste of the chocolate cookie and creamy frosting. "I don't think there are many men who would want me as a wife, though."

"Nonsense, Sabra. You're a beautiful, poised young woman, with everything to offer a man. You have brains and strength."

"Not many men are looking for that combination," Sabra said dryly, pouring tea into the waiting cup. "They may see the beauty, but that's all."

"Hmm, well, yes, there are those types out there. I won't disagree with you. But my late husband, Alfred, always said that somewhere on this globe, he knew the perfect mate was waiting for him. When he saw me, he knew it was me."

"He knew?"

Marie smiled fondly in remembrance. "I was eighteen. He was twenty-five and in the diplomatic corps here in Washington. I worked as an assistant to a senator. Alfred came in to the senator's office one day, angry and upset. He said he saw me sitting at my desk and forgot everything—even his anger."

Sighing, Sabra said, "I wish love were that easy. That uncomplicated."

"I know it is." Marie frowned. "Today's generation has grown up making it far more complicated than it needs to be, you know. Love is about being the best of friends. Of course, there's sexual chemistry, that's a given. Love means being a team and working off each other's strengths. I think if the children of today understood that, there wouldn't be so many divorces. Alfred and I were married thirty-two years before he died of a stroke. It was a wonderful marriage."

"Listening to you makes me want to get married."

Marie laughed and walked to the door. "Now you're teasing me. You're one of this generation, you know. Always reading so much into things—perhaps being too realistic for something as magical as love."

"I don't have to worry about it," Sabra said with a grin. "I don't exactly have any men looking at me as marriage material."

Shaking her finger, Marie said lightly, "Mark my words, when the right man walks into your life, you're going to know it."

Sadness filtered into Sabra's heart. Marie knew a great deal about her because of her position in Perseus. But she didn't know everything. "I think the man I could have loved has come and gone, Marie. I realized too late, I guess."

"That's because you let your head get in the way. I've always said this generation works too much from the head and not enough from positive emotions."

"Maybe that's so," Sabra agreed, her voice lowering with feeling.

"You enjoy your tea, dear. Jake and the rest should be back any moment."

The door shut quietly, and Sabra held the cup of tea in both hands, its warmth like a balm to the old anguish that lingered in her heart. *Joshua.* The name still brought her

pain. She'd tried to forget about him. About her love for
him—too little, too late. Was Marie right? Did her generation see too much of the harsh reality of life and let it prevent them from getting involved? She certainly fit that
particular bill of goods.

Sipping the tea, hoping to ease the ache in her heart, she
tried to close the emotional door that had been flung open
unexpectedly by Marie's well-meaning counsel. Captain
Joshua David had been a fighter pilot in the Israeli Air
Force. One of the best—destined for a career of military
greatness. He had been everything Sabra was not: extroverted, a joker who teased her unmercifully, in love with life.
He'd lived solely in the moment—and he'd wanted her to do
the same—to live with him.

The sugar she'd stirred into the tea was sweet against the
bitterness of her memories. She'd been shy and introverted
in comparison to the outgoing, ebullient Captain David.
He'd swept her off her feet, wooed her without apology, and
all she'd done was back off, finding reasons not to date him,
not to open up to him. Josh had been so emotionally open
that it had scared the hell out of Sabra. She still wondered
how he had been able to do that. She'd suffered too many
hurts, too many disappointments over the years to parade
her vulnerability about as he had. The hare and the tor-
toise. He'd always accused her of being the turtle in their on-
again, off-again relationship, which had ended suddenly.
Shockingly.

Biting down on her lower lip, Sabra closed her eyes and
felt the rending loss. Felt the old pain that somehow never
quite went away. After that, she'd left Mossad. Left Israel.
Perseus had become her new life—like a second family. And
bless Terry, her older, more-mature partner. He'd been forty
when she was teamed with him, and she'd been an injured,
disillusioned twenty-seven. Terry had been more father than
friend to her, if she was honest about it—everything she'd
ever wished her own father would be. In five years, Terry
had in his own safe way helped her to heal. He'd treated her
with respect, as an equal—something she'd always wanted
from the men in her life but had never before experienced.

Sabra knew Terry would retire now, and she would miss him terribly. He was an introvert like her, philosophical and quietly worldly. He'd been a mercenary all his life, and he'd noticeably mellowed over the years. Terry had been able to impart the wisdom of his life experience to her; and to her own credit, Sabra had assimilated it, had grown from his lessons. He'd taught her to be a risk taker, within reason—not going off half-cocked with some half-baked plan. He'd taught her the importance of attending to details, meticulous details that could save their lives. But his caution and common sense didn't make him a coward. If a risk had to be taken, Terry would be out in front of her, his life on the line as surely as was her own.

Slowly opening her eyes, Sabra felt the ache in her heart deepen. Terry had been more than a partner. He was part sage, part mentor and mature beyond his years. She already missed him terribly. And until this moment, she hadn't realized just how much she'd relied upon his experience and wisdom.

Well, whoever they teamed her with now she wouldn't dare compare to Terry. He'd been called the Old Man in the merc business, and he had the scars—both physical and emotional—to prove it. What would her new partner be like? Would he be older? Sabra hoped so. She had an easier time getting along with older men than with those in her own age group. They lacked the sort of maturity she'd learned to rely on.

The door opened unexpectedly. Sabra set her teacup back on its saucer and stood up. Instantly, her intuitive side was awake, picking up fragments of impressions, assessing body language and facial expressions. The big man dressed in a wrinkled, white short-sleeved shirt and dark brown chinos was the leader. His scowl was set, and his eyes missed nothing. His gaze pinned hers.

"Sabra Jacobs?"

"Yes."

"I'm Jake Randolph. Welcome."

He extended his large, scarred hand, and Sabra felt an immediate liking for his directness and warmth. She gripped his hand firmly. "Hello. Where's Morgan?"

Jake turned and stepped aside. "We'll get into that in a moment." He gestured for the rest to enter.

Sabra felt her eyes widen as Laura Trayhern entered the room after the two other mercenaries.

"Laura!"

Laura smiled wanly. "Hi, Sabra." She opened her arms.

Caught off guard by her unexpected presence, Sabra gave a hesitant hug to the smaller woman, then pulled back a step. "What are you doing here?" Sabra's radar was going off; she'd never seen Laura at Perseus, and she knew, as all the operatives did, that Morgan didn't want his family involved in his company—for a lot of good reasons.

"Sit down," Jake invited, as Wolf Harding closed the door, "and we'll fill you in."

Stymied, Sabra slowly sat. She was shocked by how pale and thin Laura was. The small-boned woman, who slipped into the chair opposite her, looked haggard and drawn. Sabra's heart began to pound a little faster, with dread. Something had happened. But what? She pursed her lips to stop herself from blurting out her troubled questions. She watched warily as Jake sat at the head of the table—in Morgan's habitual seat.

Obviously Morgan wasn't here. Sabra's glance cut to Laura. Although she was dressed in a navy suit and white silk blouse, her blond hair neatly in place as always, falling in soft curls around her shoulders, the lipstick coloring her mouth seemed almost garish against her unhealthy pallor. Sabra clenched her hands, picking up on an incredible grief surrounding Laura. The other woman's eyes, usually shining with life, were dark and shadowed.

Never had it been harder to keep a hold on her always-limited patience. Sabra had hoped that as she got older, her patience would grow with her, but so far she wasn't having much luck. Her mother was terribly impatient, and Sabra seemed to have inherited that family trait with a vengeance. As her gaze skittered from one face to another, she realized how grim and somber they all were. But she was especially disturbed by Laura—by the unknown tragedy written clearly across her tense features.

"We're glad you're here," Jake said heavily. "And what we are going to share with you doesn't leave this room. Is that understood?"

"Of course," Sabra murmured, frowning because Morgan would never question her confidentiality.

"Good." Jake opened his hands. "I'm going to make a long story very short for you, Sabra, because time is of the essence. About a month ago, Enrique Ramirez, the Peruvian drug lord Perseus has been battling off and on for the past five years, kidnapped Laura, Morgan and their son, Jason."

With a gasp, Sabra nearly came out of her chair, then caught herself and forced herself to sit back down. Her gaze was riveted on Laura, her senses reeling. "My God..."

"We had no teams available when we managed to trace Laura's whereabouts, so we brought in two outside people for her rescue. Thankfully, they were equal to the task, and we owe them a great deal of gratitude. Now you've come in off a busted assignment, and we have got another team member in. Thanks to Killian here, and the CIA, we've managed to pinpoint where Jason Trayhern is being kept, or at least where we *think* he is."

Jake got up and crossed to the wall, pulling down one of the many well-used maps—this one of the Hawaiian Islands. Punching his finger at the map, he said, "We have reason to believe that the boy is on Maui. Killian intercepted a cryptic message via satellite relay, suggesting that Jason is being held on the island. After a lot of investigation, we discovered that Ramirez has a well-concealed, multimillion dollar investment in condominium holdings on Maui.

"As you may know, one of Ramirez's right-hand men is Garcia, and the CIA was able to provide documents showing that Garcia has a hideaway near Kula, a small town in up-country Maui, on the side of the big, inactive volcano, Haleakala."

Sabra sat very still, her fingers wrapped around the arms of her chair as if to hold back her surging emotions. No wonder Laura looked so ill. The darkness in her eyes *was* grief—her husband and son were prisoners.

"Is Morgan there, too?"

"No. We're still working twenty-four hours a day covering satcom links, trying to get a clue to his whereabouts, as we did with Jason. The Maui police will be helping you. We've got full approval from the state, and they will provide us with whatever we need. But they can't get a warrant to enter Garcia's estate because no one has actually seen Jason."

"So all of this is circumstantial?"

"Yes, I'm afraid so. We're asking you and your new partner to go into Maui posing as a husband-and-wife team, there on assignment to photograph the flora and fauna of Haleakala. You'll set up on the hillside and covertly watch Garcia's estate until we can confirm whether Jason is there. We've cautioned the police not to put Garcia under surveillance, because we don't want to raise his suspicion. If Jason is there, we don't want Garcia to panic and move him. If he does that, we could spend months trying to locate him."

"I see," Sabra whispered. She turned her head to hold Laura's tragic gaze. "I'm so sorry, Laura. So sorry...." And she was. She loved Jason and Katy almost as if they were her own. And she knew how much Laura and Morgan loved them. Family meant more to Morgan than anything, and Sabra had often seen his children pull him out of one of his dark moods. Their innocence and enthusiasm were like sunlight to him. And no one was a better mother than Laura. Sabra hurt deeply for her friend, almost unable to believe that a terrible tragedy had once again cast its pall over the Trayhern family.

Laura managed a brief, wan smile. "What I'm thankful for, Sabra, is that it's you who will be on this assignment. Jason loves and trusts you. If anyone should be there to rescue him, it's you."

"Yes," Jake agreed heavily, "it's definitely in our favor for the boy to know one of the team members."

"Do we know anything of Jason's condition?"

"Nothing."

Sabra looked at Laura. "What did they do to you?"

Laura shrugged. "They drugged me...."

Sabra turned her attention back to Jake. "Jason could be drugged, too."

"Yes." Jake glanced at Laura, a worried expression on his face. "They nearly killed Laura with an overdose of cocaine. We're concerned that Garcia might do the same with Jason."

Anger chilled Sabra as she met Jake's concerned gaze. "I had a run-in with Garcia three years ago. He's an ugly little man with a depraved mind. If I know the bastard at all, his idea of getting even with Morgan and us would be to make his son an addict."

"Oh, dear..."

Sabra turned at Laura's small cry of alarm.

"Laura," Jake said quickly, "we don't know that." He gave Sabra a warning look, obviously telling her to say nothing more.

Sabra gazed down at the table. She should have kept her mouth shut. Laura had turned even paler, if that was possible. Looking back up at Jake, Sabra said quietly, "Laura, I don't think you should be here. You need to go home and rest. It won't help you to hear the details of this mission—a lot of them 'what-ifs' that may never happen. You've been through hell. Don't sit here and keep hurting yourself."

"I think that's a good idea," Jake rumbled. "Come on, Laura, Sabra's right. Her remark was only a possibility, but all these ideas have to be put on the table and discussed. And it's only going to tear you up to hear them. Come on, let's go...."

Sabra felt terrible as she watched Jake help Laura to her feet, then walk her to the door. As he opened it, Laura turned back toward her.

"Promise me you'll see me before you go, Sabra?"

Sabra nodded. "I'll see you."

"I—I have Jason's favorite toy, a little gray squirrel. If—if you could take it with you, maybe—"

"Laura, she'll come by and see you," Jake reassured her gently, placing his hand on her arm and leading her out of the room.

"My God," Sabra whispered as the door closed. She looked up at the two remaining mercenaries. "I didn't . . . I didn't know. . . ."

"It's okay," Wolf grunted, placing his hands palm down on the table. "Laura should never have been in on the planning anyway, but she insisted."

"She's too wounded to hear all of this," Killian rasped.

"I should have kept my mouth shut," Sabra murmured.

"Don't blame yourself," Wolf insisted.

"Jason. Jason's kidnapped. But why him? Why hurt a child?"

"We think," Wolf offered, "that Ramirez took Jason because he's Morgan's only boy. You know how South Americans emphasize the importance of the oldest son."

Closing her eyes, Sabra felt the shock moving through her. "And Jason is such a sweet, curious little boy. He's so trusting. . . ."

"Too trusting," Killian said. "Garcia will use that against him."

"What a horrible thing," Sabra whispered bitterly. "Those drug lords will stoop to any level for revenge."

"That's why we've removed Laura from her home. We're afraid of further reprisals," Wolf answered. "She's staying at a safe house we've arranged, with Killian's wife, Susannah—her cousin. Just for your info, Laura is on tranquilizers and seeing a therapist twice a week."

"She looks so fragile. No wonder. . ."

"We're all worried about her." Wolf grimaced. "What you don't know yet is that Laura was repeatedly raped by Garcia."

Pressing her fingers to her lips, Sabra stared at Wolf in shock. A combination of revulsion, anger and hatred twisted through her. It took her several minutes to wrestle the explosion of feelings back under control. Until then, all she could do was stare at Wolf's dark features.

Jake entered the room and quietly shut the door behind him, his mouth set in a grim line. "Marie is going to take Laura home. She'll be better off there."

Sabra nodded. "Jake, I—"

"Don't apologize," he said, sitting back down. "You're walking into this mess cold. Laura knew the risks when she came to this table. She's not dumb."

Bowing her head, Sabra whispered, "I know how much Jason means to her. If we can't get the boy back..."

"One step at a time," Jake cautioned, holding up his hand. "First we need to introduce you to your new partner. Then we need to do some detailed planning. The Hawaiian police are waiting for you, but I don't want to go into the details of the mission until Talbot arrives." Jake glanced at the clock on the wall. "Marie got word that he landed. He should be on his way."

"Talbot—is he my new partner?"

Jake opened a dossier and slid it across the table toward her. "Yes. Craig Talbot. He's been with Perseus for six months. Study his file while we wait."

Sabra felt their interest, on her reaction to the information on Talbot. She looked down at the open folder and was greeted by an 8-by-10 color photo of her new partner. True to her training, she carefully masked any overt reactions, but inwardly, her heart gave an unexpected thump. Talbot's oval face featured a strong jaw and a hawklike nose. What drew her, though, were piercing, dark blue eyes with large, intelligent black pupils, eyes that made him look more like an imperious eagle than a man. He looked in his early thirties—near her own age—and something about his mouth, a thin slash that seemed to be holding back so much, touched her heart. On the left side, a scar at least six inches long extended down his lean cheek, and that whole side of his face had an unusual shiny quality.

His hair was black with blue highlights, cut military short, and his black brows straight, emphasizing the glittering eyes that even in a two-dimensional photo seemed to miss nothing. Sabra hid her initial reaction. Talbot was neither good-looking nor bad, but he had seen perhaps too much in his relatively short life. He was deeply tanned, and though he'd obviously shaved, a darkness shadowing his jaw gave him a dangerous look—and a dangerous appeal.

Sabra had met many mercenaries in her years of service with Perseus, and she was familiar with military men and their demeanor, but this man put her on guard. She stared at the photo, trying to keep her brain at bay and allow her feminine instincts to tell her why. Talbot possessed an animal-like quality, as if he lived life on a very thin edge that could crumble at any moment. The set of his mouth, his compressed lips, hid a great deal. But what was he hiding? The scar on his left cheek appeared fairly recent.

All Sabra could receive intuitively was that Talbot was unsettling to her on every level. But why? Was it the frosty challenge in his bold blue stare? The secrets protected behind that well-shaped mouth? The boxerlike set of his jaw, defying anyone to try to hurt him? Sabra was sure he had been hurt.

The crow's-feet at the corners of his eyes reminded her of Josh. Aviators always had crow's-feet from squinting against the sun. She sensed a hidden vulnerability to Talbot, though when this photo was taken, he'd obviously been doing his best to camouflage it. As she stared into the eyes, she saw a darkness there, just as she had in Laura's eyes. Grief, perhaps? Pain? The feeling around Talbot wasn't inspiring Sabra to any greater insights. He was a man of many secrets—unlike Josh. Unlike Terry.

Forcing herself to casually push the unexpectedly provocative photo aside and look at his personnel record, Sabra saw that Talbot was thirty-two—her age. His birthday was May 22, making him a mere two months older than she was. He'd been born in Fort Wingate, New Mexico.

Before joining Perseus, he'd had a career as a marine helicopter pilot. Her heart skipped a beat: he'd been a pilot just as Josh had been. Her heart aching, Sabra compressed her lips. Talbot was single. Why had he resigned his commission shortly after Desert Storm? Sabra had a lot of questions, but decided to hold off on them until he arrived.

When she realized that he took only low- and medium-risk assignments, she lifted her head and looked at Jake, surprised. "This is a high-risk assignment. He doesn't have the background for it."

Jake's mouth became a slash. "Yeah, we know." He opened his hands. "We don't have a choice in this, Sabra. Talbot's the only person available for the assignment right now. It takes all three of us to stay on top of things here—I don't know how Morgan did it alone. We're scrambling just to keep communications open between the State Department, the CIA, Interpol and the FBI on these kidnappings. If we could, one of us would go with you, but it's not possible."

Sabra frowned. "He's only got six months with us, in low- or medium-risk missions. There's no comparison between those and a high-risk assignment."

"Talbot is ex-marine. He knows how to handle himself and weapons."

"I'm sure he does," Sabra said, her voice deepening with concern. "But we're going undercover. Has he ever done that?"

"No."

Frustrated, she looked at Jake for a long moment. "So you're saddling me with a green team member. Talbot might as well have walked in off the street."

"He's not our ideal pick," Jake admitted heavily, "but Sabra, we don't have a choice. Right now, it's most important that we verify that Jason is on Maui, don't you think?"

"Of course," she said. "But if we do verify it, Talbot and I will have to go in after him. I don't know Talbot, and I don't know how he'll react if and when we're faced with a potentially life-threatening situation." She took a deep breath. "I'd rather do the assignment alone than with a rookie, Jake. I really would."

"I understand your concerns, Sabra. But Talbot has the capacity to live up to our expectations for this mission. We've just never asked him to do it before."

"Does he know he's being asked to do it now?" she asked, sarcasm in her voice.

Jake glanced away. "Not yet. He will shortly."

She glared at him. "This really smacks of loose planning, Jake, and I don't like it. I don't mind risking my life to find Jason, but I'm not about to add the burden of teaching someone who isn't prepared for this kind of assignment."

"Why don't we wait and see?" Wolf pleaded. "None of us knows Talbot. After all, he went through Desert Storm as a combat helicopter pilot. That says something doesn't it?"

"Yes," she conceded unwillingly, "it does."

"And he was in the Marine Corps since graduating from Annapolis, so the man must have tactics and strategy training down pat," Jake reasoned.

Sabra stood up. "Maybe I'm jumpy," she murmured in apology. "I mean, if Jason wasn't involved, I probably wouldn't be so concerned about my teammate's qualifications."

Jake nodded. "I feel," he said gently, "that because you know and love Jason, your emotions are clouding your judgment."

Sabra sighed. "I won't disagree with you, Jake. I'm terribly upset. And you're right—I love Jason as if he were my own son. I've baby-sat that kid since he was born. I've taken him to the zoo...." Helplessly, she shrugged. "Maybe I am blowing things out of proportion. But I die inside every time I think about Jason being with Garcia. I want to cry...."

"We all do," Jake assured her, his voice rough with emotion.

"You have to realize we're going to help you every way we can," Wolf vowed. "Talbot is the unknown in this. Aside from his file, no one here knows anything about him. You're being thrown into an off-balance situation with him, we know. But we believe that with your time in grade with Perseus, and your background, you'll be able to take charge and find Jason."

Sabra glanced at Jake. "I'm in charge of the mission?"

"That's right."

She stood a long time without moving. Terry had always been the team leader. Now the shoe was on the other foot and she was in charge. Of what? A man she didn't know, who lacked the experience to work with her at the level she had to demand.

Releasing a long sigh, she whispered, "I reserve the right to say whether or not Talbot goes with me after I've had a chance to meet him and assess his abilities."

Jake scowled. "No, Sabra, you don't have the privilege of that decision."

"I demand it."

"No."

"It's my life on the line," she said hotly. "And Jason's! I'm not going to take on someone who may not have the guts to get close to Garcia to rescue Jason. What if Talbot is squeamish? What if he can't pull a trigger to defend himself? Or me? In high-risk missions we have to be concerned with that question. I know Garcia," she added, her voice trembling with emotion. "I know what the bastard is capable of doing. He raped and drugged Laura. He may have drugged Jason. If he catches me or Talbot, we're as good as dead. How do I know if Talbot has what it takes? Can I trust him? Why is he a merc in the first place? Can he shoot to kill? Would he? And is he really a team player?"

Pacing the length of the room, Sabra muttered, "I reserve the right to decide whether or not Talbot goes, and that's all there is to it."

Jake slowly stood up. "Then you're off this assignment, Sabra."

She halted and jerked around, her mouth falling open. "What?"

"You heard me." He frowned. "Under any other circumstances, I'd probably agree with you. But we don't have that luxury. All our other teams are out in the field, and it's too late to try to recruit from outside Perseus. The government isn't about to loan us a SEAL team or Delta Force. We're on our own with whatever we have at hand. We have you, we have Talbot. Look at it as a marriage of convenience. You don't have to like this guy, you just have to work with him on one mission. I hope we find Morgan alive and that he'll return to get Perseus back on line. Until then, this organization is reeling. We're all off-balance. We've been caught off guard in the worst kind of way.

"Sometimes," he added, a note of pleading entering his voice, "we have to settle for seconds. Nobody likes it, Sabra, but that's all we've got. That's life."

Shaken, Sabra said, "Where's Talbot's partner, then?"

"She died in an auto accident two days ago."

"Are you sure it was an accident?"

"As sure as we can be. It was a low-risk assignment."

Eyeing him angrily, Sabra muttered, "That's just great. Talbot's going to be upset about losing his partner on top of everything else. Do you really think he's got the emotional stability to hop from that into something like this?"

"We're all going to find out the answer to that together," Jake stated firmly. "Now, are you in or are you out?"

Glaring, Sabra said, "And if I'm out, what will you do?"

"Assign it to Talbot."

"You're crazy!"

"That's the choice we're faced with Sabra. You've been here five years. You know how the system works."

"You can't put someone like Talbot on this assignment alone. That's guaranteeing failure."

"Then agree to be the leader of the team."

Frustrated, she raked them with an angry look. "I don't like this, Jake. I don't like it at all."

"Give yourself some leeway, Sabra. Wait until Talbot comes in and we've had a chance to talk to him about it. Assess his responses."

"What if he doesn't measure up in your eyes, Jake?" Sabra challenged. "What then?"

"Then," he said heavily, "I'll ask you to go alone. I won't like it, but I'll do it."

She smiled grimly. "That's the better of two evils in this case. At least with me, you know what you're getting."

"I don't disagree."

There was a knock on the door. The room fell silent. Sabra turned, her fingers resting on the oak tabletop. It had to be Talbot. Her heart was beating erratically, and she tried to calm it—tried to calm herself. Jake was right: she was personally and emotionally involved in this assignment in a unique way. Since Jason's birth, she'd fed him his bottle, changed his diapers, watched him learn to crawl, then walk. Jason was like the son she'd always dreamed of having—the dream that had died five years ago with Josh. Whether he knew it or not, Jason had eased her pain simply by being himself. Sabra could live the dream of having a dark-haired little boy with beautiful gray eyes, though she would never admit it to anyone else. Jake had no idea exactly how close she felt to Jason—and why.

Moistening her lips, she whispered, "I'll stay on the mission."

Jake nodded. "I'm glad, Sabra. Thank you." He walked to the door and twisted the polished brass doorknob. "Come in," he said gruffly.

Sabra's eyes widened. Her heart contracted. Automatically, her hand went to the top of her chair, and she gripped it, feeling suddenly dizzy in the wake of Craig Talbot's silent, lethal entrance.

Chapter Two

Craig halted wearily in front of the War Room door. No one had been at the reception desk, which was highly unusual. Marie was such a calming, constant presence at Perseus. Exhaustion pulled heavily at him, and he ran his hand across his jaw, the prickly whiskers there reminding him he'd been without shower or shave for forty-eight hours— since the tragic loss of Jennifer.

His heart gave another twinge of guilt as her young, eager face danced once more in front of his smarting, bloodshot eyes. He shouldn't have allowed her to tail the suspect by herself. He should have listened to his gut instead of allowing her to talk him out of his decision. Once again he'd been a leader—and once again, he'd gotten someone killed.

His mouth tasted bitter from too much coffee on the flight from Europe, and he wiped it with the back of his hand, then knocked on the door again. Where was everyone? If he wasn't so damned tired, his internal radar might be picking up on something.

The door swung open, and he stared at the tall, burly man standing there in a white shirt and dark chinos. "Where's Marie?" Craig demanded.

"She's on an errand. I'm Jake Randolph, one of the Perseus mercs. Come in, we've been expecting you."

Confused, Craig stepped through the door. Two other mercs nodded greetings from the other end of the table, their faces set and unreadable. Although his senses were muddled by changed time zones and lack of sleep, Craig swung his attention to his right. His eyes widened slightly. There, on the other side of the table, stood a young woman of incredible exotic beauty. Craig stared at her. She was dressed in a silk T-shirt patterned with cinnamon, dark blue, lime green and black flowerlike colors. A cinnamon skirt draped her long thighs revealingly and hung gracefully around her slender ankles and sandaled feet.

Impressions of her assailed his numbed senses. Was it her large gray eyes, framed by thick black lashes, that entranced him? Or the soft set of her lips, unmarked by lipstick. She wore no makeup, but she certainly didn't need any. Her skin had an olive cast and her wide-set eyes were slightly tilted at the corners, giving her an exotic Egyptian quality. She reminded Craig of a statue of Queen Nefertiti he'd once seen in a museum.

Tearing his gaze from her, he followed Randolph into the room. One of the other mercs got up and quietly closed the door behind them. Randolph pointed to the chair next to him.

"I imagine you're tired, but have a seat. We've got a crisis at Perseus and I'm afraid you're one of only two mercs available for the assignment."

Stymied, Craig sat, his joints aching in protest as they always did if he had to stay too long in one position, ever since— He coldly squashed the rest of the paralyzing thought. Trying to push the threatening past from his mind, he watched as the operative who'd closed the door came around the table and sat opposite him. The woman also took a seat. Who was she? His mind was mushy, and thinking was difficult. All he wanted was sleep, but he didn't dare doze off here, so he fought to remain awake.

"Killian, would you mind getting Talbot some coffee?" Jake asked, understanding tinging his voice.

The Irishman rose in one fluid motion and left the room.

Jake jerked a thumb toward the door. "That's Killian who just left, and this is Wolf Harding."

Craig nodded, but his gaze was pinned on the woman across from him.

"And this is Sabra Jacobs."

"A merc?" He heard the disbelief in his voice. As soon as the words were out, he was sorry he'd said them. Her slightly winged, thick brows drew down in displeasure, her eyes mirroring irritation. Despite her expression, he liked the way her thick, black hair fell gracefully around her proud shoulders. A strand dipped prettily across her brow, further emphasizing her oval face and high cheekbones. For a moment, her cheeks flushed a dull red at his unfortunate comment, and the flash of anger in her eyes stunned him. Why did it surprise him that her emotions would be revealed in them? Maybe, somewhere in his Neanderthal mind, he thought beautiful women were always poised and never showed their true feelings. Craig almost laughed at the absurdity of his clashing thoughts. Like every other man in the military, his ideas regarding women had come under fire. He was trying his best not to look at them in terms of their relative beauty of body or face, but it was nearly impossible not to appreciate Sabra Jacobs on that level.

Disgusted with his weaknesses, which were many, he disengaged his gaze from hers and returned his attention to Randolph, who seemed to be in charge. "What's going on? Where's Morgan?" Morgan always greeted returning teams, no matter what time of day or night they came in from a mission. It was one of many things Craig admired about the man—a sign of his abiding loyalty to his people. Not many bosses felt that level of care and responsibility toward their employees.

Jake opened his hands. "Talbot, a lot has happened in the past few weeks. Ramirez, a Peruvian drug lord, sent a team up here and kidnapped Morgan, his wife, Laura, and their son, Jason. The good news is we pulled an outside team together to rescue Laura, who is back home with us. Now we've got a lead on where Jason might be."

Craig sat up, stunned. His mouth dropped open. He snapped it shut. Though he remained silent as Jake filled him in on the kidnappings, his weary eyes betrayed his shock.

When Jake had finished the initial briefing, he gestured to Wolf, who leaned forward and shoved a sheet of paper across the table. "This is Garcia's estate. We got a fax of the floor plan from Honolulu FBI. Every developer that builds there has to apply for a building permit and submit a copy of the plans. This place is situated on roughly three acres of rich Maui real estate on the side of an inactive volcano. You been to Hawaii?"

"No." Craig blinked his burning eyes and tried to focus on the paper in front of him.

"Sabra's been there," Jake said, "so that's good. Anyway, we want you two to fly there, take up residence at the Westin Kaanopoli, then drive to Kula, set up your long-range cameras and keep watch. We need confirmation that Jason is there, which may mean manning cameras twenty-four hours a day on a hillside near Garcia's estate. We've got the necessary credentials in order, including confirmation of the assignment by Parker Publishing in New York, should anyone get snoopy."

Craig looked up at Randolph. "So say we spot Jason— then what?"

"Then you'll go in and rescue him."

Scowling, Craig said, "I don't do high-risk missions."

"I know that's usually the case," Jake said steadily, "but what you have to understand is that all the high-risk teams are tied up with assignments. We can't break any of them free. Sabra is a high-risk merc, but her partner isn't available. You're the first person to come off the line. We're sorry about Jennifer's accident, and I'm sure you're as upset about her loss as we are. But right now we're operating under emergency conditions, Talbot, and you're the only merc we've got.''

Craig sat straighter, feeling his gut begin to tighten, a rolling, painful sensation. He wanted to lean forward to ease the pain, but all eyes were on him, the gazes seeming to eat into his raw emotional state. "So, you want to pair me with a high-risk merc for a high-risk mission?"

"If Jason's there," Jake said reasonably. "He may not be, and if he isn't, then this is classified a medium-risk assignment. You may not have to do more than sit on a Hawaiian hillside and watch through a lens. There's no danger in that."

"But if we spot the kid, we go in," Craig persisted.

Jake nodded, watching him warily. "We have grave concerns that Garcia might shoot the kid up with cocaine and hook him on the drug as part of getting even with Morgan. When we rescued Laura, she was drugged so heavily that we nearly lost her. If we hadn't had an emergency medical team standing by on that Coast Guard cruiser, she would have died. The boy is in danger."

Running his hand around the smooth surface of the heavy white coffee mug, Craig tried to think coherently. The part of him that wasn't injured wanted this mission. He'd always had a soft spot for kids. "The son of a bitch shouldn't be hiding behind a little boy," he muttered angrily.

"Only a drug dealer would," Killian intoned.

"Normally," Jake said, "you don't interface with drug dealers as the high-risk mercs do, Talbot. Believe me when I tell you from personal experience that Ramirez and his worldwide cartel are just about the worst kind of human beings you'll ever run into."

"I've had dealings with Garcia," Sabra interjected, "and he's like an Israeli viper—lethal."

Craig looked up at her, surprised by the sudden change in her face from utter serenity and confidence to emotional intensity. She was leaning forward, her elbows on the table. Again he was struck by her beauty, the black hair framing her face to emphasize her slim nose, soft mouth and riveting eyes.

Reluctantly returning his gaze to Randolph, he said, "Who would be in charge of this team?"

"Sabra would."

Craig frowned.

"She's got five years of experience on high-risk assignments," Jake said.

Craig looked at her. "And has she headed up a team before?"

"No," Sabra said steadily, "I have not."

"Well, I have."

"Look," Jake said more firmly, "Sabra will be in charge. She has knowledge of Hawaii and of high-risk assignments."

"Then I'm not taking the mission."

Sabra gasped and stood up. "You'd let the fact of a woman in charge get in the way of a little boy's life? Where are your morals?"

Craig glared at her. "Lady, my personal integrity is none of your business." He hated his own icy, defensive tone. If he hadn't been so tired, so emotionally beaten by the sudden loss of Jennifer, he might have handled this situation better. At least, he wanted to. But, as usual, he was a miserable failure; the thought wounded him as nothing else could. He saw her mouth snap shut, her gray eyes blazing with hurt disbelief. She stood tensely, tall and proud, and he could find nothing to dislike about her, even in her anger and disappointment. Sabra took his breath away, though it panicked him to admit it, even to himself. Why *was* he turning down the assignment? Fear of dying? Yes. A fear of her? He sighed. Yes. Or, more accurately a fear of himself—his naked, raw response to her. That was the truth, and that was one thing Craig still had; his honesty with himself, even when the truth hurt.

Sabra felt as if she'd been stung. She halted just across from her would-be partner, who glared up at her with a defiance that made her want to slap his insolent face. "Admit it—you don't like having a woman for a boss," she challenged.

"That's part of it."

Her heart wouldn't stop pounding. She wanted to hate Craig for his decision. In her book, no one worthy of being called human would turn away from saving a helpless child, whatever the risk. "How can you?' she demanded. "How can you sit there when there's a vulnerable boy at the mercy of a bastard like Garcia? Have you no heart? No soul?"

Fury shot through Craig, and he slowly stood, holding her blazing glare. Her cheeks were bright red, flushed with righteous anger. Sabra was at least five feet seven, maybe a little taller, and probably weighed around a hundred and thirty pounds, if he was any judge. She was tall, graceful and defiant. No matter what she did, he couldn't dislike her. She was too beautiful, and maybe that would prove to be his Achilles' heel. "Look," he rasped unsteadily, "I'm sorry Jason got kidnapped. I don't like it any more than you do, but—"

"Then come with me on this mission!" Sabra said huskily. "Forget that I'm a woman. Just hold this boy's plight in front of you and know that you're doing it for him."

The urgent plea in her low voice tore at Craig. He could feel it—and see it in her large eyes, her huge black pupils ringed by a thin crescent of gray. She held her hands in front of her, clasped to her small breasts.

He looked away from her. "I've never been on a high-risk mission. I'd be a detriment to this assignment, and everyone here knows it," he said, struggling to keep the bitterness from his tone.

Jake sighed and asked Sabra to sit down, then returned his attention to Craig. "Please take a seat," he entreated him in turn. "Yes, there are problems in pairing a high- and medium-risk merc. But we don't have the time to wait for another high-risk team to come in, Talbot. I know it's not the best of all worlds, but Sabra is right—there's a little boy who is completely blameless in this whole thing, standing in the middle. Can't you put aside your personal prejudice for his sake?"

Craig gripped the coffee mug, staring down at the black contents as he mulled over Randolph's plea.

Sabra sat very still, holding her breath, praying that Talbot wouldn't take the mission. She knew she could do this on her own, and she would rather work alone than with someone whose priorities were so mixed-up. Yet, as she stared at Talbot's darkly bearded face, saw his brow kneading, his mouth compressed as if to hold back pain, she recanted her feelings. Despite the aura of animal danger he projected, a part of her wanted him on the mission. The feral quality in his shadowed blue eyes told her he would miss nothing—that he possessed an extraordinary sentience about him that would work in their favor.

Torn, Sabra kept her mouth shut. She wanted to tell him to forget it, to go home and get some sleep. That tomorrow was another day, a safe day. Her heart told her differently. Talbot appeared excruciatingly bare emotionally as he considered Jake's request. She saw the man in him, the warrior, but she also saw vulnerability. A crazy urge to lean across the table and smooth those rebellious, dark brown strands of hair off his wrinkled brow caught her off guard.

Wrestling with a turmoil of feelings that seemed too much like an out-of-control roller-coaster ride, Sabra stared hard at Craig, hoping to find the reason for her uncharacteristic confusion. She'd never experienced this strange combination of uncertainty, giddiness and challenge. What was going on?

Talbot was obviously exhausted. She saw the darkness beneath his bloodshot eyes, and the way his broad shoulders slumped—shoulders fully capable of carrying very heavy loads.

Forcing herself to disconnect from him emotionally, she looked at him through new eyes. Talbot was at least six feet tall, with a lean, cougarlike body. He was pure muscle, fit and trim. She took in his navy long-sleeved shirt—then suddenly noticed a lot of small scars on his large-knuckled fingers, and some angry pink skin that covered the backs of his hands and disappeared beneath the cuffs, as if he'd been badly burned. As her gaze ranged upward, she saw a sprinkling of dark hair peeking from the neck of his shirt. His masculinity was powerful—and beckoning.

Sabra swallowed and found that her throat was constricted. Talbot wasn't pretty-boy handsome. But the photo in his file didn't do him justice, either, because as he sat opposite her, she felt a powerful, swirling energy emanating from him that was utterly masculine—and utterly compelling to her senses as a woman. She was shocked by her unbidden desire to lightly run her fingers across his arm and feel that latent power. Talbot sent her senses spinning as no man had ever done before.

Reeling at that revelation, Sabra sat back in her chair, more confused than ever. What she saw in Craig and what was in his personnel file seemed diametrically opposed. The man sitting here was all-warrior. So why did he take only the lower-risk missions? And something else was missing. Sabra sat up as she realized that it was his confidence. Yes, he looked strong and capable, but he lacked that gleam in his eyes that she'd seen in other warriors—a look of utter assuredness about themselves and their abilities.

She told herself that he had jet lag, and that his partner had just died—enough to snuff out, at least temporarily, any person's confidence. Sabra knew how close she was to Terry. Had Talbot been that close to Jennifer? Or perhaps emotionally involved on an even deeper, more-personal level? Sabra had heard how from time to time a man-and-woman merc team would fall in love. Studying Talbot, she could understand how any woman might be drawn to his rugged looks and those dark blue eyes that burned with inner torment. Any woman might choose to know him—to explore him like a dangerous hidden treasure.

Finally Killian leaned forward. "I think you have to separate your personal feelings from what's important, Talbot. The target is a boy. He can't protect himself. He can't escape. He's too young to realize what's happened. I'm sure he wonders where his father and mother are, but Garcia could lie to him and make him believe anything. If we don't get someone in there to help Jason, the boy could be lost to us even if he's allowed to live. I don't think you want that to happen."

Sabra released her held breath. She didn't know Killian very well, but she agreed with his bottom line. This wasn't about Talbot. He had to look to what was really important: a lone, defenseless five-year-old. She moistened her lips, exchanged glances with Jake, then covertly watched Talbot. His expression had changed instantly with Killian's statement. The anger in his eyes was doused and replaced with—fear? Sabra started to lean forward, but caught herself, forcing herself to sit back and appear relaxed. She knew the value of body language, and Talbot was feeling penned in anyway, without her silent challenge to hurry up and decide.

But why the instant of fear in his eyes? It seemed an odd response to Killian's reasonable statement. She saw Craig's mouth work as his hands caressed the mug in front of him. She had to admit he looked absolutely tortured. But couldn't he put his personal demons aside for the sake of a little boy? Sabra knew she could. A child in jeopardy spurred her to an instinctive, fierce desire to protect. She had to remind herself that almost any woman would respond similarly because it was genetically programmed into them, while some men, she knew, didn't care much for children. Was Talbot one of them?

Finally, she could stand the tension and silence no longer. Reaching slowly across the table until her fingers were bare inches from the cup Talbot held, she whispered unsteadily, "This mission is more than that for me, Craig. I helped raise Jason. This is personal. I happened to be coming off a task as Laura gave birth to Jason, and I got to hold him shortly afterward. Over the years, I've baby-sat him, and later Katy, their daughter. Jason knows me. He calls me 'Auntie S'...." Tears stung her eyes, and her voice cracked as she said, "Please, put aside whatever personal feelings you have toward me. Jason is what's important, not you or me or the ghosts we carry with us."

Talbot's head snapped up, his eyes narrowing dangerously. Sabra felt the intensity, the heat and the torture instantly as his gaze met and locked with hers. She was

shamed by the tears that leaked from her eyes and began to
trail down her cheeks, but she no longer cared. "I—I'm
begging you, as one human being to another, to come with
me on this mission. It's true, I've never led a team, and I'll
value your experience and input. Whatever you have to offer to help us get to Jason." She stretched her fingers toward him. "Please...."

Shock snaked through Craig as he stared down at her
outstretched hand. His throat went dry. His mouth tasted
bitter. The instant he looked into her lustrous, tear-filled
eyes, it was as if she'd torn a layer out of his heart. He *felt*
her pleading. For two years he had felt little, as if caught in
an imprisoning cocoon, cut off from his emotions. But
looking at Sabra's begging eyes, as the deep honey of her
voice flowed through him like light in the darkness of his
agonizing existence, seemed to pull him—if only for a moment—out of his personal hell.

He gripped the mug hard, feeling all eyes on him. Sabra's fingers were long and beautifully shaped, the nails
blunt cut and without nail polish. If nothing else, she was
herself, and Craig respected that discovery. She was confident enough in herself that she needed little outside adorn-
ment, he realized, slowly raising his head. As he met and
drowned in her lustrous gaze, he felt such an incredible
warmth flow through his heart that it startled him—as if the
look in her eyes was capable of melting the glacier of ice
he'd been trapped in for so long. The past half hour in this
room with her had made him feel like living again, reviving
a trickle of hope he'd believed destroyed forever.

Craig had no idea how Sabra had unlocked his heart, but
he had to acknowledge that she wielded some kind of power.
Did she realize her effect on him? No, not judging from the
haunted look in her eyes that tore so effectively at him. Was
she using her exotic beauty to persuade him? He didn't think
so. There was nothing coy or flirtatious about Sabra. She
was bold and straightforward in a way he could admire—
and respect.

More than anything, Craig found her diplomacy appeal-
ing. She could have acted like a man and told him that

whatever she said went, since she was the leader of the team. Instead, she had appealed to him on a personal level, asking for his help and counsel.

Craig delved deeply into her gray gaze, trying to ferret out her reasons for the diplomatic invitation to share her power. But all he found was grief—a plea for a child's welfare. His instincts told him she wasn't the kind of person to put on an act.

"I think," Jake said, rising slowly, "we ought to leave you two alone for a few minutes."

The other men rose and left the room. The door shut behind them. Sabra pulled her hand back to her side of the table and sat, watching Craig in the gathering silence. He was burdened by something so terrible that he couldn't get past it to make a decision. She had no idea where that knowledge came from, but she trusted her senses.

Quietly, she said, "I know high-risk missions can be life threatening, Craig. I don't know if this one will be. There's so much we don't know yet about Garcia, or where Jason is, or how he might be guarded. I can use your help and experience on this. I—I had a wonderful mentor for five years—Terry Hayes. He was in his forties, and he'd kicked around the world for years as a merc before coming to Perseus. He taught me his craft and he taught me well. I'm not sitting here saying I know it all, because I don't. Terry taught me a whole new version of teamwork. We talked over every detail of our plans together. He listened to my ideas, and I listened to his. Sometimes—" she spread her hands as Craig slowly raised his chin and pinned her with his gaze "—I knew something from my past in the Mossad that we could use. Sometimes Terry's past would be of help."

"I don't question your sincerity about enlisting my help or experience in this mission," Craig said roughly, breaking his long silence.

Sabra stared at him, puzzled. "Then what's stopping you from saying yes? I can feel you wrestling with something— something almost insurmountable...." She held his angry, confused stare and watched his generous mouth become a dark slash against his face.

"My past is none of your business," he said in a grating tone. "None of it."

"I wasn't trying to pry...."

Shaken by her insight, Craig felt anger temporarily replace his fear. "Is there flying involved in this mission?"

Sabra reacted to the unexpected question as if he'd physically struck her in the face. Reeling from his sudden fury, she stammered, "Well—yes, the flight to Hawaii."

"What about once we're there?"

"I...don't know. I've been on Maui. Kaanopolis is at the west end of the island and Kula is to the east. A rental car should be sufficient."

"No helicopter flights?"

"Why—no...not that I know of. At least not right now."

Craig pushed the chair back and stood, glaring down at her. "Good, because I *refuse* to fly a helicopter. I refuse to even climb in one. You got that?"

Stunned, Sabra stared up into his tortured, stormy features. "Y-yes, I've got that." *Why?* Her mind spun. He'd been a helicopter pilot in the Marine Corps. Why would he refuse to even ride in one? And she hadn't asked him to fly a helicopter—it wasn't in the plan.

"Perseus owns a Learjet," she said, rattled. "That's all."

Craig paced the length of the room, his hands behind his back. "I don't like being squeezed into this mission. I can't help it if the kid got nailed by Ramirez and Garcia." He stopped and twisted to look at her over his shoulder. Sabra's face was filled with desolation at his statement. "Don't play on my sympathies about kids, because it won't work. I don't like high-risk missions. There's too much that can go wrong."

"Yes," Sabra said in a strained voice, "there's no question of that. It will no doubt require a lot of creativity and flexibility on both our parts, but I feel you have that. So do I."

"You know what your problem is, Ms. Jacobs?"

Sabra blinked once, feeling the full force of his intensity, which rattled her as nothing ever had. "Excuse me?"

He gave her a lethal look. "Your problem is that you're one of these gung-ho types that goes around saving the world. You've got confidence. You've got a lot of experience under your belt. There's one problem though—you've never hit bottom. You've never paid the price for what you do."

"What are you talking about?" she demanded throatily. "I've paid plenty of dues working with Perseus! Do you think I see my job as a game? As fun?"

He shrugged and placed his hands on his hips. "I don't know, and frankly, I don't care. You're a fresh-faced kid to me. I see the excitement in your eyes over this mission. I hear it in your voice. What worries me most is that you'll do something foolhardy just because you're personally close to Jason. Being a merc means being disconnected from everything." He jammed his thumb into his chest. "I'm about as disconnected as I can get, but you aren't. And don't sit there and tell me you can put your feelings for this kid on the back burner and behave rationally when the chips are down. You won't be able to, and you'll jeopardize us because of it."

Anger surged through Sabra, and she stood suddenly, nearly tipping over the chair. She caught it, set it firmly back on the carpeted floor and whirled toward him. "Who do you think you are? You think you know me so well, but you don't know me at all! And disconnected? I've never been disconnected from any mission I've undertaken. You're dead wrong about how that plays out in me. It makes me careful, and it makes me care."

"Care—" he spat the word savagely "—is going to be your undoing, Ms. Jacobs. And I'm sure as hell not going to be there to see it happen."

Sabra felt the heat rush into her face as she stood, shaking in the aftermath of his attack. "How dare you," she whispered hoarsely. "How dare you think you know me and my heart, or the kind of care I put into every mission. I didn't join Perseus because I was running away from something, Talbot. I joined because I knew I had certain talents and skills, and I cared one heck of a lot about people in trouble. I love my job, because it's about my heart and my concern for others. That's why I do it.'' Her nostrils flared, and she walked to the end of the table, stopping within a foot of him. He was glowering down at her, and she glared back.

"Your reasons for being a merc are obviously very different from mine,'' she continued warningly. "I work from my feelings, my intuition. Evidently, you're just the opposite. While we're on the topic of why we're here, why don't you tell me why you joined Perseus.''

"That's none of your business," he insisted doggedly.

"Oh, yes it is. If we're going on this mission together, I have every right to know.''

Breathing hard, Craig turned away from her. "It has nothing to do with this mission.''

Choking back her fury, she whispered, "What are you running from, Talbot?''

He spun around, eyes blazing. Sabra stood like an avenging angel in front of him. It was the look in her eyes, lustrous with compassion and the need to understand him, that was nearly his undoing. Something deep inside him moved, cried out. He squelched the sudden desire to tell her exactly what he was running from. But the compassion in her eyes was genuine. She was concerned about him. About his ghosts. A bitter bile coated his throat and mouth. "You don't want to know," he rasped harshly.

Without thinking, Sabra reached out, wrapping her fingers around his lower arm. His skin felt chilled, as cold as the look in his eyes, the sound of his voice. "I don't care what you tell me. It won't change my mind about you.'' She tightened her warm grip on his arm as he tried to pull away. "No! No matter what you say, I know you care about Jason, about this mission! Come with me, Craig. Please. Maybe somehow I can help you with your past—with your fears, whatever they are. A team is only as strong as the trust two people share. You know you can trust me—I see it in your eyes. You know I won't let you down, and I know you're the same way. I trust you, even if you don't trust yourself.''

With a snarl, Craig wrested his arm from her grasp. "That's the trouble," he said in a shaking voice. "You've never been hurt in the line of duty, Sabra. It makes you starry-eyed, idealistic and full of hope." He jabbed his finger at the map of the islands on the wall. "I'm gonna tell you something—this mission could get us both killed. Drug dealers place no value on life. Jason could already be dead, for all we know. You're waltzing into this situation like Joan of Arc on a charger, thinking you're going to save the day." His mouth tightened as he grabbed her arm and gave her a small shake. "The hell with the idealism. Forget wanting to save the world. I won't go in there with you unless you let me call the shots. You're a risk taker, and I'm not. I've been shot at too much, seen too many men die around me. I don't want to end up that way, and I don't want my partner ending up like that, either."

He monitored the amount of strength he used on her arm, Sabra noted through reeling senses. Craig's eyes were wild looking, haunted, the past overlaying the present and their situation. She stood very still, intuitively understanding how deeply shaken he was by whatever nightmare he'd experienced. Sweat stood out on his furrowed brow, his voice trembled with emotion and his hand was damp against her skin.

"I won't," she said in a low, steady tone, "jeopardize you or myself, Craig. I don't see myself as saving the world. I've had one partner for five years on high-risk missions, and neither of us has ever been hurt. I think that says something, don't you? How many partners have you had since joining Perseus?"

He released her, fighting the urge to simply throw his arms around her, drag her against him and hold her, as if doing so could keep at bay a world that was closing in on him. Craig looked down, startled by the calm in her husky voice. Just her firm, steady nature was pulling him back from that uncontrolled emotional edge that haunted him, especially in the dark hours of the early morning. Swallowing hard, he honed in on her voice letting it soothe him, tame his frantic fears, release him from the grip of his sordid past and the debilitating shame that accompanied it.

"I've had four partners." He saw the shock in her eyes. "Look," he said defensively, "how many partners you have says nothing." It did, but he wasn't about to admit it to her. In fact, Craig was surprised and pleased to hear Sabra had had only one partner. It told of a good, reliable, steady relationship. Something he'd never had with any of his partners.

"Why don't you have a partner now?" he demanded.

"Terry had a heart attack in Prague. He's alive, and he's going to recover, but he'll never be able to work again, at least not in our business."

"I see. . . ." Craig turned away and took a deep, shaky breath.

Sabra waited in the silence, feeling the tension, seeing it in every line of Talbot's body. He stood like a man already beaten. Why? She had so many questions for him, yet she knew she didn't dare ask. Right now, her only concern was to get him to agree to the mission, though a huge part of her was afraid of him. How could she stay in the same hotel room with him, night after night? Being close to Craig was unleashing every emotion, good and bad, she'd ever experienced, and that was frightening to Sabra. But she knew she had to forsake her own misgivings and put Jason's life first.

"Do you have brothers or sisters?" she asked softly.

"What?" Craig looked at her warily.

"I just wanted to know about your family, whether you had siblings."

"Do you?"

She accepted his challenge. Okay, if Talbot wanted her to open up first, she didn't have a problem with it. "I'm an only child. I never had brothers or sisters, though I wanted them. What about you?" she persisted.

Craig stared down at his leather shoes and shrugged. "I have an older brother and a younger brother."

"Oh, you're the middle child." She smiled a little, hoping to disarm him. "So were you the mediator?"

"I don't know."

"What does your older brother do?"

"Dan is a captain in the Marine Corps. He's a legal officer." Craig pulled out a chair. His knees were shaky, and he felt as if he was going to fall. He sat down heavily.

Sabra walked to the chair opposite him. She sat down slowly, smoothing the cinnamon silk over her thighs. "An attorney. That's impressive. What about your younger brother?"

"Joe runs the family trading post and grocery store on the Navajo reservation," he said darkly, picking up his now-cold coffee and taking a slug of it.

"So, two of you went into the Marine Corps?"

"Yes. So what?"

"My father is a general in the army, and when I was young, I realized he wanted a son to follow in his footsteps. As I got older, he transferred into the Mossad. Shortly after getting my degree in college, I joined the Mossad, too. My father wasn't very pleased about me entering the spy business, but I wanted him to be proud of me." Sabra smiled sadly as Craig lifted his head to stare at her. "I spent three years there, but he kept influencing my assignments, so I quit. I came to Perseus because I liked Morgan's philosophy that getting the work done was what counted, not the gender of the worker. I've been here five years, and I nearly lost my life three different times. Maybe I'm lucky, I don't know."

Craig snorted. "Everyone's luck runs out eventually in this kind of work," he muttered, his anger dissolving in spite of himself beneath her soothing voice.

"Yours did, didn't it?"

He nodded, unable to give verbal acknowledgment to the truth. Her eyes were large with sympathy, and he felt as if he wanted to drown in them, to pull her to him and absorb her natural strength and confidence. "Someday," he said, "you'll hit bottom. It happens to everyone. It's inevitable."

"I've never denied that fact," Sabra said quietly, holding his tortured gaze. "I know that what I do could kill me."

"Then why do you do it?"

"Because people need help. Right or wrong, Craig, I feel I have something to offer Perseus as a mercenary. I'm good at what I do, but I'm not arrogant about it, nor do I fool myself into thinking I'm impervious to a bullet, which could take my life at any time."

He shook his head tiredly. "This is a crazy world. We're crazy."

"I don't think so. I'd like to think that what we do is important, if only to the people we help and to the families waiting for their safe return. We aren't in the line of killing. Our job is to save."

"It doesn't matter," he said flatly, all the life draining out of him. "Nothing matters much anymore."

"I know you just lost your partner. I'm very sorry."

He grimaced and looked down at his cup. "Yeah, so am I. She was a sweet kid. Idealistic. *Like you.*"

Sabra refused to be baited on that point, realizing that he was slowly giving in to the idea of taking the mission. It wasn't like her to rub salt in anyone's wounds, and it was obvious Talbot was not only wounded, but hemorrhaging from something that had happened in his past. That was why he felt so disconnected from the world in general. Her father had been the same way after the war.

"Will you help me?" Sabra asked gently. "Will you come with me on this mission, Craig?"

His mouth contorted. His hands tightened around the mug. The silence deepened. Finally, he lifted his head and held her warm gaze. "If I had an ounce of sense, I'd tell you no."

She managed a grateful look. "Then I'm glad you don't have that ounce of sense."

Sitting up, Craig squared his shoulders, trying to throw off the weight that perpetually saddled them. "Don't be. If Jennifer was alive, she'd tell you the personal hell I put her through." His eyes darkened and his voice dropped in warning. "I'm hell on everyone, Sabra. You'd better protect yourself from me, because if we go in together, you'll come out of this either wounded or dead."

Chapter Three

Badly shaken by the warning, Sabra said nothing as Jake knocked lightly on the door. She saw Talbot pivot, breathing hard, his fists locked at his side. Jake looked at Talbot as he entered, then at her, and halted in the doorway.

"It sounds like a damn war going on in here," he muttered. "What have you decided?"

Talbot glared at Randolph. "I'll go."

"And you can follow Sabra's orders?"

"I'll follow them as far as I think they should be followed."

Jake grunted and walked into the room, Killian and Wolf behind him.

Sabra swallowed hard, wishing her heart would settle down. They had no more than closed the door and sat down when the phone rang. The unexpected sound shattered what was left of her nerves. Talbot was back in his place opposite his shadowed gaze trained on her. He made her nervous and frightened yet strangely excited at the same time. Why this crazy quilt of feelings. She had no time to seek an answer. Jake answered the phone.

"Laura? Yes, we've got a team in place. No... I don't think you should meet with them. You're fragile enough under the circumstances. Yes, Sabra is going—it's as we discussed."

Sabra saw Jake's scowl deepened. "Laura, I don't think—" He slowly settled the receiver in its cradle and looked gravely at them. "Laura is coming over. She wants to meet and talk with both of you."

"She's just hurting herself all over again," Sabra whispered in a strained tone.

"That's what I tried to tell her," Jake said irritably, waving his hand in frustration. "She says she has something Jason will want."

Instantly, Sabra realized it was Jason's favorite stuffed toy, the gray squirrel she had mentioned earlier. "Maybe it's better this way," she said.

"It's not," Talbot retorted sharply. "Morgan never allowed his wife into his affairs at Perseus—and with good reason. I don't want to see her. What are we supposed to say—don't worry, we'll get your son back? We can't promise that, and that's what she'll want to hear."

Glaring at him, Sabra said, "We can promise we'll try."

"Promising anything is bad news and you know it."

"Laura isn't a client. She's the owner's wife. I'd say it's a little different this time around." Again, Sabra wanted to slap his insolent face. How could Talbot be such a jerk? The last thing she wanted was him hurting Laura—she'd been hurt more than enough by this tragedy already.

"It doesn't make a difference," Craig muttered, glancing at Jake. "We promise nothing."

Jake cleared his throat and moved uncomfortably in his chair. "He's right, Sabra. When Laura gets here, don't raise her hopes. The woman's walking an emotional tightrope that's ready to shred at any moment. Just let her talk. We can only be sounding boards for her fears."

Chastened, Sabra nodded. "I understand, Jake." She didn't like it, but she understood the wisdom of his request. Still, she smarted at Talbot's harsh take on life.

"Look, why don't you two go get some coffee? The rest of us will sit here and discuss a few details of the upcoming mission for a few minutes," Jake suggested.

Sabra was more than ready to leave the tension of the room. "Fine." She was at the door before Talbot had even gotten to his feet. Outside, she drew in a deep breath of air and headed to the women's rest room. Right now, she wanted to be alone. Her feelings were raging like an unchecked flood within her and she had to try and figure out why. Maybe washing her face in cold water would bring her back to reason again. Besides, with Laura coming in, Sabra wanted to be under full control. Now was not the time to show weakness; it would only make Laura worry more.

As she walked down the long, quiet hall, she wondered if Talbot was going to be an ogre to Laura. Would he give her a good dose of his version of reality, or leave her with a shred of hope? Knowing the bastard, she suspected he wouldn't give her an inch to cling to. Anger surged in her again at the thought as she entered the rest room and turned on the cold faucet at the sink in front of the mirror.

By the time she wandered back toward the War Room, Marie had returned to her desk. Sabra's heart skipped a beat as she realized Talbot was there, too, talking with her. Marie was smiling and gesturing at whatever he'd said. And to Sabra's surprise, he was smiling back! Old Sourpuss Talbot was smiling! Sabra cautioned herself not to hold such immature thoughts. This wasn't the time or place for them. She might be angry at him for attacking her on a personal level, but she couldn't afford to hold a grudge. Jason's life was at stake, and rescuing him was all that mattered.

"Sabra," Marie called in greeting, "look what Craig brought my grandson, Chris." She held up a T-shirt depicting a boat on the canal waters of Venice. "Isn't that sweet of him?" She turned and said, "You're always so thoughtful this way, Craig. You didn't have to do it, you know."

Sabra frowned. Talbot had bought a gift for Marie's four-year-old grandson? She couldn't hide her shock. Talbot flushed under Marie's warm, genuine praise, avoiding both their gazes and choosing instead to stare down at his shoes.

"How nice," Sabra said in a choked voice.

"Every mission Craig has been on," Marie said, carefully refolding the T-shirt, "he brings back some small gift for Chris."

"That's interesting," Sabra murmured. The words came out with more sarcasm than she'd intended, and when Talbot snapped a look in her direction, she realized she'd hurt his feelings. Damn! Why was she behaving like an immature teenager? She had never done so around Terry. Never, for that matter, around anyone. What was it about Talbot that drew her full range of emotions?

"Actually," Marie continued, "Chris and his parents were in here on a visit one time, and Craig happened to meet them." She turned to him and smiled. "I believe that was right after Morgan hired you, wasn't it?"

"Yeah, something like that," Craig said uncomfortably, wildly aware of Sabra's renewed interest in him. Her face had lost a lot of his sarcasm as Marie explained the circumstances. A huge part of him felt it was none of her business.

"Chris was three and a half at the time, Sabra, and he went flying toward Craig as he came out of the War Room. That little guy took to Craig like a duck to water." Marie chuckled and reached out, touching his arm. "Your first assignment was to Germany, and you brought Chris back that teddy bear. My grandson just went crazy over the gift," Marie said in a confidential tone. "Ever since then, Craig's always brought some little gift for Chris when he comes in with his report." Her eyes filled with tears. "You're so special, Craig. I hope you know how happy you make my grandson."

Craig wanted to escape Sabra's interested gaze. He squirmed inwardly as she studied him curiously. Her face had softened considerably as Marie had continued the story. Why? Had she thought he was some kind of unfeeling mon ster who hated children? Apparently so—until now. He saw confusion and then understanding come to her eyes. He turned to Marie.

"I really don't think Ms. Jacobs is that interested in all this, Marie."

"On the contrary," Sabra said smoothly, walking toward them. "I'm very interested."

Just then, Marie's intercom buzzed. She leaned over it. "Yes, Jake?"

"Are Talbot and Jacobs out there?"

"Yes, they are. Want me to send them in?"

"Would you, please?"

Marie nodded to them. "Go on in."

Relieved, Craig was the first to the door. Out of habit, he opened it for Sabra. Old ways died hard, he reminded himself. In the Marine Corps, an officer always opened a door for a woman. Times were changing, but he didn't care. Noticing the surprise in her eyes, he smiled slightly.

"What's the matter?" he taunted.

She slowed and turned to him. "I'm surprised, that's all."

"Get used to it."

Sabra held his challenging stare and started to give a flip answer in return, but decided against it. Jake and the others were listening, and she had no desire to continue to dig at Talbot. It was time to put her responses toward him away and get on with the business at hand. She seated herself and watched as Talbot shut the door, then reclaimed his seat.

Jake folded his hands in front of him and looked gravely at each of them. "We've got some real reservations, and I think we should put them on the table for discussion."

Craig waited.

Sabra frowned.

"We feel there's a lot of antagonism between the two of you. That's not good for the mission. I'm worried, frankly, that you aren't going to listen to Sabra, Talbot. Tell me I'm wrong, will you?"

Craig shrugged. "I said I'd follow her orders. If I feel there's a different way, a better one, we'll discuss it."

"Sabra, how do you feel about that?"

"I don't have a problem with communicating, Jake. It's absolutely essential on a mission like this. I want to talk everything out beforehand."

"All right," Jake said, his features reflecting a degree of mollification. He turned to Talbot. "We all have the impression you don't really like Sabra."

Craig smarted at Jake's statement. "Then you're wrong," he snapped. "I neither like nor dislike her."

"Something's eating you about her," Jake prodded. "You tell us what it is."

Wrapping his hand around his cold cup of coffee, Craig said, "I don't like her high level of confidence. It could get us killed."

Sabra glared across the table at him. "My 'high level of confidence' has often kept me and my partner from getting killed, Mr. Talbot. I think you've got this all wrong, frankly." Damn! Why couldn't she just stick to the facts? Why keep rising to his bait? Sabra closed her eyes for a second. When she opened them, she held up her hands. "Hold it. We've got to stop this bickering. I have to stop making digs at Talbot." She opened her eyes and held his blunt stare. "I don't like it that you seem too careful. That can hurt our efforts as much as going off half-cocked."

"Neither of those ways will serve you," Jake warned darkly. "You two are going to have to talk at an impersonal level with one another and hash these things out. Sabra, you're right—you can't afford to pick at Talbot. He has a different operating procedure than you do, is all. That's not to say his way is bad. It's just different from yours."

"I know that," she said irritably. "And I promise to make the necessary compromises to ensure this mission is successfully completed and Jason is returned to Laura. That's all I want, Jake."

"I know," he murmured. "What about you, Talbot? Do you think you can compromise with Sabra, if it comes down to that? Or are you going to shove your way of doing things down her throat?"

Talbot's mouth quirked. "I'll compromise, Randolph."

"Then we have your word on this—both of you," Jake said, relief now evident in his voice.

A light knock sounded at the door. He scowled. "It's probably Laura." He looked at them darkly. "Keep your war between yourselves. Show her your best side. I don't want her worrying any more than necessary."

Craig stood as a small, thin woman with blond hair was ushered into the War Room by Marie. He was shocked by her haggard appearance—and felt an unwanted pang at the sight of the small blue blanket and stuffed squirrel she clutched to her. When Jake introduced him, Laura gave him such a warm, grateful smile that he temporarily forgot everything. Her blue eyes swam with tears as she reached out toward him.

"Marie says you're wonderful, Mr. Talbot," she whispered. She gripped his hand. "I'm so grateful you're taking on this mission. Here, I wanted to give you this. This is Jason's 'blanky.'"

Craig gently took the very worn, obviously much-loved blanket from her. The figure of Winnie-the-Pooh was embroidered into one corner of the soft blue fabric, though it, too, had lost some of its color over the past five years. "Sure," he whispered, touched by her intense emotions, "we'll take it with us, Mrs. Trayhern."

"Oh…" Laura choked, pressing her fingertips against her lips and reaching out to touch the blanket one last time. "I pray you'll be able to give it to him. How upset he must be by now. Jason waited every night until his father got home. They are so close, Mr. Talbot. If—if you can give Jason this blanket, I just know it will help him. I know it…"

Sabra came around the table and gently placed her hands on Laura's frail shoulders. "We'll do our best, Laura. No one loves kids more than we do, believe me." She saw Talbot shoot her a dark look. Well, maybe he didn't like them as much as she did. Still, she felt intuitively that Craig loved children more than he let on. Why else would he keep bringing home gifts for Chris? He was such a strange, quixotic mixture of qualities, she had to admit she couldn't really read him. Talbot was highly complex—a man with a lot of secrets.

Sniffling a little, Laura patted Sabra's hand. "I know you'll do everything you can to bring Jason back to me. I know how much you love him, Sabra. Here's his favorite toy."

Sabra felt tears in her eyes and swallowed against a lump as she held the stuffed toy in one hand and gripped her friend's shoulders more firmly. "We'll bring him back, I promise you."

Embarrassed by her tears, Laura whispered, "I'm sorry, Jake. I—I know I shouldn't be here, but I had to meet Sabra's partner. I—I had to be sure...."

Jake nodded and eased Laura out of Sabra's grasp. "We all understand, Laura. You can see that Sabra and Craig are the best people for this mission."

Taking a handkerchief from the pocket of her suit, she dabbed at her eyes. "Y-yes, I do see that."

"Come on, you need to go home now, Laura. You need to rest." Once again Jake led her out of the room. Killian and Wolf followed.

The minute they were alone, Craig rasped angrily, "You had no right to promise her anything!"

At the intensity of his whispered words, Sabra felt as if she'd been struck. His eyes blazed. Taking a step back, she retorted, "It's too late to take it back, isn't it?"

Craig gripped the small blanket in his fist. "You've set her up. You know that."

"For what?" Sabra flared huskily. "I just wanted to re-assure her."

Bitterly, he thrust the blanket at her. "All you've done is foolishly raise her hopes. What if we can't get Jason? What if he's already dead? How have you helped her by being Miss Goody Two Shoes?"

"I was trying to help her, that's all!" Sabra's heart was pounding furiously in her breast. "I'm not the ogre you are, Talbot. Maybe you don't believe in hope. Well, I do! And I'm damn well glad if I can give some to Laura."

"It's one thing to offer hope," he snarled, "and it's another to promise something we may not be able to deliver. You crossed that line, Ms. Jacobs."

Breathing raggedly, Sabra held his stare. In that moment, she realized she was coming up against the hard-bitten warrior—a man who wasn't about to back off. In some ways, his harsh response was reassuring, because Sabra wondered if he had the guts to remain staunch when a situation demanded it. On high-risk missions, that kind of endurance counted. She turned the blanket in her hands. "Okay," she whispered, "maybe I did go overboard. Laura is more than an employer to me. She's been my friend for five years. I love Jason as if he were my own boy...."

Craig placed his hands on his hips and watched her face soften, heard her voice went low with pain. "I hate it when missions involve children."

Sabra looked up and was shocked to see his undisguised anguish. The change was as startling as it was breathtaking. No longer was he the avenging warrior, anger blazing in his eyes. Looking down at the blanket and touching it softly, she whispered, "I'm so scared, Craig."

Craig frowned. His hand twitched with the need to reach out and touch her. But he stopped himself. "Of what?" he demanded hoarsely.

"Of—" Sabra risked everything and looked up at him as she crushed the blanket to her breast "—of failing. Oh, God, I know how much Laura loves Jason. I know what the boy means to her and Morgan. What if—what if he's dead?" She searched Craig's stormy eyes for an answer she knew he didn't have.

"Look," he said roughly, placing his hands on her shoulders, "you can't flail yourself with that stuff. Just shut it off. We've got work to do." He gave her a small shake. "You can't blame yourself, whatever happens." He stared deep into her moist eyes. "You know that, don't you?"

Sabra felt the bite of his hands on her shoulders, felt his courage, his steadiness, for the first time. It was shocking, his touch, which communicated strength as well as gentleness. She hadn't thought Talbot possessed those qualities.

As she forced herself to look up into the deep blue of his eyes, she recognized in him a unique type of strength that was different from—and complementary to—her own. His hands were warm against her blouse, and she felt their heat radiations through the silk to touch her frightened heart.

"I—I want you to know," Sabra said brokenly, "that this is the first mission I've been on that I've had a personal stake in. I've never had a connection with the people on a mission like I do with Jason... with Laura. I felt for the families involved, of course, who hoped we could help them. But this is different, Craig."

"I know," he murmured wearily. Forcing himself to release her, because if he didn't, he was going to do the unthinkable—wrap his arms around her and crush her tightly against him—he allowed his hands to slip away. The need for Sabra, for her raw strength and courage almost overwhelmed him. Craig took a step back. "Look, I'm rummy with exhaustion. I can barely stand, and I sure as hell can't walk straight anymore. I need to get over to my apartment in Fairfax, shower, change clothes and shave."

Sabra felt bereft when his warm, strong hands lifted. She stood, swaying slightly, the child's blanket pressed tightly to her. The look in Craig's eyes startled her. Heated her. For just a moment, there had been a change from darkness to gold in their depths as he'd looked down at her. Her mouth dry, she stammered, "Why—why don't I drive you? You're too tired to drive yourself. Everything I need is here and I've had two days' rest. Maybe when we get on that flight to Hawaii, you can sleep."

His mouth twisted, and he rasped, "Planes and I don't get along, remember?" With a shake of his head, he added, "Let's saddle up. You'll drive my car for me?"

"Sure," Sabra said, gently folding the toy up in the blue blanket.

Craig was too tired to think or feel anything. "I'll give you directions. Let's go."

Sabra stood in the living room of Craig's small, one-bedroom apartment and looked around. Yes, he had furniture, but somehow the place felt empty. She spotted a couple of photographs on the television set and went over to look at them. As she leaned down to inspect them, she felt someone else in the room. Turning, she saw Craig watching her darkly. He'd come out of a quick shower, a towel wrapped haphazardly around his waist.

Sabra straightened, her pulse bounding. She hadn't been wrong about Craig Talbot looking dangerous. His chest was covered with a mat of dark hair, emphasizing his primal, animal side. His shoulders were thrown back with natural pride and grace. Her mouth went dry as she realized that the stark whiteness of the terry-cloth towel dipped provocatively below his navel, hugging his narrow hips. In a physical sense, he was beautiful, lean and very fit. Her gaze went to his arms. The pink burn scars were not only on the backs of his hands, but claimed at least half the skin up to each elbow. She wondered what terrible fire he'd been in and somehow survived. If he realized she was staring at him, he didn't show it as he rubbed at his dripping hair with another, smaller towel.

"Those are my brothers," Craig said, walking toward her. He told himself to stop—to turn around and leave. Sabra stood like a tall, graceful willow in his apartment—so wonderfully alive. He couldn't decide whether it was her exotic beauty, the sudden flush on her cheeks or the shyness in her eyes that drew him. As he realized she was blushing over his dress code—or lack of it—he smiled to himself. Should he tell her he walked around draped in a towel after every shower? That it was one of his many eccentricities?

The look in Sabra's eyes spoke of more than shyness; he saw a pleasure in them, that made him feel powerful and good. It was nice to be admired—especially by her. Still, he was touched by that shyness. Despite her many strengths, Sabra was vulnerable, he discovered. How did she balance that against the cruel realities of their work? A desire to sit down and talk with her at length overcame him as he walked toward her. She was the kind of woman he usually liked— intelligent and her own person, with a good sense about herself as a human being.

Sabra tore her gaze from Craig's beautifully sculpted form. The ache to reach out and touch him, to see if he was real—if he was as dangerous as her spinning senses told her he was—was almost her undoing. Gripping her hands together in front of her, she forced herself to turn back to the photos. She could literally feel him coming toward her as a strange, flooding warmth enveloped her like a blanket, triggering her senses. Merely standing and waiting for his approach was excruciating.

Craig draped the smaller towel around his shoulders and picked up one of the gold-framed photos. "This is my older brother, Dan, and his new wife, Libby."

He handed the picture to Sabra, and as their fingers touched, she inhaled sharply. If Craig noticed her reaction, he didn't show it. Holding the photo, she tried to concentrate on it. Dan Talbot wore his Marine Corps dress summer uniform; his beautiful bride was dressed in a pale blue suit. "They look very happy," she murmured.

Craig managed a nod of his head, wildly aware of her closeness. He picked up the faint, lingering scent of her perfume—spicy and tantalizing, like her. "Dan deserves some happiness. He went through hell with his first wife, who turned out to be a closet cocaine user for seven years of their marriage."

"Oh, no..." Sabra spun toward him and was caught by his blue eyes, which were banked with some unknown emotion as he studied her. A wild sensation bolted through her and she momentarily lost her train of thought at his smoldering inspection. How close she was to him. She merely had to lift her hand and reach out a few scant inches to tangle her fingertips in the dark mat of hair on his chest. She exhaled shakily. This man was virile in a way she'd rarely encountered.

Craig forced himself to talk. If he didn't, he was going to reach out and stroke that wonderfully rich black hair tumbling across Sabra's proud shoulders. Would it feel silky? Warm, like her? "Dan didn't know it when he married her," he said stiffly instead. "He discovered it after they'd been married a year. He went through hell and back for her. I told him there was nothing he could do to change her if she didn't want to quit. He got pretty angry with me when I advised him that the only recourse was to divorce her. But eventually he was forced to see I was right."

Sabra fingered the gold frame, trying to concentrate on the photo. She could smell the fresh pine fragrance of the soap he'd used and feel the natural warmth of his body because he was standing so close. Her voice went unintentially husky as she said, "A dose of your usual blunt realism?"

He slid his fingers through several damp strands of hair plastered to his brow. "You could say that, I guess." Craig saw unexpected panic in her eyes. Over him? Was he too close? Consciously, he stepped back, creating a safer distance between them. He longed to study her face as minutely as a scientist looking through a microscope, but didn't dare.

"Have you always had this hard sort of realistic take on life?"

"Yes." He stared down at her clean profile. Sabra had the most beautiful lips he'd ever seen. They were soft, slightly full and gently curved at the corners—and he had this wild desire to touch them with his own, to explore and savor the taste of them. Would she be pliable and as hot as he suspected? The insane urge to find out nearly unstrung him. Craig took another step back, pretending to dry his hair some more, desperate to keep his hands busy—and away from Sabra.

He cleared his throat. "My brothers are idealists, like you," he said dryly. When Sabra snapped a look in his direction, he smiled a little. "It's only a comment."

"You make it sound like a disease."

Shrugging, he said, "Sometimes it is."

She turned, holding his still-amused gaze. "I couldn't live the way you do," she said honestly. "If I didn't have some hope, some idealism, I don't think I'd survive."

"The world is made up of realists and idealists." He poked a finger at the photo. "My brother's idealism made him hang on to that marriage and suffer for nearly seven years before he got a reality check.''

"He must have loved her," Sabra said simply. "That's different from idealism. You don't just bolt and run when your partner has a problem.''

"I won't argue with that. But Dan's idealism prevented him from forcing her to get help or do something that could have saved the marriage. He dragged his feet, hoping that talking with her would help. It didn't, of course.''

"It sounds as if, in his place, you'd have dropped the marriage in a heartbeat.''

With a shrug, Craig said, "I don't believe in wasting time where I'm not wanted. His ex-wife wanted her habit more than she did him. Dan didn't want to believe that. His idealism got in the way of reality.''

Sabra set the photo down and picked up the other one. "So who's this? Your younger brother?''

"Yeah, that's Joe. Our folks retired to a small place called Cottonwood, Arizona, and he stayed on to run the family trading post and grocery store at Fort Wingate. It's on the Navajo reservation in New Mexico.''

"You two look a lot alike," Sabra said, studying the man dressed in a pair of well-worn jeans and a blue-and-white-checked cowboy shirt, a black felt cowboy hat pushed back on his dark brown hair. He stood by the store, smiling broadly, a border collie at his feet. But despite his similar features and coloring, Sabra realized Joe actually looked very different from Craig—both brothers did. What was the difference?

It took her a moment to realize that Craig looked battered in comparison to his siblings, as if he'd been beaten down by life more brutally. It was only conjecture, but Sabra instinctively felt she'd hit upon the truth.

"Joe's the joker of us," Craig said as she placed the photo back on the top of the television. "He's the wild cowboy from New Mexico.''

"And he never went into the military?''

"No, not him. He doesn't do well with too much discipline and organization around him. I think he inherited our mother's love of the land and earth. The Navajo people love him, and he's worked hard to see they have a better quality of life."

"He sounds very humanitarian."

"As opposed to me?" He saw her flush at his insight.

"Well . . . I meant—'

"It's okay," he told her, turning away. "I'm used to being the heavy in the family. Once, Joe was engaged to an Anglo." He stopped and twisted to look at her. "Anglo is how the Navajo describe a white person. Anyway, Joe fell head over heels with this Anglo teacher, Rebecca, on the res. He fell for her hook, line and sinker. When she told him she was pregnant, I laughed."

"Why?"

"Because the woman was pregnant when she met him, just looking for some idealistic jerk to marry her so she could have security and money. I happened to be home on leave, and I saw her coming a country mile away."

"Did Joe?"

"No." His mouth twisted. "She turned on her arsenal of charm, and he fell for it. I asked him if it was possible to really fall in love that fast. He said he thought so, but I warned him she wanted something from him. Something she wasn't telling him."

"So what happened?"

"I was around for thirty days, so I did a little investigating. I knew all the locals, since I'd been born and raised there. Old Doc Conner, an obstetrician from Gallup, came out to the res to see someone. On a hunch, I asked him if Rebecca was one of his patients. He said he'd been seeing her for three months, so I told Joe. He might be blind when he's in love, but he's not stupid."

"How did he take it?"

"At first he was angry with me for suggesting she was pregnant with some other man's child. We got in a fistfight over it and both ended up with broken noses. But eventually, he went to her and she spilled the truth. He broke their engagement."

"He must have been devastated," Sabra murmured.

"Yeah, he was. He really thought he was in love with Rebecca." Shaking his head, Craig said, "Love doesn't happen overnight. It takes time."

"Not always," Sabra challenged.

His eyes glittered. "There you go again—your idealism is showing. You think love is that easy?"

"I didn't say it was easy," Sabra retorted. "But my folks fell in love the moment they set eyes on each other. They've been married over forty years now, and they're still happy."

His smile was cutting. "Don't pitch one experience against the statistics, Ms. Jacobs. One out of every two marriages fails within a couple of years of tying the knot."

"Well," she said tightly, "that doesn't mean people can't fall in love quickly."

"That's romantic love, not the real thing," he drawled. Stopping in the doorway, he said, "As soon as I shave, I'll pack some clothes and we'll leave."

Sabra stood in the middle of the room feeling angry and cheated. Craig was so sure of himself when it came to love. Well, what the hell did he know about it? Very little, she was sure. With his kind of attitude, he'd probably never been involved with a woman beyond an occasional one-night stand when it suited his needs.

Sabra shook her head. That wasn't fair of her and she knew it. Wandering around the living room, she finally sat on the overstuffed couch and crossed her legs. She felt bothered by Craig's harsh view of the world. Yet his vision had helped his younger brother avoid entering a marriage based on a lie—and helped his older brother get out of one.

Maybe she was too used to Terry's easygoing ways. Terry was a realist, too, but he didn't rub his viewpoint like salt into an open wound. Talbot had so many hard edges to him. She wondered if they were edges life had placed there through experience, or ones that life hadn't yet knocked off. Either way, she felt under fire from his unyielding view. But somehow she was going to have to deal with it—and him. She rested her head in her hands. On a purely physical level, Talbot was incredibly male, a teasing masculine to her feminine desires. Yet on an emotional level, he was abrasive. Complex. Craig Talbot was highly complex, and she hadn't a clue how to handle him—or how to adequately defend her vulnerable emotions against him. What was she going to do?

Chapter Four

Sabra got up and wandered nervously around Craig's apartment. Shaken by the masculine power he exuded, she wondered if she'd assessed him correctly. Even nearly naked, he was a man no one would trifle with willingly. She shook her head, mystified by his many contradictions.

The apartment was pitifully decorated, if you could even use that word for this starkly utilitarian place. The living room held one sofa and one overstuffed chair, in an early American style, while the glass-topped table and chrome-legged chairs in the kitchen were strictly contemporary. Worse, the kitchen windows had no curtains. *Barren*. That was how the apartment struck her. The only evidence of life were those two photos on his television set.

Forcing her thoughts back to the essential business at hand, she walked back into the living room. Marie had given her a large manila envelope containing a great deal of information. The airline tickets were in there, and their hotel confirmation. Two passports gave their own first names with ''Thomas'' as a last name. Even driver's licenses in the new names, issued from the State of New York, were there. Automatically, she began organizing the credentials into her purse. Then, digging to the bottom of the big envelope, her hand touched something else, and she pulled out a small, white envelope.

What was in it? As Sabra carefully opened it, her heart dropped. Inside were two plain gold wedding bands—sized for a man and a woman. What would it be like to be married to Craig? The unbidden thought sent a spasm of panic through her, coupled with an unwanted surge of heat and desire. No question, the man appealed to her on a strictly physical level. But in every other way, he was enough to confound the wisest of women.

"Those the wedding rings?"

Sabra jumped. She'd been so intent on the rings in her palm that she didn't hear Craig approach. Angrily, she turned, upset at allowing herself for allowing her to lose the outer awareness she took pride in—and depended on. If she continued in this unaware mode, she could easily get one or both of them killed.

"I—uh, yes, they're wedding rings." Swallowing, Sabra tried not to stare as Craig came around the end of the couch. He wore a casual, short-sleeved navy shirt with white chinos, the blue of the shirt emphasizing his dark looks. Shaven, he looked less threatening, but that potent animal power still swirled around him. *He even walks like a cougar,* a little voice inside her whispered.

Craig saw shock and anger ignite briefly in Sabra's eyes. He took a seat on the couch about a foot away from her. "Well, like it or not, we're married," he said, taking up the larger, thicker gold band from her palm and slipping it onto his left ring finger. "Hmm, Marie did a good job of picking the size." The ring fit snugly, but moved onto his finger easily. Looking up, he saw that Sabra still held her ring, betraying emotions flickering in her shadowed gray eyes. He gave her a cutting, one-sided smile. "Don't worry, this isn't for real. Go ahead, put it on. It won't bite."

Sabra's palms were damp. Grimacing, she slipped the ring on. It fit perfectly.

"Not bad," Craig murmured, reaching out for the long, slender hand sporting the shiny new band. Her skin felt warm and slightly damp as he captured her fingers, admiring the ring. Her gaze snapped to his. What lovely eyes she had. Suddenly he wanted to tell her that—wanted to express her the pleasure that touching her, even briefly, brought to him. Did Sabra realize the island of calm she offered in his chaotic life? Probably not, judging from the panic in her eyes.

"You look like a woman who just walked in front of an oncoming car," he noted wryly, releasing her hand. She snatched it back and quickly got to her feet.

"It's not that," she whispered nervously, smoothing her silk skirt.

"You've gone undercover before, I'm sure. You said 'Terry' was your partner's name?"

Sabra stood a good distance away from Craig, still feeling like a target beneath his hooded gaze. She felt stripped before him, as if he could look inside her heart and read her fear—and her crazy longing for him. "Yes," she said, her voice clipped with wariness.

"I'm sure you posed as man and wife many times."

"We did."

"This won't be any different, Sabra. Quit looking at me like I'm some kind of monster who'll make you come to bed with me."

She stared at him, openmouthed. "I—I didn't think any such thing!"

His smile was sad as he rose. "Really?" he taunted softly. "I know you don't like me, Sabra. That's all right. A lot of people hate my guts. So what's new? You can add your name to a very long list." He held out his hand. "Where's our dossier?"

Hurt by his remarks, Sabra pointed to the envelope on the couch. "In there."

"Okay," Craig murmured. He pulled some papers out and studied them intently. "I suppose you've got your part memorized already."

"I'm Sabra Thomas, wife to Craig Thomas," she recited. "We're professional photographers on assignment from Parker Publishing out of New York City. They want a book on the flora and fauna of Haleakala, Maui's inactive volcano." She pointed to the envelope next to him. "Your driver's license, passport and credit cards are in there."

"This is new to me," he admitted, looking over the information. "On my assignments, we've always kept our own identities."

"In high-risk," Sabra murmured, "we never put our real identities in jeopardy."

"No doubt," he agreed, sliding the new driver's license into his wallet and taking out his own.

She crossed her arms over her chest. "Our cameras and other equipment will be waiting for us at the airline desk."

He looked up. "Do you know much about photography?"

"Not really."

"I'm surprised. You strike me as a woman who could do anything."

Sabra glared at him. "And I suppose you're a camera expert?"

"Only with your basic, all-American snapshots." He saw the pain in her eyes. "I didn't mean to hurt your feelings, so stop looking at me like that."

Sabra stood very still. Was she that readable? Scrambling internally, she muttered defiantly, "I'm not hurt."

But she was, Craig knew and he tried to modulate his tone of voice. "I'm exhausted, Sabra. I've been two nights without sleep, and I'm a little raw around the edges. Sometimes I say things that wound other people."

His apology—as close to one as he probably ever got—soothed her. "I—it's okay. I understand."

He glanced at her. "You're awfully forgiving. Are you always like this, or is it part of your wifely act for the mission?"

Tempering her sudden anger, Sabra moved to the couch and picked up her shoulder bag. "It's me. Like it or not."

He caught and held her mutinous look. His mouth pulled into what he hoped was a smile. "I like it." He liked her—way too much. Taking his various papers from the folder, he wadded up the empty envelope. "Let's saddle up. I've packed a bag. We need to get going."

Sabra walked to the door. "I'm ready." But was she? Keeping Jason's plight in front of her, she tried to ignore the reality of her situation. Once they left the safety of his apartment, they would assume the demeanor of husband and wife. She watched Craig walk down the hall to his bedroom to retrieve his single piece of luggage, tucking his ticket and passport in an outer pocket. When he returned and met her at the door, she said, "I need to understand our married relationship."

He set his bag down. "In what way?"

"Well..." Sabra hesitated. "Are we a couple that's close or distant? In the dossier, it says we've been married five years." She cleared her throat and had a tough time holding his amused gaze.

"What's comfortable for you?"

"Uh, maybe holding hands in public from time to time?"

He shrugged. "Okay."

"What about you?"

Craig placed his hand on the brass doorknob. He could see the depth of wariness in Sabra's eyes. "My parents held hands in public, kissed a little here and there and made no apology for the fact that they loved each other very much." The panic in her eyes mounted. "But," he said, "judging from your reaction, I might as well be the Hunchback of Notre Dame, so I'll keep my distance. Occasional hand-holding it will be, Ms. Jacobs."

Avoiding his gaze, Sabra whispered, "I don't think you're the Hunchback!"

"Really? You look scared to death of me, Sabra." He lost his smile. "Don't worry, I'll keep my hands off you. If there isn't a second bed or couch in our room, I'll be more than happy to sleep on the floor. That way, you can feel safe from your frightening husband." He opened the door, gave her one last penetrating look and stepped into the hall. "Come on, Mrs. Thomas. We have a plane to catch."

Sabra was quiet, mulling over a number of apologies as they sat in the first-class section of an airliner speeding across the country. They'd been in flight for over an hour and had been served food and drink. The first-class section was nearly empty, and for that she was grateful. No one sat near them, and when the flight attendant had passed, Sabra leaned over and said, "I'm sorry."

Craig had been pretending to read a magazine. He lifted his head and met her gaze. "For what?"

She licked her lips. "For what happened at the apartment. I don't think you're ugly, and I'm not uncomfortable around you. Okay?"

He saw the sincerity in her eyes. "Don't fix what isn't broken, Mrs. Thomas."

"What does that mean?" Sabra's voice was very low and taut.

Craig picked up his glass of wine and took a sip. "It's okay to admit you don't like me. I understand."

"But I don't dislike you!"

"Really?" He set the glass aside and devoted his full attention to her. Sabra had changed clothes and now wore a loose, light green silk top with dark green silk pants—completely tasteful, yet provocative as hell on her, Craig thought. She really didn't seem aware of her stunning beauty, or the grace that had made nearly every man in the airport twist his head for a good, long look at her. She had caught her hair up in a French roll with soft, wispy bangs across her brow, making her look very cosmopolitan and accentuating the emerald green earrings in her delicate ears. He had a mad urge to caress her flushed cheek as she leaned closer, her shoulder barely touching his.

"It's just that—well, I don't know you."

"I see...."

"No, you don't!" Her eyes flashed. "You don't make anything easy, do you, Craig?"

"I've been accused of that," he said agreeably. Deliberately, he reached over and picked up her left hand, then pressed a light kiss to the back of it. Her skin was soft and fragrant and suddenly he wanted to turn her hand over, run his tongue provocatively across her palm and watch her eyes grow dark with desire. Laughing at his own unexpected idealism, he released her hand as shock registered in her eyes.

Sabra jerked back her hand, her skin tingling wildly where he'd kissed it. Of all things! She looked at him angrily, her hands rigidly clasped in her lap, and saw the laughter in his eyes. He'd known full well she would overreact to his deliberate kiss. But she'd seen a pleasure in his stormy eyes, too, as he'd touched his lips to her skin. She wondered what it would be like to feel that strong mouth against hers, to explore those lips with the one corner turned slightly upward in a sad, sardonic expression.

Her heart was pounding in her breast, and she absently raised her hand to her chest, realizing belatedly that she was blushing furiously. She heard Craig chuckle and snapped her head toward him.

"What's so funny?"

"You." He smiled a little. "You don't like my touch, Sabra. I wanted to see if you were lying, and now I know the truth."

"You are infuriating!" she said through gritted teeth. "You have no idea how I feel toward you."

"The way you jerked your hand back," he rasped, leaning forward till his mouth was mere inches from her ear, "told me more than any words could ever do."

"I hope," Sabra rattled under her breath, "that you don't use the same kind of faulty judgment once we're on Maui, or we'll both be dead."

Craig eased back into an upright position, pondering Sabra's words. But if she liked his touch, why jerk her hand away? And why should he care one way or another? Something in him wanted to goad her. She invited that response, and Craig found himself wanting to kiss her again—only this time on the mouth. Well, she was right about one thing.

He had to pull his attention away from her and stay head's-up on this mission. Once they got to Maui, the games would stop and they'd get down to business. And when they got on the jumbo jet in Los Angeles, he could try to get some sleep—maybe.

Sabra tried to pretend indifference to Craig when they'd boarded the second jet. But no sooner had the jumbo jet taken off from L.A., heading out over the deep blue Pacific, than he pulled a prescription bottle out of his shirt pocket. Unlike the other flight, the first-class section on this one was completely filled. Sabra watched out of the corner of her eye as Craig opened the bottle and dropped two capsules into his palm.

Leaning over, she whispered, "What are those?"

"Sleeping pills." Craig saw the surprise in her eyes. "You got a problem with that?"

"Yes, I do."

He snapped the lid back on the bottle and slowly put it back into his pocket. "Why?"

"What if I need you? You'll be out!"

He looked around the cabin. "It's a five-hour flight. Unless there's a hijacking, I think we're safe up here."

Sabra gripped the arm of the chair between them. "Craig! Don't take those pills. Can't you sleep without them?"

He gave her a deadly look. "At one time I could. But now I can't." He popped them into his mouth and took a slug of water. The fury on her face was real. "Don't be so damned judgmental," he rasped. "I need to sleep. I'm dead on my feet. And don't you or the flight attendant touch me or try to wake me after I go to sleep. Understand?"

Sabra frowned. "No, I don't."

"I can see that." He kept his voice very low. "Look, Sabra, if someone touches me while I'm sleeping, I'm liable to strike out. I don't want to hit you or anyone else by accident. Now do you understand?"

The anger Sabra had felt dissolved. She saw a shadow in Craig's eyes, the nameless horror that stalked him. The use of sleeping pills—or for that matter, any prescription drug—

was condoned by Perseus, but sparingly as the individual situation necessitated. As tough as Craig was, she felt a sudden compassion for his plight. "You have a bad time sleeping?"

He put the seat back and tried to get comfortable. "That's an understatement. Just leave me alone, Sabra. I'll wake up before we land, on my own. Whatever you do, don't touch me."

"Okay...." Sabra was glad he had the window seat and she was on the aisle. What was it that haunted him to the point of sleeplessness? Worriedly, she glanced at him. Craig had turned to his right, facing the bulkhead after lowering the window shade against the evening light. He had crossed his arms over his chest, his back to her—to the world. Holding at bay, perhaps? Chewing worriedly on her lower lip, Sabra felt more concerned than angry. He was right, of course, that they were relatively safe on this flight. Still, what if something did happen? Craig would be too groggy to deal with it.

While the professional part of Sabra was irritated over Craig's less-than-stellar response to her concerns, her human side ached at the thought of a suffering so deep he couldn't sleep without the use of drugs. How long had he been using the pills? she wondered. She knew they became addictive at some point. And he'd drunk wine on their earlier flight. Sleeping pills and alcohol didn't mix. *Slow down,* she cautioned her cartwheeling mind. He'd had only one glass of wine.

Curiosity ate at Sabra. When she looked over at Craig, he seemed to be asleep, but she couldn't really tell. The fabric of his shirt was stretched taut across his shoulders, revealing their latent power. A hour after he'd taken the pills, a flight attendant came by with a blanket, and Sabra quickly snatched it from the woman with a smile of thanks. She set the blanket aside, afraid to place it over Craig for fear of waking him and having him come out of his drugged stupor swinging.

* * *

The noise of a chopper droned into Craig's exhausted slumber. He frowned as he heard the faint, familiar sound. *No. Not again. God, please, don't let me see it again.* He groaned, the sound moving through him like an earthquake, but the whapping blades grew closer. *Oh, God, no....* The darkness was complete. He was sitting at the controls of his helicopter, his copilot to his left, his helmet heavy on his sweaty head, as if his neck were being shoved down through his aching, tense shoulders.

His hands were slick with sweat through his gloves, and they ached and cramped as he gripped the controls. The reddish glare of the instrument panel glowed up at him as they flew through the night. Craig's copilot, Brent Summers, was droning off numbers. They were fifty feet above the desert floor, skimming swiftly through the night. SCUD missiles were everywhere and nowhere. At any moment their aircraft could be shot down by a rocket launcher from an undetected Iraqi force below. No one knew where the enemy forces were hidden in this godforsaken desert.

The helicopter shook around him. The safety harness bit deeply into his shoulders, holding him snugly against the seat. Shaking. Everything was shaking. Craig was trembling inwardly, his guts so shaky that he wanted to cry out with the fear that raced through him like a spreading, deadly disease. Two teams of Recon Marines were in the rear of his helicopter, trusting his flying abilities, trusting their lives to him. It was so dark, dark as the pit of hell. And below...the enemy below was just waiting for them to fly close enough so they could blow them out of the sky, waiting behind some camouflaged sand dune, their rocket launchers aimed.

Groaning, Craig felt a clawing sensation snake upward from his tightly knotted stomach into his constricted throat. Closer...they were getting closer.... *Oh, God, please...no, not again...not again....* He felt his throat tighten. He couldn't breathe. Struggling for air, he turned, gripping his throat and panting. The darkness was complete. He was lost. And then the screams began....

Craig sat bolt upright, gasping. He dug at the collar of his shirt with badly shaking hands and gasped for air. Sweat ran down his temples. He could feel dampness at his armpits and sweat trickling down the center of his chest.

"Craig?"

A woman's voice. *Who?* He was completely disoriented, caught up in the nightmare and groggy from the pills he'd taken. Again he heard his name. The voice was husky with concern, but he could see only darkness. Were his eyes open? Was he asleep? Awake? A hand tentatively touched his shoulder, and he squeezed his eyes shut, honing in on that gentle touch. His senses were spinning out of control. He wanted to scream along with the cries reverberating inside his head. Doubling up, he pressed his hands to his ears.

"Craig!" Sabra leaned over, sliding her hand along the expanse of his shoulders. His shirt was soaked with his sweat. He'd bent over, his arms wrapped tightly across his belly, his head shoved between his legs. Alarmed, she sat up. Three hours had passed, and he'd seemed to be sleeping deeply. Then he'd started to toss a little and had turned over suddenly onto his back. Sabra had seen the sheen of sweat on his frozen features and had heard the animal-like groan that came from deep within him. He'd started breathing hard.

Anxiously, she unbuckled her seat belt and scooted forward, leaning over him, her arm tight across his shoulders as he remained in the bent-over position. Luckily, the cabin was in near darkness, with most of the passengers asleep. Craig gasped for air. More alarmed, Sabra gripped his shoulder with her other hand.

"Craig? Craig, answer me! Are you all right?" She realized her voice was raspy and off-key. He was soaking wet! Feeling him trembling, she held him even more tightly.

"Can I be of help?" the flight attendant asked, bending over, worry on her face.

"N-no," Sabra said, "he's having a bad dream, that's all."

"I see." She straightened. "Perhaps some water?"

Desperately, Sabra nodded. "Yes." She was afraid Craig would scream or strike out, as he'd warned. But as the flight attendant left, his breathing began to even out to a series of ragged gasps. Slowly, he eased from his hunched position, his arms loosening from around his stomach. As he leaned back, Sabra released her grip on him. The look on his face terrified her. He was utterly without color, his skin shiny with sweat, his eyes open but vacant looking as he stared into the air above him, his head tipped back against his seat.

Gulping, Sabra reached out again. Would he strike her? She had to take the risk. Her fingers barely touched the scars on his forearm. She felt the tautness of his skin beneath her fingertips. Even the dark hair, which grew in uneven patches, was damp with perspiration. "Craig? It's Sabra. You're all right. You're safe," she crooned unsteadily. Her eyes never left his frozen, twisted features. The shocking change in his expression tore at her heart. She increased the pressure of her touch, gently running her fingers across his arm in a soothing motion. At least she hoped it was soothing.

"Craig?"

Craig blinked rapidly, sweat running into the corners of his eyes and making them smart. *Sabra.* It was Sabra. The nightmare slowly released him as he honed in on her husky, tremulous voice. Still, he saw nothing but darkness in front of his open eyes. He struggled valiantly to hear her voice over the shrieking screams echoing crazily inside his throbbing head. The moment she touched him, he reeled internally from the contact. Her hand was warm and steadying on his arm. As she tightened her grip, he was able to pull away from the virulent nightmare holding him captive in its unforgiving talons.

He squeezed his eyes shut and opened his mouth, taking in great drafts of lifesaving oxygen. He heard another woman's voice, but things became confused in his head as he lay there, breathing raggedly. A warm cloth touched his forehead, and his eyes flew open again. He jerked upright, pulling away from the unexpected contact.

Sabra gave a small cry and watched as Craig wrenched away, pressing himself against the bulkhead and staring at her with dark, unseeing eyes. The flight attendant had brought a warm cloth, and stupidly, Sabra had followed her suggestion of laying it on his brow. Handing the cloth back to the attendant, she told her to leave them alone, that Craig would be all right in a few minutes. But would he?

Sabra turned back to him. In the low lighting, the shadows emphasized every frozen line in his tortured face. She saw him close his eyes again, still breathing in gulps through his mouth, his hands clenched into fists against his stomach. Softly, she began speaking to him, realizing belatedly that her voice had a soothing effect on him.

"Craig, it's Sabra. You're all right now. You're safe. I want you to just sit quietly. Try to control your breathing. Breathe in and out. In and out. You're safe...safe...." Without thinking, she reached out, barely touching his cheek. His skin was clammy beneath her palm. Even as she touched him, she froze, preparing for him to lash out at her. Instead, her touch had a mollifying effect, and she saw him sag heavily against the bulkhead, his head tipping back. She maintained the contact.

She continued talking to him in a low voice, no longer caring what anyone thought; her focus was on Craig. Eventually, he opened his eyes once more. This time he looked at her. She tried to smile. "Craig?"

"Yeah..." he said roughly, his voice trembling. Sabra's touch was steadying. She kept caressing his cheek, and he absorbed her tentative strokes like a man starved for touch. Well, wasn't he? Craig wanted her to never stop touching him. She made the nightmare recede—her touch had made it let go of him a hell of a lot sooner than usual. He felt the perspiration dribbling down the sides of his face, smelled the fear sweat bathing his body. Craig hated that powerful, raw odor. Through it all, Sabra's voice remained low with genuine concern. Clinging to her dark, anxious gaze, he drowned in her eyes, savoring her life, her touch, like a greedy thief.

Slowly, Sabra eased her hand from Craig's cheek. She briefly touched his left shoulder, her fingertips trailing down his left arm until she tangled her fingers with his. He was shaking like a baby and the urge to throw her arms around him nearly undid her. She remembered his warning about touching him. Did she dare risk it? Looking deep into his nearly black, stormy eyes, Sabra didn't think so. Instead, she kept talking in a low tone, gripping his hand to give him a point of reality to concentrate on.

Gradually, his breathing calmed, and the perspiration on his face began to dry. Sabra could smell the fear around him, and her heart opened at the unknown torture he'd seen or endured. Memories of her father slammed into her, and she wondered if Craig had suffered some terrible event as he had. When Craig raised his hand to wipe his face, she released his fingers. Sitting uncertainly on the edge of the chair, she clasped her hands in her lap. The flight attendant had left a glass of water, and Sabra picked it up.

"Here," she offered, "drink this. It might help you feel better...."

Craig stared at the glass and at the hand that held it. Sabra had such lovely, slender hands. He slowly reached for the glass, his fingers curving around it, curving around hers. Her skin was warm with life, while his was cold with death. For a long moment, he gripped her fingers and the glass, holding her worried, compassionate gaze.

His mouth was gummy, with a bitter, metallic taste that reminded him of the taste of blood. Sabra eased her hand away, and he brought the glass slowly, jerkily, to his lips. The cold water was shocking to him, but he gulped it down like a man who'd been in the desert far too long. He laughed at himself. He was a man in the desert all right. A desert called hell.

Closing his eyes, he handed her the empty glass, then sank against his seat. "Just leave me alone. I'll be all right in a little while," he heard himself rasp. Though he had shut his eyes, he could feel her nearness, smell the faint fragrant scent of her skin. How Craig ached to simply turn over, slide his arms around her, draw her against him and hide from the world. His need for Sabra was so great that he felt like crying. Crying! Hardly appropriate for a marine. This was the first time since the crash he'd come even close to wanting to cry.

Craig hid in the darkness behind his tightly shut eyes, his hands gripping the arms of the chair, for a long time. Every muscle in his body was screaming with tension, the ache in his shoulders and neck particularly severe. Sitting up at last, he turned to her.

"Would you mind massaging my neck and shoulders a little?" It was the first time he'd ever asked for help. The first. He saw the care in Sabra's eyes. Her lips parted, and he knew she would do that for him. Slowly, he turned his back toward her, anticipating her healing touch. Craig knew she didn't realize just how much he needed her hands upon him. It didn't matter.

Sabra gently settled her hands on Craig's back. His shirt stretched tightly across its breadth, damp beneath her palms. She had wanted to do something, anything, to help him. But no one could be more surprised at him asking for help than she was. She moved her fingers in a light, caressing motion up his spine, then slid them across his shoulders. His muscles were rigid. Concerned, Sabra began to realize the true depth of the nightmare's effect on him.

"Just try to relax," she whispered unsteadily, her lips near his ear. "Lean back on me and I'll help you...."

Biting back a groan of pleasure, Craig surrendered to her touch as her strong, sure fingers eased the pain and tension he carried. Every stroke wreaked a magic on him he'd never experienced. As she worked the knots from his shoulders, he groaned softly.

"I'm sorry...."

"No," he rasped, "it feels good. Damn good. Don't ever stop...."

Heartened, Sabra continued sliding her hands across his shoulders, kneading and coaxing the tension out of them. Just being able to touch him quelled her worry. It was on the tip of her tongue to ask him about his nightmare, but she realized it would be poor timing. She couldn't believe that he'd taken two sleeping pills and three hours later was completely awake. What kind of nightmare could rip him out of a drugged sleep that way?

Biting her lower lip, Sabra concentrated on loosening the dream's hold on him. With each stroking sweep of her fingers, Craig leaned a little more heavily against her. He was trusting her, and that knowledge sent a shaft of hot, sweet discovery through her. Craig didn't trust anyone, she'd realized early on. But now he was trusting her—with himself. A euphoria flooded her, chasing away her fear and anxiety. Touch was underrated by Americans, Sabra had realized many years ago. Human touch was healing, and Craig was allowing her an intimacy she would never have dreamed of.

Chapter Five

"Is there anything I can do to help Mr. Thomas?" the flight attendant asked as she leaned over and smiled, her eyes trained on Craig.

"Uh, no," Sabra said, "it was just a bad nightmare, that's all." Craig was sitting up, his elbows planted on his thighs, his face buried in his hands, unmoving.

"Are you sure?"

She strengthened her voice and put an edge in it. "I'm very sure. Thanks for your help."

The flight attendant nodded and left, disappearing into the gloom of the cabin.

Sabra sat tensely, her hands clutched in her lap. What else could she do? Reach out and try to comfort Craig? Say something?

"Craig?" Her voice was low and unsteady.

Craig opened his eyes and savagely rubbed his face with his hands. Shame wound through him, along with the remnants of the horrible nightmare. Despite Sabra's ministrations, he could hear the screams echoing faintly. Feeling as if he were going insane, he rasped, "Talk to me. About anything. Just talk to me. . . ."

Sabra swallowed hard, her mind whirling. She twisted her head and looked around the cabin. Anyone who might have been awakened seemed to have gone back to sleep. She riveted her attention on Craig who remained in the same rigid position.

"When I was a little girl," she began huskily, unsure it was something he wanted to hear, "my mother would take me to Dublin to visit my grandparents. I have wonderful memories of being in their home. They really didn't live in Dublin proper, they lived outside of it on a small plot of land that had been in their family for six generations."

She looked around, then concentrated on him again. As she spoke, she saw him slowly begin to relax. "Since I was an only child, my grandparents doted on me. I remember my grandmother, Sorcha, teaching me how to knit. She was a wonderful crocheter and knitter. I used to sit by the hour on an old footstool at her feet. She would knit in her wooden rocking chair, her fingers flying, and I would struggle with a pair of small knitting needles my grandfather, Kerwin, had made for me."

Hesitating, Sabra went on, beginning to relax herself at recounting the happy memories. "Grandfather Kerwin had been a potato farmer, like his father and grandfather before him, until he hurt his back. Then he turned to carving and making furniture. He became locally famous for his rocking chairs. I remember his hands—large, with a lot of little scars on them, much like yours. I would stand in his small garage and watch him for hours as he took a piece of fruit wood and shaped it. I was amazed at how gentle he was with a carving knife or a rasp. The wood seemed to melt to his will." Sabra moistened her lips, glanced apprehensively at him and went on.

"My mother loved visiting her family. Israel is desert dry. In Ireland, she always said she felt reborn."

"How often did you go?"

Craig's voice was rough, and Sabra checked the urge to reach out and touch his sagging shoulder. Somehow, her story had helped bleed away his tension. "Well..." She hesitated, not having expected him to ask questions. "We went when we could afford it. My father was in the army, and the paychecks were small. But my mother was a wonderful seamstress. People hired her to make dresses, and she saved her money until we had enough to fly to Ireland." Lifting her hands, Sabra murmured, "I think we visited about every two years."

"Where were you born?"

"In Jerusalem."

"And did you have your mother's love of Ireland?"

Delighted that Craig was taking an interest in something other than his nightmare, Sabra said, "I was born in a hot, dry place, but I feel, in my soul, I'll always love Ireland's moist greenness. I never saw much rain until I started visiting my grandparents. I have this memory, when I was about three, I think, and it was raining outside my grandparent's home. I toddled outside, and my mother panicked because she couldn't find me." Sabra chuckled, the memory still strong. "There I was—standing outside in that pouring rain, my little hands stretched skyward for all they were worth, my face upturned, laughing. The rain was wonderful, and I felt like a thirsty sponge. My mother, of course, was upset to find me soaked to the skin and shivering, but I was oblivious. That rain just felt so good."

Craig took a deep breath. Sabra's voice was like an angel hauling him out of hell itself. Finally, he had the strength to lift his head and sit up. He could feel the cold rivulets of sweat still trickling down the sides of his rib cage, the dampness of the fabric now making him chilly. He shivered, unable to hide the response.

"You're cold," Sabra whispered, getting up.

Before he could say or do anything, she opened the overhead compartment and retrieved a blanket. In the shadowy gloom, he saw concern burning in her eyes as she leaned over and settled the blanket around his shoulders. Unable to look at her, he turned away.

"Thanks," he muttered roughly. Pulling the ends of the blanket tightly about him, Craig wished he had a warm shower to climb into. That's what he did after every nightmare, letting the water drive out the last of the inner trembling that kept him in its poisonous grip. Well, he didn't have that luxury this time, and he was feeling confused and groggy from the damn sleeping pills he'd taken earlier. Usually, when he took the pills, he could grab four or five hours sleep—enough to survive on. Tonight it didn't work, probably because of the stress of the mission and the flight.

"Better?" Sabra asked, sitting down and rebuckling her seat belt.

"Yeah," he said. "Thanks."

She stole a glance at him. "Would some coffee help?"

The corners of his mouth cut upward. "Coffee? No. A nice warm shower would, but that isn't available."

"Oh . . ." She laced her fingers together nervously. "I remember my father getting nightmares when I was growing up. Before he transferred into the Mossad, he was on the front lines, protecting Israel's borders. I think I was fourteen when he started having these horrible nightmares. My bedroom was down the hall in our small apartment, and I used to wake out of a sleep and hear him screaming."

She gave Craig a sympathetic look, noticing how bloodshot and exhausted looking his eyes had become. "The first time it happened, I leapt out of bed, thinking someone was attacking us. I ran down the hall and into my parent's bedroom and saw my mother holding my father. He—" she grimaced "—I had never seen my father cry before. I just stood there in shock, watching him weep, hearing terrible animal sounds tearing out of him. It was awful. . . ."

Craig saw the pain in Sabra's eyes. "Anyone who fights in a war gets that way eventually," he muttered, wiping the sweat off his brow and allowing his elbows to rest on his long thighs. He felt weak, with even the effort of talking draining him.

"At the time, I didn't realize that," Sabra admitted quietly. "My mother, bless her heart, told me to go back to bed, that Father was all right and that things would be fine. The next morning, before I went to school and after my father had left for work, she tried to explain what had happened. I remember crying because I was so frightened.''

Craig twisted his head to look in her direction. "And despite that, you joined the army.''

"In Israel, everyone has to join the army for a period of time. I served at a kibbutz as a communications specialist. Kibbutzim are like outposts, and the work wasn't dangerous.''

"Did you want it to be?' Craig's gaze clung to her soft, shadowed features. How beautiful and calm Sabra looked. He wanted to turn and bury his head against her breasts and just be held—if for a little while. She fed him strength— something that had never happened between him and any woman before. Stymied, he kept his hands where they were.

"No, not really. My father's nightmares were many, and over the years, I learned to sleep through them, because my mother was always there to help him when he woke up from them.''

"You don't have nightmares?''

Sabra raised her eyebrows. "Not often.''

"I would think with high-risk missions, you would.''

"Maybe it was because of my partner,'' Sabra offered quietly. "Terry was a wonderful teacher. One of the first things he taught me was to talk about anything and everything that bothered me. If I was scared, he wanted to know about it. I think he realized that talking helped bleed off some of the adrenaline that built up over the stress of whatever had to be accomplished.''

"He was older?''

"Yes, he was forty when I was teamed with him.''

"You were like a baby to him.''

She smiled a little. "I'm sure I was. He used to tease me that I was awfully green around the edges.''

"Was he a merc all his life?''

"Yes. He told phenomenal stories of his adventures before joining Perseus. Originally, he'd been in the British Army, part of a very secret and elite commando troop. After that, he kicked around the world, getting hired out by small countries, and I'm afraid he did a lot of killing.''

"Have you?" He held her startled look.

"No."

"And yet you're in high-risk."

"Usually that means we're liable to get shot at or killed, not that we're doing the killing, Craig. I couldn't do that. That's why I like Perseus so much—we're in the business of rescue, not murder."

He stared at her. "Have you been shot at?"

"Yes, a number of times." She held up her hand and pointed to a small, round scar on her forearm. "A bullet went through me there. I was lucky. It could have hit a bone and shattered my arm."

"How did it happen?"

"The first year I was with Terry we were trying to rescue an American child from kidnappers in Italy. He was the son of an American diplomat. The U.S. government called Morgan and asked for help, though the Italian police and the CIA were trying to locate the son, too. Terry was very good at finding local contacts. He speaks at least eight languages fluently, including Italian. An old man in a village outside of Rome gave us reliable information. We found the child at a villa owned by a mafia leader in that country. Under cover of nightfall, we scaled the walls and saved him. During the escape, the guards discovered us and started shooting." She shrugged. "I took a hit climbing over the wall."

"What did you do?"

"Nothing, at the time. I felt a sting on my arm. I was carrying the boy and Terry was behind me, returning fire. We made it down a hill to where our car was hidden in an olive grove, and took off. It was dark, and I was so concerned about the boy's safety that I honestly didn't think anything about my arm until much later. By dawn, we reached Rome and returned the child to his parents. It was only afterward, when Terry pointed to my arm, that I realized I had been bleeding."

"Did you go into shock then?"

"Actually," Sabra whispered, avoiding his gaze, "I did something very embarrassing."

"What?"

"I fainted."

"Not an abnormal reaction."

"I guess not, but can you imagine? I'm supposed to be this tough mercenary, and I take one look at my bloody sleeve and drop like a ton of rocks to the floor." Laughing quietly, Sabra added wryly, "I found out later that Terry picked me up and carried me to a chair and plunked me down. They called an ambulance, and I remember waking up in it on the way to the hospital. Terry was with me, holding my hand, reassuring me I wasn't going to die. Later, I found out it was little more than a flesh wound, and I was embarrassed by my reaction. At the time, it seemed a lot worse to me."

"Experience teaches you to minimize or maximize your reaction."

Sabra nodded, absently rubbing the small scar on her arm. "That's what Terry told me. I was in the hospital, and when he came to visit me the next day, I started to cry. I mean, this was no small amount of weeping. I felt horribly embarrassed at my lack of control over my emotional state, but Terry just laughed. He assured me it was a healthy reaction and encouraged me to keep on crying as hard and long as I wanted."

"He sounds like a good man."

"He is. I hope," Sabra murmured, "you can meet him someday."

"Maybe," Craig muttered. "First we have to survive this mission."

Nervously, Sabra picked at her slacks. "Craig?"

He turned, seeing the question on her face. "Look, I'm not the talking type. I don't want to discuss what happened to me."

"But—"

"No."

She saw the flat glare in his eyes; the warning was clear. "Then answer me this—do you have to take sleeping pills every night in order to sleep?"

"Yes. So what?"

Her lips curved downward. "You can't do that on this mission, Craig. From the time we land on Maui, we have to be alert. If you take those pills, you might not hear something that could save our lives. I can't be expected to stay up and be alert enough for both of us. I'm going to need your help."

"I don't think we've got to be on guard twenty-four hours a day. We have to be heads-up when we check out the estate, but not back at our hotel room."

"You're wrong," Sabra said forcefully. "If Garcia even suspects us, he could send his men there to kill us."

Holding up his hand wearily, Craig rasped, "Let's discuss this later. Right now, all I want to do is try to get a little more sleep."

Chastened, Sabra realized belatedly it wasn't the right place or time to discuss the issue. She knew better. Terry had taught her the importance of timing talks. "You're right."

Craig lay back in his seat. "I hope I don't wake up like I did before. If I do, just talk to me, okay? It helps."

She managed a strained smile. "Sure...." Sabra watched him turn on his side again, his back to her, the blanket wrapped tightly around him. She felt such an urge to lean over, gently stroke his tousled hair and reassure him that everything would be all right. But she couldn't do that. Worriedly, she leaned back in her chair, wrapped her arms around herself and closed her eyes.

Sleep wouldn't come. Part of her waited for Craig to have the nightmare again, while another part of her searched frantically for the reasons behind his responses. Something terrible had happened to him, and judging by the violence of his reactions, not too long ago. Did the burn scars on his hands, arms and cheek have anything to do with it? The scars still looked relatively fresh. Sabra sighed and tried to clear her mind. In two hours, they would land. Perhaps the magic of Hawaii's ephemeral beauty would ease his pain. She hoped so.

A policeman in civilian clothes—a bright Hawaiian print shirt and white cotton slacks—met them shortly after they'd

retrieved their luggage. Sabra had spotted the man immediately as they'd walked to the luggage area to wait for the
items. He appeared Chinese in heritage, with short black
hair and dark brown eyes that were constantly roving,
missing nothing. Craig was groggy, and Sabra walked
closely at his side, remaining alert for both of them. They
had no weapons, because it was against the law to carry
them onto the islands.

The crowd of tourists who had been on the flight milled
around them. Children cried from being awakened too early.
Jet lag was compounded by the fact that it was 3:00 a.m.
Hawaiian time, and Sabra felt exhaustion pulling at her, but
forced it away. The warm dry air of Hawaii felt good, almost reviving, to her.

As soon as they'd retrieved their luggage, the same man
she'd noticed made a beeline toward them. Automatically,
Sabra went on guard, unsure if he were friend or foe, and
put herself in front of Craig. She felt him stiffen and become intent behind her.

"What?" he demanded.

"That man," she said in a low voice, keeping her eyes on
the approaching figure, "is either a cop or a hit man."

Craig squinted against the lights, groggy and not at all
alert. Gripping Sabra's arm, he forced her to step aside.
What the hell was she doing, putting herself between him
and potential danger? He used enough force to let her know
that and saw the anger leap to her eyes as he drew her aside.

"You're not my shield," he growled.

Sabra rubbed her arm where he'd gripped it. Before she
could say anything, the man stopped in front of them.

"I'm Detective Sam Chung." He dug out his badge case
as inconspicuously as possible and held it open to their inspection. "You're from Perseus, right?"

"Yes," Sabra said, "we are."

"Great. Come with me."

Sabra gave Craig a glare and jerked up her single piece of
luggage, hefting photographic equipment in her other arm.
He glared back at her and did the same. Together, they
braved the crowds of excited tourists and headed outdoors.

Maui's early morning warmth struck her full force. She inhaled deeply as she hurried to keep up with the short, wiry detective. Overhead, stars twinkled in a soft ebony sky. Palm trees hugged the asphalt road around the airline building, starkly silhouetted against the glare of the area lights.

Chung opened the trunk of his car. The parking lot was comparatively empty this time of morning as they settled their luggage in the compartment.

"Once we get in the car, I'll give you weapons that are registered with us," he told them in a low tone. "Then I'll drive you to the car-rental area, where you can pick up your vehicle."

"Good," Craig said, shutting the trunk. "Let's go."

Sabra climbed into the rear seat, while Craig sat up front with Detective Chung. The policeman was in his forties, but he looked much younger, a toothy smile in place as he turned and laid his arm along the back of the seat to speak with both of them.

"We still don't have conclusive proof that Jason Trayhern is at Garcia's estate. We haven't tailed any of Garcia's men, because we don't want to arouse suspicion." He reached into his pocket and handed Craig a piece of paper. "Here's a detailed map of Garcia's estate and suggested locations where you can set up your camera equipment to watch for the boy. There are two hills you might use. One is pretty steep and rolling, with lots of eucalyptus trees and tall grass to hide in. The other hill is pretty brushy, with shrubs and fewer trees, so you'd have to be more careful. Both are about a mile from the estate, right off the Kula Highway. Most of the traffic stops at nightfall, so you don't have to worry too much about headlights interfering with your infrared equipment."

"Does Garcia have any idea we're around?"

"No," Sam said, shaking his head. "We know who his guards are, and there's been no unusual activity. We're fairly sure Garcia isn't on to the fact that we know something. We've deliberately stayed away from his area. We have a police cruiser that normally drives the road to Kula daily, so we've maintained that schedule but nothing more." He reached into the glove box and handed Craig an envelope. "There are photos in there of Garcia's hoods, the boys who do the damage, as well as some of his chauffeur, the maids and other people in his employ that we've managed to photograph over the years. His hit men have criminal records, so their photos are real clear. The rest tend to be surveillance shots, so they can be a little fuzzy."

"It's good to have these," Craig said.

Sabra leaned forward. "Is Garcia at his estate now?"

"As far as we know. If he leaves by jet, we know it."

"How?" Craig demanded.

"Garcia keeps a Learjet at this airport. He uses it to fly to Honolulu on the island of Oahu, then takes a commercial flight from there to the Mainland or wherever he's going."

"I see," Craig said.

"But," Sam added, "Garcia also has a helicopter with long-range fuel tanks. So he could fly from his estate to any of the other islands, leaving his Learjet behind. We may or may not know about those flights."

Frowning, Craig said, "By federal law, he has to file a flight plan."

Sam chuckled. "Listen, there are so many interisland flights here, the FAA can't track all of them down. Yes, the small airline companies do file flight plans, but these helicopter businesses don't. Most of them have commercial trade. For instance, there's a helicopter service in Kula that offers flights up to the Haleakala crater and the rest of the island. They don't file flight plans."

Sweat broke out on Craig's brow and he wiped it away with his fingers. "Do you have a photo or ID on the helicopter he uses?"

"Yes. It's all in there. You'll probably see it on Garcia's private landing pad at his estate, anyway. If you want my opinion, I think it's going to take you three or four days of surveillance to find out anything."

"I don't disagree," Sabra murmured. "Sam, can you take us to the rental agency? We're really exhausted."

"Sure." He pulled two weapons in leather holsters from beneath his seat. "You're going to need these. Both are registered with our department. When we get your luggage out of the trunk, I'll give you some boxes of ammunition." He frowned. "Garcia jets between Maui and his Caribbean kingdom frequently. He's been here for a week this time. Usually, after two weeks at the most, he'll fly out of Maui, then return a month or two later. If the Trayhern boy is with them at Kula, you may not have much time."

"If Garcia tries to take the boy on his Learjet, will we have your help to stop the flight?" Sabra asked as she carefully checked out her weapon, making sure it wasn't loaded. She saw Craig handling his similarly.

"Of course," Sam said. "We'd like to nail him on kidnapping charges and put his rear in prison for a long, long time." He handed Sabra a radio. "This will put you in touch with us twenty-four hours a day. The thing is set on a special frequency, so transmissions between us can't be detected. If you see anything, call it in. We have a special SWAT team unit standing by in case you need help."

"If things go as planned," Craig said, slipping on the shoulder holster and positioning it beneath his left arm, "we'll break into Garcia's estate, grab the boy and get out without detection."

"Good luck," Sam snorted. "Garcia's got goons carrying submachine guns all over his estate. Look, I'm not saying you can't do it, but if you see the boy and can't get to him, we'll get a search warrant and go in."

Craig nodded. "Fair enough. Let's get going."

Sabra was too tired to appreciate the beauty of the Westin Hotel at Kaanapoli. It was a sumptuous place, with expensive Oriental carpets and a huge waterfall right outside the registration area, nearly empty at four in the morning. She stood fighting off tiredness, looking around the deserted place as Craig checked them in, but saw only a few hotel clerks.

"Aloha, Mr. and Mrs. Thomas," the desk clerk said with a smile. "We'll have your luggage taken up—"

"No, we'll carry it," Craig said tersely, picking up the plastic key card for their room. "Thanks." He turned to Sabra. Shadows lingered under her glorious eyes. He forced a smile he didn't feel. "Let's go, sweetheart."

Sabra nearly choked on the endearment, but forced a returning smile as she picked up the photographic equipment. "Of course, darling."

The carpeted hall was filled with expensive sculptures and paintings from around the world. Sabra felt as if she were in the Louvre in Paris than in a hotel. The brass elevators at the end of the hall ran quietly. Craig punched the button, one of the doors whooshed open and they quickly stepped in. Once the doors had shut, Sabra leaned wearily against the wall as the elevator sped upward.

"I'm so tired I could sleep on my feet," she muttered.

Craig nodded. "You take the bed."

She nodded. The doors opened and they stepped out on the twelfth floor. The halls were eerily quiet, all the guests asleep. Craig slid the card key into the door and opened it. The room was a suite, with a huge picture window facing the Pacific and overlooking the hotel beach. The aqua curtains were filmy looking, part of a decor comprised of soothing pastel colors. Sabra placed her luggage on the huge bed.

Craig dropped his luggage in the smaller room, which sported a couch, a coffee table, two overstuffed chairs and a refrigerator.

"Why don't you take a shower?" he suggested, walking back into her bedroom.

Sabra put her finger to her lips. First she wanted to check out the room for electronic bugs. She moved from lamp to lamp, checking them out, top to bottom. Then she crossed to the phone and unscrewed the receiver. She ran her fingers along the window, but found nothing. She saw Craig frowning at her, as if disapproving, but she didn't care. First things first—she had to make sure there were no hidden devices, including cameras in the ceiling, watching them. She wondered if Craig had ever made such a search, because he just stood there and watched her as she made her efficient rounds.

The bathroom seemed clean, too. Craig entered and shut the door behind him, then gripped her arm and moved her to one side while he leaned into the shower and turned it on, full force. The sound of falling water filled the huge, tiled room.

"What are you doing?" Sabra demanded, wresting her arm away.

"What are *you* doing?"

"Checking the place out. What did you think I was doing?"

"I could have done that. Why don't you get showered and go to bed?"

"It's my responsibility, Craig, to make the place is safe for us." Sabra was relieved to see Craig knew enough to turn on the shower to create noise to cover their conversation if there were bugs. She saw his face darken.

"Okay, so it's checked. So how about getting that shower and going to bed?"

She hesitated. "What are you going to do?"

"Reconnoiter a little. I'll be in and out of the room for a few minutes. I want to check where the emergency exits are—things like that."

"Okay. . . ." She slipped past him and opened the door. Just being with Craig in such a small space made her feel unaccountably panicky. She'd seen the burning look in his eyes as he'd studied her, and despite her best intentions, her gaze had lingered too long on his strong, male mouth. Swallowing hard, she fled into the main room.

Dawn was barely crawling up the horizon, revealing the still-dark Pacific Ocean, as Sabra closed the drapes to prevent morning light from spilling into the huge bedroom. She'd taken a hot, relaxing bath, washed her hair and pulled on a pale pink silk nightgown that fell to her knees. She'd loaded her pistol and placed it beneath the pillow next to hers. She could hear Craig in the next room and had deliberately left the door open. She heard his suitcase unzip and realized he was unpacking.

Walking to the connecting doorway, she saw him throwing his folded clothes into a dresser near the couch.

"Craig?"

Craig turned. His eyes narrowed. Sabra's hair fell in glossy waves around her shoulders. Recently washed, it glinted in the low light, framing her face. His heart sped as his gaze moved downward. Her silk nightgown lovingly outlined her every contour. He started to take a step forward, but forced himself to remain where he was. He could see the swell of her small breasts outlined by the smooth fabric, the front of the nightgown curving in a graceful scooped neckline to reveal smooth skin. An ache filled him. He longed to walk over, slide his hand across those finely outlined collarbones and trail a series of hot kisses downward until he met the softness of her breasts.

"*What?*" The word came out harsh.

"I—I'm done in the bathroom." Nervously, Sabra said, "I'm leaving the door open between our rooms. I don't think it's a good idea to shut it, do you?" She felt the smoldering intensity of his gaze burning through her nightgown, scorching her breasts. The look on his face was primal. His eyes burned with desire—for her. Unconsciously, she touched the nightgown. She hadn't meant to tease him. Terry had never given her this kind of look. Her mouth went dry as she plainly read the hunger in his face. Shaken, she whispered, "I'm sorry. I should have worn my robe...."

"No," Craig whispered thickly. "It's all right." He turned away, forcing himself to stop staring at her tall, slender form. The ache in his lower body intensified to a painful level. Every inch of her spoke of beauty and grace, and she wore the silk nightgown like a lover's hand. He wanted to run his own hand over her hills and valleys, experience her softness, her giving way beneath his exploration. Savagely, Craig reminded himself his feelings were a one-way street. Sabra didn't desire him as he did her. Somehow he had to quell his need of her.

Feeling the familiar flush flow into her face, Sabra turned and fled. Her body seemed heated wherever his gaze had touched her. Switching off the light, she quickly crossed to the bed and threw back the covers. She heard the door to the bathroom open and close. Sabra took a long, unsteady breath. What was going on here? Why did she feel so trembly every time Craig looked at her? She slipped into bed and turned her back toward the door, embarrassed at her stupidity. She had a robe. Why hadn't she worn it when she went to talk to Craig? Obviously, he was upset with her.

As exhausted as she was, Sabra couldn't fall asleep right away. She heard the shower being turned on full force. At least Craig would get the shower he'd wanted so desperately. Her heart twisted with compassion. He was a man chased by invisible demons—and how badly she wanted to comfort him. Turning onto her back, she stared up at the darkened ceiling, a bone-deep weariness finally forcing her lashes closed. How much she'd wanted to kiss him! The thought was heated, filled with promise and panic. Turning angrily onto her side, Sabra pulled the covers up over her shoulders and sighed loudly. Not since Josh had she thought of a man this way. For so long, men had ceased to exist in her life—until now. Until Craig.

The thought sent Sabra sitting bolt upright in bed. Clenching her fists in her lap, she released a ragged breath. What was wrong with her? She pushed several thick strands of hair away from her face. She was acting like a lovesick teenager. But her feelings were real and vibrant and clamoring to be heard and acted on. Even Josh had never made her feel this way, she admitted grudgingly. No man had.

Great, all she needed was to be attracted to trouble like Craig Talbot. And he was trouble with a capital *T*, no doubt about it. He wasn't anything like Josh. In fact, he was the opposite, closed up tighter than a proverbial clam. He was an introvert, going beyond her own range of shyness. He wasn't a talker, and he was abrasive to her feelings. He was a man on the run, and she had absolutely no experience with someone like that. Josh had had goals in life, dreams he wanted to fulfill and he'd known exactly where he was going. Sabra didn't think Craig had any dreams—or hopes.

Maybe she was wrong, Sabra chastised herself as she lay back down on her left side. Just because she'd seen hunger for her in his eyes didn't mean he liked her. A man could want a woman on a purely physical level. The idea that Craig might not really like her—probably didn't, when it came right down to it—made her feel pain as never before. She had an attractive body and face—that's where his interest lay. Well, that was hardly an excuse to give in to her own desire for him—which went beyond physical superficialities.

He did have such a wonderful mouth, though, with strong, well-shaped lips. She wondered again what it would be like to press her mouth to his. Would he kiss her hard? Claim her as if he owned her? Or would it be a gentle kiss, filled with exploration and tenderness? Groaning, Sabra put an end to her wild fantasies. It was time to go to sleep and stop thinking about the difficult, complex man in the room next door.

Craig slowly walked toward Sabra's bedroom. He'd taken the longest shower of his life. Water dripped from his hair, and he absently toweled it off as he halted in the doorway. From the light that came from his room he could see Sabra sleeping, a pale blue sheet draped across her hips and waist. Her hair pooled around her, and he had to fight an urge to walk in and look more closely at her as she slept. Checking his idiotic desires, Craig turned away. He couldn't have Sabra anyway. He'd seen the revulsion in her eyes.

Switching off his light, he dropped the damp towel on the coffee table. The other towel rode low across his hips as he padded over to the sofa. He'd found a blanket in the closet and a spare pillow. Now he threw them on the couch in a makeshift bed, then went to the door and made sure the dead bolt was engaged. His eyes stung from lack of sleep, and his head ached as if hammers were pounding his temples. Sleep. Precious sleep. That was all he needed—and the last thing he was likely to get.

Ambling back to the couch, he loosened the towel and allowed it to drop to the carpeted floor, then tugged on light cotton pajama bottoms. Sitting down, he shook out the blanket. His pistol lay on the coffee table. Leaning over, he took it out of the holster, fed a bullet into the chamber and put the safety back on. Placing it gently on the carpet near his head, he lay down.

Everything was quiet. Sabra had opened the window in her bedroom earlier, and he could hear the waves crashing on the beach outside the hotel. The sound was lulling, and he closed his eyes. If only he could sleep. If only... Now was not the time to take any more sleeping pills. Sabra was right: Garcia could already have staked them out—could be watching and waiting for the right moment to nail them. His eyes drooped closed, as if weighted. Without the pills, he knew he'd spend hours tossing, turning, moving between raw wakefulness and the terror of the nightmare. God, if only he could get up, slide into the bed and draw Sabra to him, he was sure he could sleep for the first time in two years. She could give him the solace to surrender to the darkness.

Craig's mouth tightened, and he turned onto his side, burying his head in the soft pillow. Maybe if he pretended Sabra was in his arms....

Chapter Six

By concentrating on the image of Sabra's face and recalling her soothing voice, Craig found an element of comfort in his usually chaotic night. Soon his fear of the nightmare returning had dissolved, and he plummeted into a deep sleep. He'd always been a vivid dreamer, but this time his dream visions were of something beautiful: Sabra. Her expressions fascinated him—the quirk at the corner of her mouth when she was irritated or didn't quite agree with him, the lowering of her thick, black lashes when she was shy, and, more than anything, the changing of her gray eyes from light to stormy and dark.

He was lost in her small gestures and the way she used her hands when talking. Moment by moment, he reexperienced her touching him, massaging the tension from his shoulders and back. She'd been strong yet gentle, monitoring the pressure as she coaxed the rigidity out of his muscles....

On some far boundary of his peripheral senses, Craig heard the blades of a helicopter. No. It couldn't be. In his sleep, he struggled to shut out the approaching sound, which sent an icy shaft of fear through his gut. Sabra's touch, her face, began to dissolve, to be replaced by the *whap, whap, whap* that grew louder, closer with every passing moment.

Groaning, Craig turned over. *Not again. No...* The sound intensified, and he began feel the tiny tremblings a helicopter pilot experiences when his bird starts up. The vibration began in his booted feet and, like small currents of electricity, moved up his legs, into his thighs. As the blades whirled faster and faster, he could feel his whole body swinging in time with them, until he became a part of the machine and it a part of him. Where did flesh and blood leave off and cold steel begin?

Craig felt sweat running down his temples from beneath his helmet. He was gripping the controls through wet Nomex gloves. He always sweated on a dangerous mission— everyone did. Lieutenant Brent Summers, his copilot and one of his best friends for three years, called off their altitude.

It was dark, so dark out. The reddish glow of the control panel glared up at him, while before him stretched endless desert.

"We're in Iraqi territory," Summers warned.

"Indian Country."

Summers laughed, but the sound was strained. "Yeah. Got to watch for those arrows, buddy."

Wasn't that the truth? Only this time the arrows were rocket grenade launchers. Craig compressed his lips, feeling moisture form on his upper lip. He had a wild urge to scratch at his temple, where the sweat tickled unmercifully. He couldn't, of course. Both hands were fully involved on keeping his aircraft straight and level.

The machine vibrated around him, vibrated with him, and he felt the heart of it beating in time with his own pounding heart, which was throbbing with unleashed adrenaline and fear. Behind him was their precious cargo: two marine reconnaissance teams they were to drop close to the enemy line. Their mission: to destroy their defenses and put such a scare into them that they'd hightail it and run. What Craig had heard about the elite Republican Guard was that they weren't cowards; they'd stand and fight.

They flew lower, and Craig strained his eyes, trying to focus on the screen located at the front of his helmet, revealing through a series of radar images the rolling desert dunes, now dangerously close. He could hear Summers's altitude information, the twenty-five-year-old's voice tighter than usual. This wasn't a practice run. No, this was for real. They'd already made one run—and had a harrowing close call—but had managed to drop their human cargo at precisely the right place and time.

This was the second run, different and more dangerous, as far as Craig was concerned. He knew the men of these recon units. They had come from Camp Reed, where he was based, and he'd trained nearly a year with them—dropping them off, picking them up. Always before they'd been training runs, with no real danger beyond him screwing up at the controls and crashing them into a hill. It was his greatest apprehension—his only one. Still, he was known as the pilot in his squadron who took the most chances.

He'd been the only pilot willing to dangle his chopper dangerously close to some high electric power lines in order to rescue a Recon who had busted his leg in the middle of nowhere. He'd hung in midair as the man was hoisted to safety, then had flown him to medical help at the nearby base hospital.

Craig concentrated so hard on the all-terrain monitor in front of him that he felt as if his head might explode with pain. The hills of Camp Reed were far different from the shifting sand dunes of Iraq. The winds here were haphazard, constantly changing the dunes' height and size. There was no such thing as stable terrain in this war, he thought as he felt the harness bite deeply into his shoulders, his hands cramp as he gripped the controls. Desert Storm was a crap shoot, in his opinion.

His mind shifted back to the cabin and his precious cargo. He'd gone drinking and carousing with these Recons. The man who had broken his leg last year was Captain Cal Talbot—not related, but since they shared a last name, Craig had volunteered for the rescue. It had been a windy day, and a gust could easily have thrown his chopper into the high-tension lines. After the delicate rescue, his friendship with Cal had begun. Now they were closer than brothers, and Cal was back there with his men, greasepaint concealing their white skin, wearing the most technically advanced equipment in the world, ready to be dropped behind enemy lines.

Cal was married. Craig had visited him at the Camp Reed hospital when Cal's wife, Linda, had delivered their second beautiful red-haired daughter. Craig had stood outside the window of the maternity ward with Cal while his friend cried and laughed, pointing to the tiny girl wrapped in a pink blanket. He'd stood, big hands pressed against the glass, smiling with pride and telling Craig they were going to name her Claire, after Craig's mother, with the middle name Lynn, after Linda's mother.

Craig had been dumbstruck that Cal and Linda would name their new baby in his honor. But Cal had laughed, brushed the tears out of his eyes, and put his hands on Craig's shoulders and told him they'd wanted to do something to thank him for rescuing his miserable neck that day he'd broken his leg and nicked an artery out in the bush.

"But," Craig rasped, shaken, "I didn't do anything anyone else wouldn't have done."

"Hey," Cal chided, sliding his arm around his friend's shoulder and pointing to the baby in her crib, "if it hadn't been for you, Talbot, I wouldn't have been here to make that kid, much less see her born. No, Linda and I wanted to surprise you. We can't name her Craig, but when I found out your mom's name was Claire, we thought it was the next best thing." Cal turned, tears in his eyes. "To remind us of the man who risked his life to save mine."

Craig stared openmouthed at Cal, not knowing what to say or do. "Well...no one has ever done something like this for me..."

Patting him on the shoulder, Cal released him. "That's okay, pardner. In my book, you're the best damn leatherneck pilot there is. There are three things I love more than life in this world, and that's my wife and my two daughters." He poked a finger at the window, becoming very serious. "Craig, you don't get it, do you? You're standing there with that funny look on your face again. There are pilots and there are *pilots*. I've flown with you nearly two years now at Reed, and you're the best. Why shouldn't I honor you in some way? That little girl will know why she's named Claire when she can understand it all. She'll be proud, too, the way Linda and I are of you."

Craig felt embarrassment mixed with a deep satisfaction as he stared down at the tiny baby with the thick thatch of red hair. Cal stood by him, sharing a profound, awed silence as they watched his daughter sleep.

"You know," Cal said in a low, off-key voice, "I was never much one for kids. At least, not until I met Linda and married her. I came out of a pretty rugged family—my folks got divorced, and I was a pawn between two war camps after that. I told Linda I was afraid to have children, but she convinced me otherwise. She came out of a real stable family, just the opposite of mine. She was one of six kids. Can you imagine? Six kids?"

"No, I can't," Craig answered.

"Big family," Cal said with a laugh, "and a happy one. When Linda got pregnant with Samantha, I freaked. I was afraid I couldn't be a good father. I was afraid I'd end up like my old man, a kind of absent shadow, you know? Linda just laughed at me. I remember the first time she took my hand and pressed it against her belly to feel Sammy moving. I was kneeling next to the couch, and I just busted into tears, of all things. I mean, to feel that little thing inside her moving around... Man, it was a miracle or something."

Craig stole a look at his friend's somber profile. "What do you mean?"

Chuckling, Cal said, "From the moment I felt Sammy kicking, I began to lose my fear. Linda had a lot of long, serious talks with me. Yes, I'd be absent from time to time because of my Recon work. But at least I'd be home after my watch. By the time Sammy was born, I wasn't panicking anymore."

Propping his hands on his narrow hips, Cal grinned proudly. "Linda helped make the transition from wild bachelor to father easy for me."

"That's saying a lot," Craig teased. He knew Cal had been known by the nickname Wild Man, earned in his earlier years in the Corps.

Sighing, Cal pressed his hands against the glass again. "Look at her, Craig. Isn't she tiny? So perfectly formed? Isn't she a miracle? Claire lived nine months in Linda and look at her. She's so pretty."

It had been hell on Craig to watch Linda and Cal kiss one last time at the Camp Reed airport before he and his team had boarded the transport plane that would eventually take them halfway around the world to a staging area in Saudi Arabia. Craig had been part of that deployment, and he'd hugged Linda goodbye, too, feeling very much a part of her and Cal's extended family.

"Bring him back home safe to me, Craig," Linda had whispered as she released him, tears in her eyes. "Please take care of him—for all of us."

Choking back tears that lodged in his throat, Craig rasped, "Don't worry, Linda, I will."

"Here, kiss the girls. You're practically their uncle." She lifted two-year-old Sammy into his arms.

Craig smiled at the carrot-topped little girl, who was a spitting image of her mother.

"'Bye, Uncle Craig." She'd thrown her small arms around his neck and hugged him as hard as she could with her tiny strength.

"'Bye, sweetheart," he'd whispered, kissing her on the forehead and blinking back tears as he gently set her down next to her mother. He didn't dare look into Linda's tear-swollen blue eyes as he eased three-month-old Claire from Cal's arms. The tiny pink bow in Claire's hair made her look even more feminine.

"Say goodbye to your goddaughter," Cal had said, slapping him on the shoulder.

Babies, Craig had discovered, always smelled good. Sometimes they smelled of baby powder; sometimes their skin possessed a sweet fragrance like a newly blossomed flower. He never got over that fact, and he loved to hold Claire close, to inhale her special scent. Claire was wide-awake. Though she had Linda's red hair, she had her father's big green eyes and gorgeous smile. Craig couldn't help smiling back as the baby reached up with one of her pudgy little arms, her fingers opening and closing against his shaven face.

"She's going to be a beauty," Craig confided in a strained voice.

"Just like her mama," Cal murmured proudly. "A real heartbreaker."

Craig pressed a soft kiss to Claire's ruddy cheek. Her skin was so delicately soft, so unmarred by life. He carefully returned the blanketed form to her mother's waiting arms. Turning on his heel, he'd whispered goodbye to Linda, unable to stand the look of anguish in her face any longer. As he walked toward the ramp of the plane, he knew Cal was holding her, saying goodbye to her one last time. He felt the weight on his shoulders, knowing that Cal's life, and that of the other Recon teams, would be in his hands once they got over there. The fear of losing them, of destroying families' lives, ate at him....

The shuddering, shaking of the helicopter continued to vibrate through Craig. He hated the darkness. He hated even more the unknowns of this second mission. The two teams were to be dropped very close to Republican Guard lines—much closer than the first teams. They were nearing the drop zone. The muscles in his body were so tight with tension that Craig felt like one huge, painful cramp. He kept praying that nothing would happen. *Let them land safely. Let them—*

"Look out!" Summers shrieked, gesturing to the right in warning.

Craig had only seconds to react. Out of the corner of his eye, he saw a flicker of light, the illumination of one of the thousands of sand dunes surrounding them. A grenade launcher! They were flying at five hundred feet, dipping up and over one dune, down into the valley then up and over the next. Called "flying by the nap of the earth," it required hard, tense maneuvering. Crashing was always a possibility, and Craig counted on avoiding that by sheer concentration, flying as he'd never flown before. But the one thing he couldn't avoid, and couldn't allow for in advance was a direct enemy attack.

The grenade hit the chopper even as Craig jerked the controls, sending his aircraft up and away. *Too late.* An earsplitting explosion sounded above him, and he knew the grenade had struck the main rotor. He heard a sharp cry from Summers and the copilot slumped forward, held in place by the array of harnesses. Craig felt pain, shut his eyes and jerked his head to one side, away from the main explosion. Hot metal tore through the cabin, shredding everything in its path. The aircraft jerked upward, mortally wounded. And then it began to spiral, tail first, toward the desert below.

Frantically, despite the fires igniting all around him, igniting on his protective clothing on his arms, Craig tried to stop the flailing fall of his aircraft. He heard shrieks in his earphones. He heard Cal's voice booming above the rest, yelling at his men to prepare for a crash landing. The bird tumbled out of the black sky toward the black ground. Wildly, Craig tried to use the controls to stop the tail-first slide toward the sand. It was impossible! The grenade had not only shattered the main rotor above them, but shrapnel from the explosion had cut through the cables that would have allowed him some control over the wounded bird.

Craig was jerked violently from side to side. He felt the bird inverting from the tail, falling slowly over on it's port side. He heard the shrieks and screams of the men in the rear. They had no safety harnesses on them; they merely sat on nylon web seats, waiting, just waiting. He knew they were being thrown around in the cabin like marbles being thrown into a huge, empty room.

Below, he saw the fire highlighting the sand here and there. He saw hot pieces of metal plummeting down before them, lighting their way. Craig knew he was going to die. They were all going to die. In those seconds before the helicopter crashed into the three hundred foot sand dune, his entire life ran past his widened eyes, as if in slow motion.

Everything slowed as Craig tried to brace himself for impact, screaming at the others to do the same. The aircraft struck the sand on its left side. Craig was jerked violently downward, but the harness held him in place, probably saving his life. They had a lot of fuel on board for the long haul to the target drop zone, and it exploded on impact, hurling liquid through the rear cabin. In an instant, fire raged all around them.... The windows on the bird shattered inward, into the cockpit, sending glass projectiles hurling like bullets through his cabin. Droplets of fire rained down on him. Frantically, Craig tried to find the harness release. It was jammed! The heat in the cabin was intense. He heard the screams of men being burned alive all around him. The helicopter was still sliding downward, on the steep side of a large dune.

His Nomex gloves had been burned off his hands as he attempted to jerk the harness free. The heat and odor of fuel choked him. He gasped. The heat funneling up his nose into his mouth burned him. Both arms of his flight suit were on fire. Craig tried to think, but it was impossible. Out of instinct, out of hours of training, he reached for a boot knife that he always kept strapped to his right leg. Gripping the handle, he jerked it upward and laid the large blade against the harness that now held him prisoner. He had to get free to help Cal! The screams of the marines were pounding against his ears. The roar of the fuel fire was spreading. The heat was intense.

The aircraft jolted to a stop, and then slowly pitched over so that Craig was thrown upside down. It rested on its top, the metal wreaking and tearing as the weight of it sank downward. The fire engulfed everything. Sobbing, Craig sawed against the straps. One by one, they freed beneath the sharpened blade. He fell hard. Frantically, he worked to get Summers free. The heat was terrible, driving him out of the shattered cockpit window. Somehow, he got to his feet, ran around the copilot's side and began to saw at the harness that still held Summers. The copilot was unconscious.

Maybe dead. He didn't know. He heard screams in the chopper. Heard men pounding against the metal skin and trying to escape.

Once he dragged Summers free of the cockpit, Craig drunkenly ran around the chopper to the door on the other side. The dune was steep, sucking at his boots, slowing down his forward progress. He heard men crying and screaming, banging on the door that had been jammed shut. The main fire was between the cockpit and cabin, stopping any escape attempts from it through the shattered windows of the cockpit. Sobbing for breath, Craig saw the burned, twisted metal that had once been the door. The grenade had landed between the door and the rotor above it.

Just as he launched himself forward to try and pull the door open, the second fuel tank exploded. There was a tremendous whoosh of heat, the sound of the explosion breaking his eardrums, and a feeling of being hurled bodily through the air. Craig remembered nothing more as he was slammed into the side of the dune, unconscious from impact.

He regained consciousness maybe fifteen minutes later. He felt very weak, disoriented, and his skin feeling like it was on fire. Barely raising his helmeted head, Craig saw his helicopter burning brightly down below him, like a torch in the darkness. A cry ripped from him as he sat up. When he tried to stand up, to run back down the slope to try and help his comrades, he fell flat on his face and lost consciousness again. Much later, he regained consciousness—only this time, it was at a field hospital behind the safety of American lines in Saudi Arabia.

Craig thrashed about on the couch, twitching feverishly. He felt a horrible fist jamming through him, and the need to cry was overwhelming. He'd never cried after what had happened. Once, after he'd gotten out of the hospital, he'd gone to see Linda and her children. . . .

He retreated into a fetal position, the continuing *whap, whap, whap* of helicopter blades threatening to drive him insane. Why wouldn't the sound stop? Why? *Oh, God, just let me die. Release me. Stop the pain. Stop the remembering....*

In the midst of his tortured anguish, Craig felt a cool hand on his sweaty shoulder. He wrestled out of his tormented state, the sound of the helicopter still in his ears. He could literally feel the vibration of it, it was so close. Had his nightmare of the crash taken a turn for the worse? He heard a woman's voice, low and husky, calling his name. Despite his disorientation, Craig realized the voice belonged to Sabra.

He concentrated on her touch, her cool hand sliding gently back and forth across his sweaty shoulder. A whimper escaped his tightly shut lips as he fought to disengage from the past and hone in on the present. He would have done anything to give up the nightmare, to bury his memories of the crash forever. Sabra's touch was healing, helping him stabilize. *Just let Cal get out of it. Please, let me go. Let me survive....*

Sabra sat on the edge of the couch where Craig lay wrapped in a tight fetal position, his blanket twisted and knotted around his drawn-up legs. It was almost noon, and light was leaking in around the edges of the drapes. She'd been awakened by a helicopter flying very close to the hotel, just outside their window, along the beach. Then she'd heard a cry from the other room—Craig's voice. It had sent her flying out of bed.

Thinking he was under attack, she ran into his room, her pistol in hand, the safety off. Shocked, she saw Craig flailing around on the couch, as if fighting an invisible enemy. He kept clawing upward, reaching for something, then making slashing motions across himself. Realizing there was no intruder, Sabra put the safety back on her pistol, laid the weapon on the dresser and hurried to his side.

Though she vividly recalled his warning not to touch him, she couldn't help herself. He was in a tight knot, his arms wrapped around himself, his knees drawn upward toward his chest. He wore only light blue pajama bottoms. As full awareness surged through her, abruptly wiping away all sleepiness, she realized the cotton fabric was soaked, sticking to him like a second skin. His face looked tortured, his mouth contorted as if in a silent scream as she lowered herself beside him, her hip barely making contact with his knees. Even in the gloomy light, she could see his burn scars. They had reddened considerably during the nightmare. Lifting her hand, she reached out, her fingertips barely grazing his damp flesh. Craig was trembling, caught in the vise of something only he could see.

"Craig?" she whispered.

She saw the effect of her voice on him. His mouth eased, and he seemed to respond peripherally. Heartened, Sabra continued talking in a low voice. She wasn't sure what she said, so caught up was she in his pain. She just continued stroking his shoulder, offering him a point of reassurance within his nightmare experience.

Slowly, ever so slowly, Craig stopped trembling. His arms loosened slightly, and his knees were no longer frozen in such a locked position. Sabra pushed her hip against his thigh, forcing his long, powerful legs to stretch downward and release the rigid tension that had gripped them. She had never been able to stand seeing someone in pain. Maybe that was a weakness, but she didn't care. With her right hand, she increased her area of contact, softly caressing his bunched shoulders. There was such terrible tension in him. She placed her left hand over his badly scarred forearm, so in case he lashed out unexpectedly, she could parry the movement somewhat.

Strands of his hair stuck against his furrowed brow, and his eyes remained tightly shut, his spikey lashes flat against his drawn, pale skin. His breathing was ragged, gasping, and his body convulsed from time to time. Sabra leaned forward, her face close to his as she slid her arm around his shoulders to cradle him. To her utter surprise, the movement worked. As she curved her arm around him, Craig huddled against her, his damp face pressing against her nightgowned body.

Gently, Sabra allowed him to find her. His head nuzzled against her; one shoulder pinned her thigh. She tightened her arms, just holding him. Words continued to slip from her. How many times had her mother held her, and soothed her this way as she lay crying, searching for protection?

Something old broke loose in Sabra's heart as she leaned forward and rested her lips against Craig's damp, short hair. He needed to be held, to be protected. She had no idea against what, but that no longer mattered. Even in the throes of his tortured sleep, caught in the predatory claws of the nightmare, he'd sought her arms and the safety of her embrace like a hurt child

Craig nestled more deeply into her lap, and in that moment, Sabra felt an incredible joy fill her pounding heart. As she continued speaking in soothing tones, her lips close to his ear, she felt him relax further, his arm unwinding to follow the curve of her hip and waist. A soft smile touched her lips as his arm encircled her and tightened. He was holding her back, his face against her belly, his breathing much less chaotic now.

Minutes ran together as her world became his. With each stroke of her hand up and down his strong spine, she felt his muscles respond. The sound of the helicopter receded, replaced by the happy noises of people at the beach. The salt breeze mingled with the scent of sweat from his body. Sabra saw color return to his face, his dark beard maintaining his dangerous look even now. Out of instinct, she leaned over and placed another soft kiss against his temple. She tasted the salt of sweat tangled in the strands of his hair. His breathing became more regular, and she closed her eyes and kissed his cheek. Something miraculous was occurring, and she didn't question it as she moved her lips against him.

This time, Sabra felt Craig move, his arm tightening even more around her. She had kissed him to ease his pain, an offering of solace and love. As she trailed her lips downward, his head moved. In moments, she felt his fingers touch her jaw and guide her down—down to his mouth. Heat purled within her as his lips, strong and hungry, slid against hers. His breath brushed her cheek and his fingers tightened, drawing her down, drawing her closer. Every place her body touched his was like wildfire to Sabra. Vividly aware of his strong, guiding hand at her cheek, Sabra surrendered to his hungry, searching mouth.

She lost all sense of time and place. The sounds of the ocean crashing onto the sandy shore, of children laughing and playing, dissolved and melted into a startling awareness of Craig moving his lips powerfully against hers. His mouth was electric, molding and stamping her with his taste, his strength. A soft sigh escaped her as she felt him turn onto his back, both of his hands now framing her face, drawing her down over him. She felt the rise and fall of his chest, the thick mat of hair tantalizing her breasts through the thin silk barrier of her gown as she rested more surely against him. His mouth was demanding, and she acquiesced, understanding on some instinctive level, that he needed whatever she had to share. There was a desperation to the feel of his lips on hers, and she allowed him to drink deeply of her, taste her and take her as she'd never been taken before.

For lingering, molten moments, Sabra lost all awareness of her surroundings. When reality finally intruded on her spinning world of light and heat, she drew back, out of his grasp. Her eyes flew open and she stared down at Craig, her ragged breathing in time with his. His eyes were open, smoldering, watching her, and Sabra saw the terror in their depths—and the desire for her overlaying those fears. She felt his hands clasp her arms, as if to stop her from leaving. His face glistened with sweat, but his cheeks were flushed with life now, not drained to the pallor of death. His mouth... She groaned to herself. Craig's mouth was wonderful. She could still taste him on her lips, a tingling sensation lingering in the wake of his branding, possessive kiss. She had been right: he was a man who claimed and took the woman he wanted. He was primal—part animal, part man.

Shaken, she stared at him, a sudden sinking feeling in her stomach. What had she just done? She shouldn't be kissing Craig. He was her partner. They had a dangerous mission to accomplish. A little boy's life was at stake. With a small cry, Sabra pulled free and stumbled to her feet.

"I—I'm sorry," she whispered. She turned and fled from the room, her hand pressed to her parted lips to stop the cry that threatened to tear out of her.

Craig slowly sat up, still caught in memories of the past that were tangled with the surprising, molten present. What the hell had happened? Confused, he tried to sort out the events. He'd relived the crash. In the distance, he could still hear a helicopter. Was it his imagination? Shaking his head, he rubbed his face savagely and sat very still, his head cocked. No, there was a helicopter nearby. Had it flown near the hotel? Was that what had triggered the nightmare?

Looking around, he slowly realized where he was. He'd just been kissing Sabra. But how had it happened? Small fragments of memory started flowing back to him. His body ached like fire itself. He'd wanted Sabra—all of her—in every possible way. He wanted to lay her on the carpet, cover her with his body, plunge deeply into her, take her, love her and make her his. It was craziness!

Rubbing his face again, Craig wrestled with his demons—past and present. He could hear Sabra moving around in her room, but he was unable to see her from this angle. Without thinking, he got up, the twisted tangle of blanket falling to the carpet. He stepped over it and headed to the doorway between their rooms. Just as he got there, he heard the bathroom door shut. Grimacing, he stood, hands hanging helplessly at his side. He'd kissed her. He'd done more than kiss her, he realized as he slowly walked to the windows and pulled back the drapes. He'd taken her. Claimed her. As he stood there, bathed in the bright noontime sunlight, he looked with unseeing eyes over the turquoise Pacific and yellow sand beach below.

The room seemed suddenly stuffy, so Craig slid open the glass door and walked out onto the small balcony. Before him stretched hundreds of bright hibiscus bushes, exploding with a profusion of color, and palm trees swaying gracefully in a slight breeze. Birds sang melodically. Frowning, Craig leaned on the wrought-iron balcony railing. Families and couples moved around below, following a number of concrete paths that connected at least ten different pools within the hotel's expansive grounds. White and black swans swam in one huge pool, next to a man-made waterfall. In a smaller pool, children played on a water slide. Ducks swam in other pools. The hotel seemed to be part zoo, part water park, and definitely aimed at entertaining the hundreds of guests who could afford what it had to offer.

Craig's emotions remained elsewhere, however, hovering sweetly on his kiss with Sabra. Her mouth... He groaned and shut his eyes momentarily, reliving their wild, hot exchange. Her mouth was like a ripe, red hibiscus blossom, opening to him. She had tasted sweet and delicious, her lips sliding across his, allowing him to brand her with his essence. She had surrendered to him completely, he realized, as he opened his eyes, a stormy mix of emotions tunneling through him. Sabra had entrusted herself to him. He laughed sharply and straightened, throwing back his shoulders as if to throw off the weight he carried.

Sabra had no business trusting him. No one did—but especially not her. Why had she been sitting on the couch where he slept? Had he screamed? Called out? Grimly, Craig turned, stared into the room and leaned back against the balcony railing, his arms crossed over his bare chest. Somehow, he had to apologize for his actions. He'd seen the sorrow in her eyes as she pulled away from him—and the terrible regret. Compressing his lips, he sighed, unlocked his arms and walked back into the suite.

He could hear the shower running as he walked through the bedroom to the smaller room. Picking up the phone, he ordered breakfast and coffee. Then he picked up his blanket, folded it and placed it with the pillow on the sofa. Always, he kept his hearing keyed. What was he going to say to Sabra? The truth? No, he could never speak the truth of that horrible tragedy to anyone. Somehow, he would find a way to apologize to her.

Sabra felt the beat of her heart pick up as she quietly opened the bathroom door. She had towel dried her hair, and it hung in damp strands against the pale green blouse she'd put on. The mirror was covered with steam, and she deliberately turned back and wiped a small clearing on the fogged surface with her palm. For the first time, she dared look at herself. She felt so different after Craig's crushing, heated kiss. Leaning closer, she touched her lower lip, seeing its lush, well-kissed look. Craig's kiss had been startling. Unexpected. Wonderful.

Why was she trying to deny the good feelings that ran through her? She studied her eyes in the mirror, seeking an answer and finding none. Her cheeks were flushed a rosy color that made her look innocent. But she was hardly that. She was old enough to know what had gone down and honest enough to admit her role in it. Bluntly, Sabra told herself it was her fault the kiss had occurred in the first place.

Determinedly, she left the bathroom, her nightgown and robe over her arm. She looked around before stepping into the bedroom. Where was Craig? Hearing nothing, she moved to the bed.

"Sabra?"

She gasped and whirled around, her nightgown spilling off her arm and falling to the carpeted floor. Craig stood between the rooms, frowning, his arms crossed over his broad, masculine chest. All words fled from Sabra's mind as she helplessly surrendered to his dark, smoldering gaze. Desire was banked like hot coals in his eyes. Was she crazy? Too long without a kiss? When had she last kissed a man? *Joshua.* That had been two years ago.

She leaned down and picked up the fallen nightgown. "You startled me," she whispered, straightening, the silk gripped in her tense fingers.

"I didn't mean to," Craig murmured, walking toward her. He had changed into a short-sleeved white shirt and a faded pair of jeans. He was still barefoot.

Gulping, Sabra took a step back as he halted within feet of her. She tore her gaze from his mouth—the mouth that had claimed her, heart and soul, in one breathtaking kiss.

"I have to apologize," he said, opening his hands in a gesture of friendship. "I don't know what happened. I was asleep, and the next thing I knew, I dreamt you were there beside me, kissing me." He ran his fingers through his hair. "It shouldn't have happened...."

Sabra bowed her head and held the nightgown tightly against her. "I—I'm sorry, too. It was my fault... all my fault." She shrugged helplessly and whispered, "I heard a noise and went to investigate." Getting up enough courage to look him in the eyes, she said in a strangled tone, "I thought someone had broken into our suite."

"That's why your pistol is on my dresser?"

"Yes... I—I saw you on the couch. You were using your arms, swinging them around, as if trying to hit someone or maybe escape. I don't know. Anyway," she rushed on breathlessly, unable to stand the sudden warmth in his gaze, "I came over, thinking you were having that nightmare again, the one you'd had on the flight...." Sabra turned and went to the bed, dumping her robe and nightgown on it. She felt herself trembling. Why was Craig looking at her like that? She couldn't stand that unexplained warmth in his eyes. Wrapping her arms around herself, she turned back toward him, strengthening her voice.

"I—I did a stupid thing. I know you told me not to touch you when you were having a bad dream. I sat down and—and slid my arm around your shoulder. You seemed so tortured, Craig." She bit her lower lip and looked away. Finally, she forced the words out. "I tried to hold you, that was all. When I put my arm around you, you were still caught up in your nightmare, I think. You crawled into my arms and I just held you until... well, I felt so awful for you. You were like a hurt little boy, and I hurt for you. I leaned down and kissed your cheek...."

Craig rested his hands on his hips, studying Sabra in the uncomfortable silence. She was flushed, her gaze darting to him and away again. Feeling her nervousness, he took a step forward. "Look," he rasped, "you didn't do anything wrong. I'm not saying that. I can't separate nightmare from reality when I'm caught up in it. I thought I heard your voice. I thought..." He grimaced. "I felt your hand on my shoulder, and I thought it was some kind of crazy overlay to the nightmare." He managed a twisted smile for just a moment, the corners of his mouth deepening. "To tell you the truth, when I went to bed last night, I didn't think I'd sleep. So I replayed the words you spoke to me on the plane and remembered your touch." He shrugged. "I fell asleep. It's the first time in a long time I've dropped off that fast." He halted, realizing he was saying too much. Clearing his throat, he added, "So, you see, I thought you were a dream. I didn't know it was real, not until later...."

Rubbing her brow, Sabra whispered, "You don't have to make excuses for me—"

"I'm not trying to, Sabra." He saw the wariness in her lovely eyes and had the urge to reach out and touch her long, damp hair, to tame away some of her nervousness. "I'm just trying to tell you what happened at my end of that...kiss."

Heat flared up into her cheeks, and Sabra died inwardly. She hadn't blushed like this in years! Craig's gentle tone was undoing her, just as his mouth had unfastened the gates to a cauldron of desire hidden deep within her. She'd had no idea of the power of her desire for him until that moment, and it frightened her. "It was a stupid mistake, that's all," she found herself rattling. "Let's just forget it, okay?" But how could she? She saw amusement lingering in his gaze. The man was going to drive her to distraction with looks like that! Did he realize his impact on her? She didn't think so. What hurt most was that he was apologizing for kissing her! If he'd meant to kiss her, he certainly wouldn't be apologizing like this.

"It's forgotten," he said huskily. He pointed to the other room. "Listen, I ordered us a late breakfast. It's here. Do you want to eat something?"

Touched, Sabra shrugged. Her stomach was in knots. Her lower body felt like it was on fire. She wanted only to throw her arms around his broad, capable shoulders and kiss him until they melted into each other. Moistening her lips, she said, "I could stand some coffee."

He allowed his hand to drop to his side. "Good. Come on."

She followed at a distance, but not because she didn't trust him. Oh, no—it was herself she didn't trust. With his day's growth of beard, Craig looked devastating, and now that she'd encountered the power of his kiss, she had to be careful not to respond to his looks, to any accidental touch. Her throat aching, she tried to put her turmoil and desire aside as she stepped into his room. Breakfast had been set out on the coffee table, and Sabra realized Craig must have done it. The coffee was already poured, her toast buttered, with jam slathered across it, waiting for her.

She sat down hesitantly at the opposite end of the couch, as far away from him as she could get. "You didn't have to do this," she murmured, motioning to the toast.

"Old habits die hard," he said wryly, trying not to stare at her too long or too much. Sabra's mint green blouse lovingly outlined her contours. Her white silk pants were as loose and flowing as her glorious dark hair. Once again, Craig was reminded of a graceful willow.

"What do you mean?" Sabra asked as she picked up the toast, barely noticing its whole-wheat flavor or the rich strawberry taste of the jam. Craig's powerful presence mere feet away from her was overwhelming.

He picked up his cup of coffee. "Back home in Fort Wingate, it was my job to butter the toast and put jam on the table for everybody." Giving her a slight smile and holding her shadowed gaze, Craig said, "Everyone at our house was assigned chores. Dan made breakfast, Joe set the table and I made sure the toast was buttered and the juice poured."

Relieved to be discussing such a safe topic, Sabra took a sip of the fragrant Kona coffee. His voice sounded low and intimate in a way she'd never experienced from him before. His face appeared totally relaxed for the first time, and she was in awe at the difference in him between their first meeting and now. How much of himself had he been hiding from her? Had their kiss made this difference? Flushing hotly, Sabra put her cup back on its saucer and stared down at the toast in her other hand.

"You said," she began, trying to keep things light between them, "that you were raised on an Indian reservation?"

"Yes. All three of us boys were born at Gallup, New Mexico, about sixteen miles from the family trading post and grocery store on the Navajo reservation. We kids were more or less adopted by neighbors of ours, the Yazzies. Alfred and Luanne Yazzie had a pretty big family of their own. I think we were lucky growing up in the wilds of the New Mexico desert with the Navajo people."

Sabra nodded and forced herself to swallow another bite of toast, then take another sip of coffee. Silence descended on them, and she scrambled mentally for some safe response. But what came out of her mouth was anything but safe. "Do you think the nightmare will come back again? Tonight?"

Craig's hands stilled on his thighs. He saw the worry in Sabra's eyes and heard it distinctly in her voice. "No," he said, "I hope not." Giving her a sad smile, he added, "You've really been lucky. Usually, the nightmare only hits about once a week. The rest of the nights I'm just restless. I toss and turn a lot, but I don't remember..." His voice trailed off.

"Maybe you're upset over losing Jennifer?"

He nodded, resting his elbows onto his thighs and clasping his hands between his knees. Avoiding Sabra's gaze, he rasped, "I'm more than upset."

"Were...you two close?"

He caught the inference. Looking up at her, he shook his head. "She was a good teammate, nothing more. We'd been on assignments together the past couple months." His mouth turned down. "I guess what hurts is that Jenny was engaged to be married as soon as we got off this last mission." Running his fingers through his hair in an aggravated motion, he muttered, "If I hadn't let her tail that suspect alone, she'd be enjoying her wedding now."

"Maybe," Sabra said quietly. "Maybe not. You can't predict future events any better than anyone else. You didn't know she would get in an auto accident."

He nodded, staring at the floor beyond his hands. "Maybe..."

Sabra set the cup down. "I could walk out of here and be nailed by a car crossing the street, Craig. It could happen to anyone."

He snapped his head up, glaring at her. "I've lost people twice in my life to things like that. I'm not about to lose you the same way."

Chapter Seven

Stunned by his sudden emotional intensity, Sabra stared at him, her cup frozen halfway to her lips.

"Look," he said angrily, "I've lost people I've loved before. Good people who didn't deserve to die. I'm like a black cloud, Sabra. Bad things happen when I'm around." He avoided her compassionate gaze and rubbed his hands together slowly, feeling the pain of the admission. "I know you're supposed to be the leader on this team," he croaked. "My head knows it, but my heart doesn't. I just lost my partner. I'm feeling damned guilty about it." He raised his chin, his eyes stormy. "I'm not going to lose you, Sabra. You're too special . . . too—"

Craig caught himself and snapped his mouth shut. He'd said much more than he'd intended. Much more. Sabra set her cup down and clasped her hands in her lap. He felt her gaze on him, and heat swept into his face. "There's no sense in you trying to give me any arguments," he told her irritably, meeting and holding her gaze. *"None."*

Gently, Sabra reached out, her fingers barely grazing his arm. She felt the tautness of muscles beneath her finger- tips, felt the same heat as when he'd been in the grasp of that virulent nightmare. "Listen to me," she pleaded softly, "I'm not your past. I'm your present, Craig. You keep for- getting, I've been through a lot of scrapes and lived to tell about them. I'm not going to do anything stupid, trust me on that. I'll look both ways before I cross the street. I al- ways drive defensively." She released his arm, though it was the last thing she wanted to do. Taking a shaky breath, she added, "If it makes you feel any better, you can drive when we go up to Kula to start snooping around." The look of relief on his face was telling, and the suffering in his eyes when she'd reached out and touched him was heartbreak- ing. She'd seen tears in his eyes. Or had she?

Craig sat for a long moment, battling his emotions. He picked up his cup, because if he didn't, he was going to slide over and put his arms around Sabra. She invited that kind of intimacy, and right now, he felt exceedingly vulnerable to her—more than ever before, because of the nightmare striking two times within a twenty-four-hour period. "Thanks," he rasped, and took a gulp of the hot coffee.

"Why don't we get going?" she suggested softly, look- ing around the room. Though the suite was large and spa- cious, she suddenly felt trapped.

"Good idea," he muttered, rising. "Let me grab a quick shower and shave. Get the map and the car keys?"

Sabra breathed a sigh of relief and stood. "Yes, I'll get them." Perhaps the tension that vibrated between them would dissolve if they were out on the road doing some- thing to keep their minds occupied. As she went to retrieve her purse, she laughed at herself. No matter what she did with Craig, she would always be highly aware of him—of the charismatic power that swirled around him and of the danger he presented to her as a woman.

Opting not to wear the shoulder holster, she placed her pistol in her purse. Wearing the holster meant covering it with some kind of jacket, and with the temperature in the eighties, that was the last thing she wanted to do. Craig headed into the bathroom to shower.

"I'll go get the car," she called from the door.

"Fine, I'll meet you there."

Good. She had something to do. Opening the door, she saw a number of people, mostly families, in the hallway. She noticed both Japanese and Americans, and she heard a smattering of German from a couple ahead of her. Hawaii drew people from all over the world. And with good reason, she thought, as she took the elevator to the main level.

In the lobby, Sabra began to appreciate the unique beauty of the hotel. A huge, concrete pool stretched half the length of the place, with a man-made waterfall cascading noisily into it right outside the registration area desk. Below the falls, graceful swans and various species of ducks swam. All around the pool, hotel guests took photos of the extraordinary place, or tossed bread crumbs to the birds.

Just getting out the room helped Sabra start to unwind. She hadn't realized the tension she carried in her shoulders until she walked into the spacious lobby filled with antiques and art. Outside, a valet approached, but she waved him away, deciding to get the car herself. The sky overhead was a pale blue, with fluffy fragments of white clouds. In the distance, she could see the velvety green slopes of Haleakala. Once it was classified as a dormant volcano, but recently, she had read smoke had been spotted in the bottom of the crater, so it had been taken off the dormant list and upgraded to inactive status. More clouds circled the top of the ten-thousand-foot peak, Sabra noted as she stepped onto the asphalt driveway in front of the hotel.

The Westin was a very busy place, with a row of limousines, plus a number of Mercedes Benzes and BMWs, speaking to the wealth of the visitors. As Sabra made her way to the parking lot, she enjoyed the high, dark green bushes that surrounded the hotel. Hibiscus bloomed in colorful profusion, like miniature rainbows. Bougainvillea climbed walls here and there, and palms trees, for which Hawaii was famous, were scattered around the huge parking lot.

Sabra's instincts took over as she approached space 121, where they'd parked the white Toyota Camry they had rented. Dredging up her knowledge of car bombs, she carefully knelt down and checked under the car, especially around the doors. Sometimes terrorists placed bombs to go off when a car door was opened. She found nothing. Moving to the hood of the car, she visually inspected the opening, then ran her fingertips beneath the hood area, searching for any unusual wires.

Next she carefully lifted the hood and inspected the engine. Most car bombs were placed either in the engine compartment or on the fire wall, near the ignition.

Her gaze ranged knowingly across various areas where the plastic explosives might be placed. Though she found nothing, Sabra never relaxed her vigil as she checked under hoses and cables, sliding her fingers along them, just in case. C-4 was completely pliable and could be taped anywhere.

Finally satisfied, she gently closed the hood and went around to the car door, noting the new-car odor that lingered in the vehicle as she slid into the driver's seat. Inside, she automatically checked under the dash and in the glove box, where someone could have planted a bug to pick up their conversations. Leaning over, she visually inspected both areas. A bug could be put almost anywhere, and she knew that although she was trained to find them, one could be hidden in the light above her, or under her seat. Or in the trunk.

Popping the trunk lid open, Sabra got out and inspected the area. Often, a transponder device could be attached beneath the trunk lid, so a car could be followed with ease—either by road or by air. Finding nothing except the spare tire and tire iron, she closed the lid and relaxed a little, enjoying the warmth of the noonday sun. The wind was sporadic, tugging at strands of her hair.

Just as she was about to get back into the car, she spotted Craig walking purposefully toward her, their camera equipment in a huge canvas bag over his shoulder. His hair was dark and sleek from its recent washing, and his face was scraped free of the dark shadow of beard. He wore the same clothes as before, but with a light blue jacket to conceal his shoulder holster. To her surprise, he held a lei in one hand

Sabra reopened the trunk. Craig met her there and stowed their equipment.

"Here," Craig said gruffly, "this is for you," and he lowered the lei over her head, settling it against her neck "It's plumaria. I liked the smell of it and thought of you...." He saw the pleasure in her eyes as he gently pulled her hair away from the flowers. Just as he'd thought, her hair was not only thick but fine, like strong silk. Though he ached to thrust his fingers through the mass of it, glinting with reddish highlights in the sun, he resisted.

"Thank you," Sabra murmured, touching the waxy pet als of the fragrant white blooms.

Craig stood for a moment, watching a blush spread across her cheeks. Her eyes shone with such beauty that he forced himself to turn and slam the trunk closed. "Come on," he said. "Let's go."

Once they were in the car, heading down the long, palm tree-lined lane that would eventually take them to the high way, Craig asked, "Did you find anything?"

Sabra shook her head. "No... nothing."

Quirking his mouth, he braked at the stop sign. The only highway that traversed Maui was busy this afternoon. He wasn't surprised. Making a right turn, he accelerated until they were moving with the rest of the traffic, heading east toward what was commonly known as up-country Maui.

Craig knew that although Sabra had no doubt gone over the car with a fine-tooth comb, there still could be a bug present, so they couldn't risk talking about anything that might make them suspect. His gaze ranged from the cars ahead of them to the ones behind, particularly alert for any that might seem to be following them.

"What do you feel like doing today, sweetheart?"

Sabra smiled a little, realizing Craig was pretending for the benefit of a possible bug. "Oh, I don't know. Part of me would love to go shopping, but the other part says we should drive around and look for photographic sights for our book." She deliberately stretched her arm across his seat and touched his shoulder. The contact was pleasurable, and she watched his mouth part slightly at her unexpected contact. Well, they were married, and such touching was expected, Sabra told herself. Only Craig reacted far differently from Terry, when they'd had to play such a role. She wondered if Craig's response was real or feigned.

"Lahaina isn't far from here," he suggested.

"Mmm, let's just sort of be whimsical today. Go where our spirits take us."

He smiled a little. "Okay." Sabra's soft touch against his shoulder again set his skin to tingling. But it was all an act, he realized, chastising himself unhappily. She wouldn't be touching him otherwise. Despite the pleasure of her company, he concentrated on the traffic around him. At the last moment, he turned off onto a side street that would lead them to Lahaina, one of the huge shopping areas on Maui. No cars followed. He went down a few blocks, made a left turn and headed back out to the highway. Again on the main thoroughfare, he continued to keep watch.

Sabra couldn't relax despite the excellent job Craig was doing driving and watching. She shifted her arm off the back of the seat and clasped her hands together in her lap. The beauty of Maui was evident everywhere. Once they'd gone beyond the main business area, the four-lane highway narrowed to two lanes. On the left rose volcanic hills of reddish black lava. On the right stretched the turquoise waters of the Pacific. As they climbed in elevation, Sabra could see a good portion of eastern Maui ahead of them.

Craig remained silent on their forty-five-minute drive to Kula, a small farming community roughly four thousand feet above sea level on the slopes of the magnificent Haleakala crater. Besides the local farmers, tiny Kula boasted its share of million-dollar estates for the rich and famous. In addition, the rare flower known as protea grew in the rich volcanic soil around Kula. The foliage was thick, and the many silver-barked eucalyptus trees that lined the narrow highway leading to Kula reminded him of Australia.

Proteas poked their huge, pincushion-shaped heads up here and there in people's front lawns bordering the highway. Craig glanced at Sabra, who had pulled out a map and spread it across her lap. Without a word, she held up one finger, meaning it was one mile to Garcia's estate. He nodded and slowed down a little more. Traffic through Kula was mainly tourists, coming from or going to Haleakala, which rose above them.

Garcia's estate sat about fifty feet off the highway on their right. Craig noted that the surrounding black, wrought-iron fence was at least ten feet tall, covered with red, pink and orange bougainvillea. Palm and eucalyptus trees grew near the iron fence, both inside and out. He didn't dare slow down too much and draw attention. Sabra had raised her camera and was clicking away as they passed the huge estate. Up ahead, he saw a small road and turned left, following it. The road was dirt and very rutted. Slowing to a crawl, they climbed its dusty expanse. Slopes of knee-high green grass bracketed them, interspersed with numerous eucalyptus trees, which dominated the rolling landscape.

Finally, after nearly a mile, Craig pulled the car to the side of the road. The slopes rose around them, all part of Haleakala's lower skirts, which flared outward to encompass most of eastern Maui. Climbing out, he opened the trunk, pulled out the canvas bag and slung it across his shoulder. He saw Sabra locking the car. Their eyes met, and he signaled her to follow him up the grassy knoll, thickly covered with eucalyptus.

The day was warm and breezy, the dark green leaves of the eucalyptus swaying in the wind. The grass was tall and thick and tangled easily around Craig's feet as he carefully made his way up the slope. The rich, black soil was composed of volcanic matter ground away over millions of years. He felt Sabra move up beside him. The climb was steeper than he'd realized.

"Did you see how secluded Garcia's estate was?" she asked, slightly out of breath.

"Yeah."

"Still," she said, continuing to look around and study their position, "it's accessible."

"Maybe." Craig halted at the top of the knoll and grinned at her. "We've got a good view."

Sabra pushed strands of hair away from her face as the breeze swirled around her. Her heart was pounding from the climb as well as the elevation, but a smile tugged at her own mouth as she stood there. A thousand feet below, the road ran like a narrow ribbon, and directly across from it lay Garcia's elaborate, multimillion-dollar estate. From here they could see not only the iron fence that completely enclosed the grounds, but a huge Olympic-size pool to the left of his sumptuous house, the helicopter landing pad to the right.

"Whew," she said, wiping her brow, "that's quite a climb."

"We'll adjust to the altitude in a couple of days," Craig said, kneeling down and opening the canvas bag. "Come on, help me get this equipment up and running."

For the next half hour, they worked together in silence. The photographic equipment was state-of-the-art. When it was assembled, Sabra could see every movement on the estate as if it were mere feet away, through the lens of the high-powered camera she'd secured to a sturdy tripod. Craig anchored the tripod to prevent the gusting wind from knocking it over. They'd placed it next to a huge eucalyptus tree that provided partial cover for them and the camera. There was no doubt in Sabra's mind that the sentries would constantly check the surrounding hills for eavesdroppers such as themselves.

Finally, everything was done. Dancing sunlight slanted across the thick green grass. Craig sat down near Sabra's feet, his back against the tree, as she peered through the lens at the estate.

"We're going to have to pull half-hour watches," he said, opening his notebook and resting it against his drawn-up legs.

Sabra slowly panned the camera. "I know."

"Give me a verbal on the exterior layout."

Pleased at his efficiency, she said, "An Olympic swimming pool, regulation size, lies to the left of the house, completely enclosed by a white, wrought-iron fence. A number of lounge chairs and some tables with red-and-white-striped umbrellas surround the pool, but no people are visible.''

"Good," Craig exclaimed, writing down the information and beginning to make a detailed map. "What else?"

Sabra moved the camera gently, panning to the right. "Wait . . . I see a man, probably a guard. Yes . . . he's carrying an assault rifle . . . no, it's a Beretta 12 submachine gun.''

"I'm not surprised," Craig muttered, writing down the information.

She followed the progress of the guard, who walked slowly around the entire pool area. "I'm not, either. I was just hoping otherwise.''

"That Beretta submachine gun can do a lot of damage in a hurry.''

Sabra's heart pumped a little harder as she watched the guard. "This guy is about six feet tall, one hundred and eighty pounds. He's got black hair, brown eyes and a swarthy complexion.''

Craig looked up. Sabra's mouth was compressed. The breeze tugged at her silk blouse and pants, outlining one side of her lithe form. She was beautiful no matter what she was doing or wearing, he decided. Tearing his mind off such things, he said, "Do you see any other guards?"

"Not yet. I want to time this guy."

"I'll do it." Craig set his watch.

"He's circled the pool, and now he's heading toward the rear of the estate, toward the fence."

"He's got a circuit he's walking. Let's find out how long it is. If we get lucky, Garcia won't have too many goons on the perimeter fence."

"Maybe," Sabra murmured. "This guy is good. He walks a few feet, then waits and listens, looks around and then moves on. He's trained well."

"See any dogs?"

She sighed. "Not yet. I hope he doesn't have any, if you want the truth." Dogs made it much tougher to enter an area undetected.

"Jake said Garcia had them at his Caribbean-island estate. Why wouldn't he have them here?"

"He probably does. I just haven't seen them yet."

For the the rest of her half-hour shift, Sabra watched, giving verbal reports to Craig. To their relief, there appeared to be only two guards on duty, each walking one side of the estate. Both were heavily armed. She'd spotted no dogs, but that meant nothing at this stage of the game.

Craig closed the notepad and reached into the canvas bag. "Hungry?"

Sabra came and sat down opposite him, the huge trunk of the eucalyptus hiding them completely from any prying eyes at the Garcia estate. "A little."

He pulled out two sandwiches wrapped in plastic. "I got these at the deli at the hotel. They're both chicken."

Her fingers touched his as she took one sandwich. Sabra found herself wanting excuses to touch him. "Thanks," she murmured, unwrapping the whole-grain bread. Crossing her legs, she began munching and looked upward.

"This tree is so beautiful."

"Like you." Craig frowned. Now where the hell had that come from? He saw Sabra's eyes widen over the compliment. Just as quickly, he saw her avert her gaze. "You've always reminded me of a willow," he said gruffly, trying to cover his faux pax. "You're graceful, like this tree."

Sabra chewed on the sandwich, no longer tasting it. "I've never been compared to a willow before, but it's a nice compliment," she said softly.

"When I first saw you, I wondered if you'd taken ballet lessons or something." Craig couldn't help himself. He wanted to know more about Sabra on a personal level. He had no right—no business asking, but it didn't matter. For the moment, they were safe, and they had gotten useful information.

"I never took ballet," she said. She enjoyed watching him lean back fully against the tree, his long legs sprawling in front of him. "But I love to dance."

Craig believed it, feeling his body tighten with desire at the thought of moving with her in his arms.

"What about you?" she asked, studying him. "Do you like to dance?"

He snorted softly and took another big bite of his sandwich. "I've got two left feet. It goes downhill from there."

Chuckling, Sabra set her sandwich aside and wiped her mouth with the paper napkin he'd provided. "I don't believe it. I think you're like a lot of men—just shy about dancing."

"It's more than that."

"Prove it, then."

He raised his head and stared at her darkly. "What?"

"If things are slow tonight, and we don't find anything to act on, will you take me dancing?"

Was Sabra playing her role of wife? Or was she sincere? He probed into her wistful eyes and found nothing coy in them. Rubbing his jaw, he muttered, "Out here, you can drop the wifely pretense."

"I wasn't pretending," Sabra said. If only Craig realized how much she valued his touch. She was sure he didn't know, and the playful, bold part of her wanted more. Right or wrong, she felt something driving her to want Craig on any level she could have him. They were both single, and it was obvious he had no one in his life at the moment. Working with him, she could see he was just as professional as she was at intrigue and espionage. Whatever doubts she'd had on that score were quickly being laid to rest.

"Oh." He swallowed the last of his sandwich and threw the wrapper back into the canvas bag. A huge part of him was hungry for any reason to be with Sabra. The idea of holding her close on the dance floor was excruciatingly tantalizing—it was the ideal excuse to hold her tight and feel her contours against him. His mouth went dry as his thoughts turned to more torrid and burning possibilities.

Trying to swallow her disappointment, Sabra realized that her attraction was only one-sided. He was frowning, settling his gaze anywhere but on her as he mulled over her invitation. With a sigh, she got to her feet and brushed off the seat of her pants.

"Forget it," she said as lightly as possible, "it was just a thought. I'm not going to hold you to it, Craig." Forcing herself to move, she went back to the camera, to begin once more monitoring activity at the estate.

Stung, Craig sat where he was for a moment, feeling pretty damned foolish. He had acted like some green, tongue-tied teenager asked to his first dance by a cute girl he had a crush on, but unable to believe she could like him enough to ask. The hurt in Sabra's tone needled him. She'd offered herself to him, and like a fool, he'd frozen....

It was nearly 10:00 p.m. when Craig said, "Let's close up shop for the evening."

Sabra was sitting next to the tree, her arms wrapped around herself against the evening chill. "Good," she said through teeth that chattered. "I didn't realize how cold it would get here at night."

Craig took the camera off the tripod and knelt near the canvas bag. "Me, neither. Tomorrow night we're bringing jackets and blankets. We're going to have to time the guards' watches from dark to dawn."

"Yes," she agreed, getting up to help him with the equipment.

It took far less time to break it down than it had to set it up. In no time, Craig was slinging the bag across his shoulder. Sabra was obviously cold, her arms wrapped around herself in an effort to keep warm. He reached out, placing his free arm around her shoulders. "Lean against me," he said. "It will help warm you up."

Surprised by his sudden gesture, Sabra found herself drawn up against his bulk. "You're so warm!"

He nodded, carefully feeling the terrain beneath his feet as they started down the steep slope. "Yeah, I'm pretty warm-blooded." Hot-blooded would be more like it, but he didn't want to get into that. Sabra fell into step with him quickly, and he bit back a groan of pleasure as she flowed against him. Her arm went around his waist, and he smiled to himself. How good she felt against him, strong and supple and inviting.

It was very dark, with only a small slice of moon in the starry sky above them. Craig balanced the weight of the equipment on his shoulder, keeping Sabra tucked beneath his other arm. All too soon, they were off the grassy slope and back on the dirt road. Reluctantly, he eased his arm from her shoulders.

"Thanks," Sabra whispered, going to open the trunk. Her heart was fluttering rapidly in her breast, and her skin tingled pleasantly from the feel of his body against hers. She stepped aside so that he could put away the equipment.

"Are you warmer now?"

"Yes..."

"Get in the car and start the engine. You're still shivering."

She was, she realized, but it wasn't from the chilly evening—it was from Craig unexpectedly claiming her once again. Getting into the car, Sabra started the engine and waited for him. As he came around the driver's side, she slid into the passenger seat, deciding to let him drive.

Once in the car, Craig said, "How about we grab something to eat at the hotel?"

"Fine," she answered.

"Are you tired?"

Sabra shrugged. "Bored maybe, but not really tired. What about you?"

"Bored." He turned the car around and eased it down the road without turning the lights on. Craig didn't want to risk detection by Garcia's people. He'd wait until they were entering the main highway before he turned on the headlights.

She laughed a little. "In our business it's hours and days of boredom punctuated by moments of terror. At least, that's the way it's been for me."

Craig was focusing on the road, not wanting to run off it. Realizing that Sabra had forgotten their playacting, he said, "Sweetheart, if you're so bored, what do you say we go dancing? I think the photos we took today of the flowers are going to be pretty spectacular. Let's celebrate."

Damn! Sabra realized her laxness and, despite the darkness, gave Craig an apologetic look. What was wrong with her? She knew better. She never lapsed with Terry. Disgruntled and embarrassed, she forced a brittle laugh. "Oh, darling, I'd love to go dancing!"

"Good, we'll do it then."

Sabra knew there were so many types of bugs available that their conversation could be easily recorded from almost any distance. Fortunately, Craig hadn't blown their cover as she almost had. What must he think of her now? She was behaving like an inept beginner in a world that didn't forgive mistakes.

"I love you," he said, picking up her hand and kissing the back of it. Craig hated himself for playing the charade. Wanting to kiss her wasn't a lie, of course, but Sabra didn't know that. He heard her swift intake of breath at his gesture. And where had those words come from? Angrily, he released her hand and turned onto the asphalt highway. Switching on the headlights, he reentered the flow of traffic, which was very light at this time of night.

Sabra sat still, her fingers resting over the spot Craig had kissed. The words, *I love you,* rang in her mind and vibrated wildly in her heart. It was all a charade and she knew it. Or was it? Craig's voice had lowered to such an intimate level when he'd spoken the words, as if an animal growl—as if he were an alpha-male wolf claiming her as his mate. Shakily, she touched her brow. She was being silly. Craig had pretended in order to cover her faux pax, that was all. When she stole a look at his profile, her pulse bounded unexpectedly.

His face was rugged, his mouth deliciously firm beneath his strong nose and those hooded eyes that could look straight into her. Sabra took a deep, ragged breath. She couldn't help herself; driven by her own needs, which Craig was completely unaware of, she leaned over and placed her arm around his shoulders. "I love you, too," she whispered, kissing his cheek.

If Craig was surprised, he never showed it. As Sabra eased back, releasing him, she watched him closely. His mouth had compressed, almost as if with displeasure. Wounded, she fell into silence. It was pretend. That was all. Closing her eyes, she realized she wanted Craig's genuine attention, wanted to know how he honestly felt about her, but it was an impossible wish to fulfill under the circumstances.

Sabra knew the routine for when they got back to the hotel. They would have to scour their suite for bugs again. And even if they found none, they still couldn't be sure they weren't being monitored. It was pretend there, too. She longed for the freedom to really talk to Craig. To find out, one way or another, if he truly liked her. She wanted to tell him how his touch affected her, how his kiss was indelibly stamped upon her lips and that she longed to kiss him again.

Miserably, Sabra sank into a well of sadness. What was wrong with her? Craig was only doing his job. Desperately, she searched for a way to talk with him—honestly and openly. But they could be followed and never know it. Someone who looked like a tourist could really be one of Garcia's hit men. Sabra knew the drug cartels had sophisticated equipment that could overhear conversations anywhere. A laser beam could be aimed from miles away to pick up the vibrations of their voices through the glass of their hotel windows. Even on a dance floor their conversations could be monitored. Somehow, she would have to swallow all these vibrant, wonderful emotions. She'd thought her feelings were dead since Josh had been torn from her life. But now Craig was bringing her to life in a way she'd never experienced before.

Though Sabra yearned for time to talk with Craig, she had to be realistic. A little boy's life hung in the balance. Her mind seesawed between worrying over Jason and wondering if he was really at the estate at all. Today they'd seen no sign of him. Still, they would need to carry out surveillance twenty-four hours a day for the next couple of days before they could say for sure.

"Look out!"

Craig's voice broke into Sabra's meandering thoughts.

A set of headlights swerved, aiming directly at them. Slamming on the brakes, he yanked the steering wheel to the right, tires squealing. The lava bank loomed close. Craig felt the car skidding against the gravel of the berm. The other car suddenly veered back to its own side of the road, as their Toyota slid to a stop a few inches from the sharp lava bank.

"Sabra, are you okay?" Craig turned, gripping her shoulder. In the oncoming headlights he could see the terror on her face.

"I—yes, I'm okay." She slid her fingers upward across her right cheek. "Oh, dear..."

"What?" He unsnapped his seat belt and turned to get a closer look at her. "What is it?"

Sabra grimaced. "It's all right. It's just a little blood. I think I hit the window, that's all."

Worriedly, Craig slid his hand along her jaw. It was hard to tell much of anything in the darkness, but he could make out a small rivulet of blood trickling down from her hairline. "Yeah, you've got a cut or something. Hang on. When we get back to the room, I'll take a closer look at it."

Closing her eyes momentarily, Sabra absorbed the roughened touch of his hand against her cheek. His voice was low and urgent, filled with genuine care. Or was it pretense? Her head seemed to spin. Opening her eyes, she pulled away from him.

"Are you—"

"I'm fine!" she assured him. Shakily, he released her.

"Damn good thing we wear seat belts."

Touching her brow, she whispered, "Yes."

"Stupid jerk," he muttered, putting the car back into gear. "Probably drunk or something."

Sabra wasn't so sure. She bit down hard on her lower lip as he eased the car back into traffic. Was it an accident? Or had it been intentional?

Chapter Eight

Sabra pressed her hand to her aching forehead. The darkness was complete, broken only by occasional headlights flashing by as they drove down the main highway toward Lahaina. Had it really been an accident? She couldn't voice her fears for fear of electronic eavesdroppers. Every once in a while, she felt Craig's intense gaze fall upon her for just a moment.

Just as they reached the outskirts of Lahaina, she heard him suck in a breath of air. She twisted to look in his direction. Too late! Sabra's eyes widened enormously as she saw a car race up beside them on the four-lane highway. As it deliberately swerved toward them, she clung to the door handle and tried to brace herself for the coming impact. The first attack had been no accident! Fear shot through her. All she could do was watch through horrified eyes.

Craig yanked the steering wheel to the right. Fortunately, traffic was light, and he took the car onto the sidewalk, where it groaned and clunked, one set of wheels higher than the other. Glass shattered around them. The other car was firing at them!

"Get down!" Craig roared, wrenching the wheel to the left. The light had just turned red, but if he braked, they were dead. He heard the *ping-ping-ping* of submachine-gun bullets stitching along the side of the car. More glass shattered inward. Hunching over, he jammed his foot down on the accelerator, and the car leapt through the light. The speedometer needle rose rapidly to fifty, sixty, seventy miles an hour. He wove between the few cars, jerking a look into the rearview mirror. Were they following? He had to assume they were.

Luckily, it was night, which made them harder to tail— unless a bug had been attached to their car so they could follow it by remote control. His head spun with options. He risked a quick look at Sabra. She had bent down, her hands covering her head.

"Sabra?"

"I—I'm okay. You?"

Craig said raggedly, "I'm okay."

She sat up and twisted to look out the shattered rear window. Her breath was coming in ragged gulps. Bits of glass tumbled out of her hair and down her front as she turned back to face the road. Her heart was pounding hard in her chest. She looked over at Craig. His profile was hard and set, and sweat stood out on his face, gleaming in the oncoming headlights.

"What are we going to do?"

"They're on to us. Whoever they are," he rasped. Slamming on the brakes, he turned the car down a darkened side street to the right. Flicking off the headlights, he guided it down the rutted, dirt road in near blackness. Houses flashed by on either side of them. Ahead, he spotted another small road, and steered the car onto it.

"See anything?" he demanded.

"No," Sabra said, watching out the rear window. "Nothing."

"We've got to ditch this car."

"Yes."

Savagely, he jerked the steering wheel, aiming the vehicle down another meandering lane with very few homes along it. Pulling into a grassy area off the road, he left the keys in the car and climbed out.

"Come on," he ordered, hurrying to the trunk.

The night air was cool and still. Craig's hands shook as he pulled the trunk open and grabbed the canvas bag. He felt more than saw Sabra reach his side as he hefted it over his shoulder.

"Where—"

"Let's get away from the car," he said raggedly. Grabbing her arm, he said, "This way." He led them up a grassy knoll toward a stand of darkened trees at the top—probably eucalyptus. Right now, he wanted good, thick cover. If those were Garcia's henchmen, they'd certainly have night goggles or infrared scopes on their weapons that detected body heat. If necessary, he and Sabra could dig shallow holes, cover themselves with dried leaves and wait it out.

Sabra dug her toes into the damp, moist earth of the hillside. She felt dizzy, but shook it off, trying to keep up with Craig. The hill was steeper than she'd thought, and by the time they'd scaled it, she was breathing hard from the exertion. Following Craig into the heart of the eucalyptus grove, she looked back, but could see no one coming down the road toward where they'd left the car.

"Over here," Craig called. He gently placed the canvas bag on the ground and with his hands raked up a bunch of leaves to hide it. "Get down and start digging a shallow grave to lie in."

Sabra nodded and fell to her knees. Her fingers felt numb; her head ached. She dug quickly, finding the soil loose.

"Do you think—"

"I'm assuming they've got night goggles," he rasped, rapidly digging his own shallow trench. "Maybe infrared. We're going to have to wait them out. We can't talk, either. They may have sensing equipment that can pick us up a mile away."

Sabra steadied herself and nodded. "I'm going belly down in my grave. Cover me?"

Craig leaned over and quickly placed dirt and leaves across her legs, back and shoulders. "I'll be close by. If you see anything, just nudge me lightly with your foot. I'll do the same. I don't know how long we'll have to stay here."

Already shivering in the damp ground, Sabra said nothing. Craig had dug his trench close enough to her that if she stretched out her right foot, her toe could make contact with his arm. Trying to steady her breathing, she studied the streets below. A dog barked somewhere in the distance. She could see the lights of Lahaina not far away, the main shopping area that was lit up in carnival-like colors.

Craig was covering himself the best he could. Night goggles allowed a person to see into the night as if it were daylight, magnifying whatever light was there, so that everything looked light green or yellow. If Garcia's men had body-heat detectors, they could find them even if they missed them with the night goggles—providing Craig and Sabra were above ground or moving around. If they remained silent, they had a chance of surviving.

His mind whirled with questions. What had given them away? Had they somehow compromised themselves by their position on the hill earlier today? A bug in their suite? Was there a leak in the police department? Had the detective, Chung, given information to Garcia, acting as a paid informant and mole? Craig didn't want to think that. Sam Chung didn't seem the type. But how had Garcia found them?

He ticked off the possibilities, among them that someone at the hotel could have become suspicious. But how? Their cover was intact, as far as he was concerned. Someone in the airline watching for flights out of D.C. to Hawaii? That was possible, but not high on his list. No, Garcia's guards must have spotted them earlier today. Damn!

His mouth grew dry as he saw a vehicle make the turn off the main highway and take the same dirt road they had. It was moving deliberately, as if searching for something—or

someone. He felt Sabra nudge his arm with her toe. She'd
seen it, too. At least they were armed; but Craig didn't want
a shoot-out. He frowned, squinting as he watched the car
crawl up the road. Its headlights stabbed through the darkness, and it slowly turned onto the smaller road where he'd
parked their Toyota.

To his surprise, he saw the lights of a police cruiser suddenly switch on. It was the cops! Watching warily, Craig saw
the vehicle pull over next to their car. He felt Sabra nudge
him strongly. Could they trust the police? Should they go
down and tell them what had happened? Sweat trickled
down his temples as he watched. But how did the cops know
about this? How could they possibly know he and Sabra had
parked there? Perhaps someone in the sparsely populated
neighborhood had called the police because the two of them
had been tearing around at high speeds on back roads late
at night. There were so many possibilities. But right now,
Craig instinctively mistrusted the police.

Anxiously, he watched as two uniformed policemen got
out of the cruiser, their flashlights on, and started investigating the bullet-ridden car. They were too far away to hear
their voices, but from time to time he could pick up snatches
from the police radio in the cruiser. He felt Sabra move. No!
Risking everything, he slowly reached out and wrapped his
hand around her slender ankle. Giving her flesh a long, slow
squeeze, he tried to impress on her that it was vital not to get
up, not to move. Would she remain still?

Slowly, ever so slowly, he felt the tension in her leg dissolve beneath his hand. Good. She was going to stay put as
he had silently requested. Slipping his fingers from her ankle, he brought his hand carefully back against his side.
Chances were the cops would check out the car, then call a
wrecker to impound it. Releasing a slow breath, Craig knew
they had at least another hour of hiding in store before they
could escape.

Sabra tried to stop her teeth from chattering. The wrecker
and police cruiser had come and gone. Their car had been
hauled away. The road was again clear of any traffic. Her

head ached, and she felt the muscles of her legs drawing up
from the dampness, wanting to cramp. Just when she
thought she could take it no longer, she heard Craig slowly
rise from his trench. Leaves fell around her, then she felt his
hands upon her body, brushing the leaves off of her. Slowly,
she turned over and sat up.

"Come on," he said, holding out his hand to her.

She gripped it and felt herself being pulled upward. Diz-
ziness assailed her, and Sabra felt herself falling forward.
Before she could cry out, Craig's strong arms wrapped
around her and brought her against him. Without a word,
she sank into him, her head hurting so much she couldn't
speak for a moment. Instead, Sabra placed her arms around
his shoulders and allowed herself the momentary luxury of
resting against his strong reassuring bulk. How could he feel
so warm? Right now, she was cramping and shivering, her
teeth chattering.

Craig groaned softly and held Sabra tightly against him.
She'd flowed against him like sunlight. He was surprised at
how strong and supple she felt beneath his hands. She was
shivering, and he realized she was very cold. Beginning to
rub her back briskly with his hand, he rasped, "Just lean on
me. I'll get you warmed up in a minute."

Sabra closed her eyes and surrendered to Craig. No longer
did she try and fight what her heart wanted. She felt the
slow, powerful beat of his heart against her breasts, felt the
warmth of his breath against her cheek and the side of her
neck as he ran his hands firmly up and down her back, en-
couraging her circulation. A soft smile touched her lips as
she nestled her head against him. How wrong she'd been
about Craig. If anything, he'd acted far more professionally in this crisis than she might have. Knowing that made
her trust him even more. His hand felt good, and she automatically tightened her arms around his neck, steadying
herself against him.

Craig forced himself not to pay too much attention to
Sabra's nearness. It was close to impossible, though their
circumstances were precarious at best. A few minutes later
he felt her stop shivering and gently eased her away from

him, enough to look down into her dark, shadowed eyes. Even in the dim light, he could see the dried blood along her right temple, where she'd struck her head earlier. Not only that, but he saw tiny nicks on her neck and shoulder where the exploding glass had cut into her beautiful skin.

"We need to get help," Sabra said in a low voice. She was glad Craig didn't let her go. Instead, he wrapped his arm around her waist and kept her leaning against him.

"First, we need a room somewhere." He pointed to Lahaina below. "There are a lot of motels along the main road. We need a room for the night."

Sabra nodded. "We can't go back to the Westin. They're probably waiting for us there."

He frowned and nodded. "We can't trust anyone, Sabra," he warned. "Not even the police."

"I know," she said sadly, searching his dark, hard features. "We need to get to a pay phone, something they can't trace, and alert Perseus."

"First things first," he rasped, leading her to where he'd hidden the canvas bag. "Let's get a room, and I'll make the call. You can wash up, get some sleep, and we'll figure out what our next move will be."

Sabra moved away from Craig as he leaned down to pick up the bag. Her knees felt wobbly. She and Craig had almost died. The rush of adrenaline had long since left her. Now, she felt weak and shaky, and she wanted to cry. She knew the reaction was a normal one for her. She saw Craig hold out his hand toward her.

"Come on," he entreated softly. He saw the surprise in her eyes and managed a twisted smile. "Whether you like it or not, we're hip deep in trouble. All we have is each other right now."

Sabra lifted her hand and slid it into his. Amazingly, Craig seemed to be unaffected by the chaos and danger of the last few hours. He must be hiding his feelings, she thought, as they carefully made their way down the slope. Right now, they had to remain alert for any possible complications. Garcia's henchmen could still be around. The cops might be looking for them.

Moving through back alleys, slipping between houses, Craig got them to Lahaina. A small motel, the Dolphin Inn, displayed a vacancy sign out front, glowing bright red in the darkness. Craig cautioned Sabra to remain in the shadows of the hibiscus bushes with the canvas bag at her feet. He brushed off his shirt and chinos the best he could before heading into the office. Sabra stood unmoving, her back against the wooden wall, well hidden by the lush greenery growing around her. It was three in the morning, and fog was rolling in off the Pacific, beginning to blanket Lahaina. She shivered, desperately wanting a hot shower. It was the kind of cold that went to her bones, and she knew she would take hours to really warm up.

She heard the door to the office open and close. Holding her breath, she watched the corner of the building. Craig came around it as noiselessly as a shadow.

He held up the key. "We've got a home." Picking up the bag, he walked back the way he'd come. Sabra followed warily, her gaze pinned on the driveway and highway in front of the small motel. There was hardly any traffic now, most of the island deeply asleep. He led her down to the end of the L-shaped motel.

"We're lucky," he said as he opened the door. "It was the last room he had."

She stumbled into the darkened room and flipped the light switch. Squinting against the sudden brightness, she put her hand up to shade her eyes. The room was dingy, with yellow paint peeling off the walls, the drapes old and thin, and the carpet scruffy-looking. But Sabra didn't care. In the middle of the small room was a double bed covered by a bright red quilt with white hibiscus flowers on it. Yellow and red. Not a great color combination, but at this point Sabra's only care was for plenty of hot water. She headed into the bathroom.

Craig closed the door and laid the canvas bag on the floor near the bed. He saw Sabra go into the bathroom. Taking out his pistol, he put a bullet in the chamber, flipped the safety back on and jammed the gun back into the holster beneath his left arm. Glancing at his watch, he saw it was 0300.

First things first. He went to the bathroom doorway. Sabra was testing the temperature of the water with outstretched fingers. Her hair sparkled with bits of glass still scattered among the thick strands. The left side of her neck was pockmarked with a number of tiny cuts.

"I'm going to locate a phone to call Perseus," he told her.

Sabra straightened. Seeing the darkness in Craig's eyes, she realized he was as exhausted as she was. "I can do it, if you want."

"No, you stay here." He smiled briefly. "You've got a nice goose egg on the right side of your head, did you know that?"

Frowning, Sabra touched it. "Ouch."

"Take your shower and get into bed. I'll be back as soon as possible. I think I saw a pay phone about two blocks away."

"Be careful?"

"Count on it." He gestured to the door. "Keep the lights out. When I come back, I'll knock three times. You let me in."

Exhaustion was sweeping over her. "Okay...."

Craig reached out, grazing her bloodied cheek with a finger. "Just take care of yourself, sweetheart. It's been one hell of a day."

Shaken by his unexpected warm, brief touch, Sabra watched him turn and disappear from view. The motel door opened and closed. Automatically, she forced herself back out into the room to slide the dead bolt into place. Next she dowsed the room lights. Craig was taking a huge risk of being spotted by going to the pay phone, but Sabra knew it was necessary. The sound of running water beckoned to her and she headed back into the bathroom.

The hot water pummeled the tense, sore muscles along her neck, shoulders and upper back. As she washed her hair, so many shards of glass fell out that she ended up cutting her feet on them. But the fear sweat was washed away and, with it, the last of her shivering. By the time Sabra finished, she felt unbelievably tired. She wanted only sleep.

She towel dried her hair. Then, looking at her soiled silk pants and blouse, she put them into a sinkful of cold water, glad she'd chosen washable silk. She wrapped a towel around herself, then scrubbed her clothes clean. These were the only clothes she had for now, and come tomorrow, she couldn't afford to have them looking soiled or bloody. For the next fifteen minutes, she washed them carefully, then rolled them up in a towel to press out the moisture. Finally, she found the room's lone closet and hung them on hangers.

Worriedly, Sabra looked at her watch. It was 0330; half an hour had passed. Craig should be back by now. A sudden lump formed in her throat as Sabra considered the possibilities. She stood in the center of the room, gripping the front of the towel that covered her, fear snaking through her.

Three sharp knocks sounded at the door. Gasping, she moved to the door. "Craig?"

"Yeah. Let me in."

Sabra breathed a sigh of relief and slid back the dead bolt. Her heart pounding, she opened the door, and Craig quickly slipped inside.

Craig stared down at Sabra. Her clean hair lay in damp strands against her face and shoulders. He saw the fear and worry in her eyes as he closed the door behind him and twisted the bolt. The white towel emphasized her olive coloring, and he had a tough time not staring. He'd never realized exactly how long limbed she was until now, her beautifully shaped calves and firm, curved thighs extending below the terry cloth.

"Did you reach them?" Sabra asked, breathlessly aware of Craig's hooded look, of his power as a man. Automatically, she stepped away.

He took off his jacket and shrugged out of the shoulder holster. "Yes. They don't know what went wrong either. Jake is sending the jet over with Killian and two FBI agents—they're going to join us."

"Good," Sabra whispered, relieved. She sat on the edge of the bed, watching as he unbuttoned his shirt. Despite everything that had happened, Craig looked unruffled with only a few tiny cuts on the left side of his neck to show for it. "It's a miracle we survived tonight."

"Tell me about it," he said gruffly, throwing the shirt on the bed. He started to unbuckle his pants, then hesitated. Sabra's eyes had widened, but it didn't look like fear. His mouth flattened and he allowed his hands to drop from the buckle. "I'm going to take a shower."

Gulping, Sabra nodded. "Go ahead. We can talk afterward." As she watched him turn and disappear into the bathroom, it suddenly hit her that they were going to have to share this small bed. Her fingers worried the top of her towel. She had no nightgown—nothing. And neither did he. Looking around, Sabra felt her heart picking up in beat. What could she do? The room was so small. There was no sofa, not even an upholstered chair—just a table and a straight-backed chair in one corner.

Her emotions were at war, a huge part of her wanting Craig's closeness and the sense of protection he gave her. She remembered how strong he'd been on the hill earlier. He seemed invincible. Whatever horror and nightmares he carried from his past certainly didn't interfere with his ability to act professionally in the present.

Sabra felt groggy. Her head hurt so much that it was troublesome to move. After a few minutes, she gave up. They were both so tired that it really didn't matter. Sleep was the priority, or they'd never be alert enough to cope with whatever was coming next. Slowly she pulled back the covers. The only light in the room was filtering through the thin, faded drapes. But it was enough to see by, and Sabra lay down. After tightening the towel around her the best she could, she pulled the covers up over her shoulders.

She closed her eyes and listened to the water running in the shower. Her heart pounded briefly at the thought that very soon, Craig would join her in bed. Or would he? He was as exhausted as she was. He couldn't sit up the rest of the night in that chair. Thinking of what it would be like sleeping in his arms, Sabra spiraled into a deep, healing sleep.

Craig emerged half an hour later after wrapping a towel around his waist. Shoving damp strands of hair off his brow, he quietly opened the bathroom door, allowing the steam that had built up to escape. Shutting off the bathroom light, he allowed his eyes to adjust to the gloom. Sabra was in bed, the covers drawn tightly across her. She lay on one edge of the small bed as he approached soundlessly on damp, bare feet.

Tonight he needed her. Desperately. Was she awake? Uncertain, he sat carefully on his edge of the bed. The springs creaked in protest. The clock on the nightstand read 0400, and Craig felt tiredness claw at him. He wanted to hold Sabra. He needed her. He removed the pistol from its holster, took the safety off and laid it on the floor next to the bed, where he could reach it in a hurry if he had to.

Turning, he sighed and carefully inserted his long legs beneath the covers. Sabra didn't move. The bed creaked again, but he no longer cared as he stretched his length across the lumpy mattress. The motel was seedy, not a place he'd stay if he had a choice. But right now, despite the lumps and sagging springs, he had to admit this bed felt damn good. Pulling the covers up around him, Craig turned onto his right side. Sabra's back was to him, and he smiled to himself as exhaustion dragged him smoothly toward sleep. Well, he'd wanted her close. Now she was mere inches away. He could feel the natural heat of her body and longed to reach out and slide his arm beneath her neck, to gently turn her till she fit snugly against him.

Dreams. All dreams, he told himself wearily as he shut his eyes. Tonight, he knew, the nightmare wouldn't strike. Tonight he could sleep. It was one of the few times in two years that Craig could know that for sure, and he knew it was because Sabra was next to him. She offered him protection in a way he didn't understand, but gratefully accepted. He was a man on the run. A man with a terrible past and no future.

Yet she was here—next to him. Somehow, fate had been kind to him for once.

Craig didn't know what wakened him. Maybe it was the sunlight pouring through the dingy drapes. His groggy attention shifted and he became aware of someone lying against him, of warmth and soft breath caressing his chest as he lay on his back in the bed.

Sabra. Her name flowed through him like hot honey. He realized that, as they'd slept, they must have naturally gravitated to each other. Keeping his eyes shut, he savored her length against him. One of her arms was thrown across his belly, her cheek resting in the crook of his shoulder. She was still asleep, he realized, monitoring her slow, steady breathing. Absorbing her nearness, he felt one of her long legs stretched across his. His arm was under her neck, curled around her shoulders to hold her close. His other arm lay across her, his hand resting on her upper arm. They were tangled together like two perfectly joined puzzle pieces.

Slowly, Craig senses awakened. His nostrils flaring, he caught a breath of her sweet scent. Her skin was firm and velvety against him, and a few dark strands of her hair tickled his cheek and nose. The rest of her hair cascaded over his shoulder and across his chest, surrounding her head like a halo. Her breasts were pressed against his chest and her hip seemed melded to his. She was only a few inches shorter than he was, and he marveled at how well her feminine curves fit against his harder planes.

Heat began to purl in Craig's lower body. The fragrance of her skin encircled him entrancingly, and he inhaled it like a dying man. He moved his hand gently against her shoulder, feeling the pliancy and warmth of her skin beneath his fingertips. The urge to tuck Sabra even closer and love her flowed through him. It was more than a thought; it was a powerful, primal urge. For the first time in two years, he'd slept deeply, without interruption, free of the screams that so frequently haunted his hours of darkness.

Carefully, Craig eased away just enough to raise himself onto his elbow. He stared down at Sabra's sleeping features. Her lips were parted, her face without tension. In sleep, she looked innocent—and vulnerable. Her hair was softly tangled around her face, and he lifted his hand to touch those thick, silken tresses. He hadn't meant to touch her at all, but he couldn't help himself. They'd nearly died last night, and the only thing he'd remembered through that hellish escape was the importance of his feelings for Sabra.

The panic he'd felt for her safety, the fear that she could have been killed, collided within him. These were crazy, stupid thoughts, Craig realized as he gently stroked her hair. She didn't even like him! As he'd huddled in that shallow trench, all he'd thought of was her. Even now, they were in danger. They could die at any moment—he knew it with a certainty that shook him to his core. Every protective mechanism in him as a man was emerging; the urge to keep Sabra safe was paramount. But that, too, was stupid, since he knew she was just as capable as he was, and probably better at surviving this sort of situation because of her greater experience. For him, yesterday marked the first time he'd been shot at since Desert Storm. The feeling was ugly. Invasive.

Lifting a strand of her hair, he leaned down and pressed his face against it. Her hair combined softness and strength as she did. There was a faint scent of plumaria, one of the lei flowers of Hawaii, to her hair and he realized that she'd washed it last night with that small bar of soap that had the same fragrance. Gently, he laid the strand back across her shoulder. The covers had slipped off during the night, revealing the swell of her breasts, and the towel she'd worn to bed had long since dropped away. They were naked, lying together, sharing their body heat.

Craig watched as Sabra took in a slow, deep breath. She moved slightly, pressing against him, as if realizing he'd moved away from her. The corners of his mouth pulled up in a soft smile. Leaning down, he touched his lips to her smooth, high cheek. He became lost in the fragrance of her, his fingers tunneling gently through her hair, easing her back just enough so he could find her parted lips. In the midst of his spinning senses, Craig heard himself say *no,* the word repeating in his head as Sabra moaned beneath him, her lips opening to receive his questing kiss.

His dreaminess turned to heat as he felt her awaken beneath his exploring kiss. Her lips parted, soft and pliant against him. Sliding his hand around the back of her head, Craig brought Sabra's mouth fully to his. She smelled of heady plumaria, her breath was coming raggedly in time with his own. Unable to stop himself, he closed his eyes and deepened the kiss, his lips moving against hers. This time, he wanted to do more than take; he wanted to share with her. In moments, he'd eased Sabra onto her back and framed her face with his hands. As he opened his eyes, Craig saw the smoky gray of hers looking up at him—filled with a smoldering desire. Desire for him. Nothing else mattered right now. Only her. Only them.

"I need you," he rasped unsteadily, moving his hand down over her collarbone to the ripe curve of her breast, feeling her skin tighten beneath his exploration. He waited, not wanting to force himself on her, not willing to take unfair advantage of their dangerous situation. He could see the sleepiness in her wonderful eyes, along with unmistakable fire. His mind swirling with new and confusing feelings, Craig hesitated, trying to focus on the harsh reality: people just didn't fall in love this fast. Or did they? He remembered Sabra telling him how her parents had fallen in love the first time they saw each other. Briefly, Craig wondered if these feelings could be something like that. Then he forced the crazy thoughts aside. Whatever the possibilities for other people, he knew he wasn't worthy of being loved that way.

Easing his hand around her breast, he saw her lashes flutter closed. Her lips parted even more, and she arched against him. Good. She wanted this as much as he did. Craig wasn't sure of Sabra's reasons, but he didn't want to talk right now. All he wanted to do was worship her, let her know in his own male way how much he needed her. She was offering herself to him, whatever her reasons, and he humbly accepted the gift.

The scorching touch of Craig's fingers as they caressed her breast, finding the tightly raised nipple, made Sabra gasp with pleasure. When his moist mouth covered the hardened bud, suckling her, she gave a small cry and pressed herself hard against him, locked in the strength of his arms. She had awakened out of a torrid dream of him skimming his hand across her naked body, igniting heat and urgency though her. Where did the dream end and reality begin? It didn't matter to Sabra. She'd only wanted Craig to hold her, to love her.

Never had she felt this kind of urgency. Never had a man's touch made her cry out with need, as she pleaded with him to complete her. She clung to his demanding hardness as he suckled her, twisting beneath him as his hands ranged downward, his roughened fingers leaving a trail of fire in the wake of his exploration. An ache built intensely within her, and Sabra moaned. As his hand slid between her damp thighs, she opened to his continued exploration. A wild, tingling sensation exploded through her at his gentle touch. Then she felt him move above her, his knee guiding her thighs farther apart. Never had she wanted a man the way she did him.

Sabra's ragged breathing caught and held deep within her as she felt Craig settle his weight upon her. Mindlessly, she thrust her hips forward. A powerful sensation filled her, and a small cry escaped her throat. She threw back her head, aching to meet him and take him deeply within her. His sliding heat filled her as she began to rock with him, melding into a oneness that left her sobbing and clinging to him. His mouth plundered hers as he thrust hard and deep into her, taking her, claiming her, making her his in all ways. Their bodies were moist, sliding against each other as his powerful thrusts went deeper. Her legs caught and tangled with his.

The fire in her culminated. Sabra felt Craig stiffen against her, his arm crushing her to him. A cry began somewhere deep within her as she tensed against him, feeling the heat unfurl rapidly through her. A wild, dizzying sensation held her captive as a hot river of pleasure coursed through her. She felt Craig's brow press against hers. He groaned, his hands digging into her shoulders as he pinned her against the bed.

A broken smile pulled at Sabra's lips as she relaxed within his grip, absorbing his weight, strength and power. The moments eddied and swirled around them, and she weakly rested her arms across his shoulders.

Ever so gently, Craig took her lips, testing them as if they were some treasured, fragile possession. Undeniable joy flowed through her, along with an overwhelming sense of protection. Barely lifting her lashes, she saw Craig looking down at her through hooded, smoldering eyes. His face glistened with sweat, his mouth strong, his gaze tender as he regarded her in the silence. She smiled a little, then closed her eyes and sighed, content to be in his arms.

She felt his fingers tunnel through her hair and gently begin to massage her scalp in a sensation as wonderful as it was unexpected. He trailed a series of small kisses from her brow to her nose, over her cheek finally coming to rest on her lips. This time his kiss was long and slow, filled with reverence. Sabra returned his kiss with equal heat and felt him smile against her mouth. Before she could ask why he was smiling, he'd eased away from her and brought her on top of him. The smile in his eyes told her everything as she relaxed against him. She placed her hands on his chest and rested her chin on top of them, caught in the unrestrained joy dancing in his dark blue eyes.

Craig tugged the covers back up and over them, then rested his hands on her upper arms. The light he saw in Sabra's eyes was clearly happiness, not regret, and for that he was thankful. Running his fingers across her silky shoulder, he collected her damp hair and smoothed it behind her graceful neck.

"You have the most beautiful hair," he murmured.

"And you're just plain beautiful."

He grinned a little. "I've been called a lot of things in my life, but 'beautiful' wasn't one of them."

Sabra luxuriated in her position atop him. Feeling his returning strength, she pressed her hips more firmly against his, to show him her appreciation of him. The change in his eyes was instantaneous; then became hooded with desire once more.

"When I first saw you, that was the word that came to mind," she said, her voice a little breathless. She slid her fingers across his brow and gently tamed several rebellious strands of his hair back into place.

"I won't tell you what I thought."

She grinned, caught up in the moment of shared intimacy. "You can tell me. I'm a big girl."

"I know you are," he murmured appreciatively, absorbing her fleeting touch, "but my thoughts were purely X-rated, believe me."

"Hmm." Sabra leaned down, caressing his mouth and feeling his immediate response. His hands ranged downward beneath the covers, outlining her ribs, waist and hips.

"You are incredible," he rasped against her lips. "Beautiful, warm and incredible."

Sabra reveled in his low, husky voice, feeling his words thrum through her as if she were a drum being struck. Every movement of his body, every breath he took she took with him.

Craig brought her close, pressing her against his length. She rested her cheek against his chest, and as he moved his hand slowly up and down her arm, she thought she'd never felt so content in all her life.

Craig took a deep breath and released it. Gently, he eased Sabra to his side and rested his chin against her hair. He knew it must be near noon and they had to get up, though it was the last thing he wanted to do. He wanted to spend the day here, with her in his arms, loving her all over again. Outside the motel room, traffic noise told of the ceaseless coming and going of tourists. The motel was right next to the Lahaina shopping district, where they all came to spend their money.

"Last night," Sabra whispered, gently moving her fingers through the thick tangle of hair on his chest, "I thought we were going to die. I was so afraid, Craig. More afraid than I'd ever been."

"Because of me?"

She eased away just enough to look into his dark blue eyes. "No."

He grazed her lower lip with his teeth. "What then?"

Her lip tingled beneath his butterfly caress, and it took her a long moment to collect her scattered thoughts. "I was caught off guard last night, Craig. I wasn't reacting the way I should have. You took over."

He smiled a little and slid his hand along her flushed cheek. "You sound amazed."

She had the good grace to blush. "Let's just say any doubts I might have had about you are gone."

"You didn't do anything wrong last night, Sabra."

She frowned and slid her hand over his. "I know. I guess . . . the nightmares you had, Craig, made me question whether you could handle the stress of a life-threatening situation."

"You had every right to question me." Easing into a sitting position, Craig brought Sabra into his arms and pulled the covers up. "Settle back against me, okay?"

She nodded, surrendering to his embrace. Was life really this good? Taking a deep breath, she whispered, "Please, tell me what happened to you, Craig." She stroked his beard-stubbled cheek and saw the pain come back to his eyes. "So many times, I almost asked you," she continued quickly. "I know you didn't want to tell me. But we're in danger here, and we may not make it Craig. Let's share ourselves with each other. I'm not the type for a one-night stand."

"I know that," he said gruffly, capturing her hand and kissing it gently. He felt as if he was drowning in Sabra's compassionate eyes. "Do you know how you make me feel?"

"No," she breathed.

"Like I want to live again," he whispered unsteadily, touching her hair, smoothing it away from her shoulder. "What I have to tell you is pretty bad, Sabra. You may not want to be with me after I tell you all of it."

She shook her head. "No. I'd never feel that way."

He looked down at her grimly. "We'll see. I've never told anyone about it. I was too ashamed, I guess." His mouth quirked, and he looked up at the ceiling, holding her a little more tightly against him. "After I tell you, I know you'll leave me...."

Chapter Nine

Craig hesitated. Once Sabra realized just how much of a coward he'd been, she'd surely leave his side, her eyes filled with accusation and disgust. Still, the gentle touch of her fingers grazing his jaw suggested otherwise. It was a chance he was going to have to take, he decided. As he forced the words between his lips they came out in a rasp.

"I was stationed at Camp Reed three years ago," he began. "A Marine Recon, Lieutenant Cal Talbot, busted up his leg on one of those rocky, cactus-strewn hills during war games. I was at the weather desk at Ops when the call came in. The wind was really gusting—maybe thirty or forty miles an hour—coming in off the Pacific. Talbot's team was calling for immediate pickup because he was bleeding to death. He'd not only broken his leg, he'd cut into an artery. They'd applied a tourniquet trying to stop the worst of the bleeding, but the situation was grim.

"I volunteered because his last name was Talbot, like mine. My copilot, Brent Summers told me we should do it—that it wasn't every day I could save one of my relatives or in the field." Craig scowled, nervously running his hand up and down Sabra's velvety arm. "He wasn't a relative, of course, but Summers and I tended to be high risk takers, so we went for it. When we reached the area, I realized the high-tension electric lines were too close to the pickup area. I couldn't land, because they were on the side of a very steep hill, and we could see that the Recons couldn't move the officer to better ground."

Sabra frowned. "What did you do?" She wasn't a pilot, but she knew the risk of strong gusts of wind. It chilled her to think that they could have been blown into those power lines....

"I ordered my crew chief to drop the litter basket we carried for such rescues. My helo was dancing all over the place, and Summers was watching out the window, telling me how close we were to the wires." He shook his head. "We had so many close calls that day, I lost count. Finally, we managed to rescue Cal. We flew him to the base hospital and saved his life. That evening, I went to see how he was doing. That's when I met his wife, Linda, who was pregnant then with their first child, Sammy."

Sabra heard Craig's voice drop, and she slid her arm around his waist, squeezing gently. "They are very lucky to have you for a friend. You didn't have to go find out how he was."

"I've always been that way," he muttered, absorbing her touch.

"Something happened, though?"

"Yeah," he whispered roughly, releasing her and pushing himself into a more-upright position against the wall. The covers pooled around his waist, and Sabra moved close, her hand on his blanketed thigh, her eyes soft with compassion. Glancing down at her, Craig said, "It happened during Desert Storm." He almost choked on the words.

Sabra's hand tightened on his tense thigh, and she held his grief-stricken gaze. "I thought it might have."

He studied her a moment. "How?"

"Terry had seen action in Vietnam, and he warned me the first day we teamed up not to touch him to waken him—just like you did."

"I see. . . ."

Sabra reached out to captured the hand that lay against his belly and tangled her fingers with his. "It's a symptom of posttraumatic-stress syndrome. I know I'm not telling you anything new. But Terry sat me down and we had a long heart-to-heart talk about what he'd seen during the war and how it affected him." Sabra shrugged, saddened. "I'm pretty used to what you think might be terrible to tell others, Craig. In the past five years, Terry has had some nightmares as bad as the ones you've had. I remember the first time he had a night terror, and I ran into his room to help him, like an idiot." Sabra touched the side of her jaw. "I forgot what he'd told me, and he nailed me with a right cross that sent me flying halfway across the room."

Craig's eyes narrowed.

"I had it coming," Sabra said wryly. "It broke the skin but didn't break my jaw. I was young and idealistic then, thinking I could change things." She studied his scarred, burned hand against her own perfect-looking one. "Terry taught me a lot about PTSD, Craig. I understand that it's hard for you to communicate what happened because you're ashamed." She fought back tears, her voice dropping to a husky, uneven whisper. "I see no shame in what's happened to anyone who's been in a wartime situation. I don't think less of you for crying out. For wanting to cry, even if you don't. . . ."

Craig tightened his fingers around her slender ones. "So you knew all along . . ."

"In a way, I did. I didn't want to make assumptions, though. I felt it was only fair to wait and let you share with me when you were ready, Craig. Terry taught me that everyone reacts differently to any given situation. One thing you have in common, though—the trauma is like baggage."

His mouth flattened and he managed a twisted smile. "Yeah, that's for sure." His terror dissolved a little more at

Sabra's understanding look, and he felt more emotionally stable with her holding his hand. He placed his other hand over hers. "I haven't been giving you very much credit, have I?"

"You remind me of Terry in some ways," Sabra admitted softly. "So it's easy to allow you the space you need. But it would help if you could share what happened."

Craig hung his head and concentrated on running his fingers across hers. Sabra's skin was so smooth and unmarred, unlike his own. But scars went beyond the visible ones; he carried the worst ones inside him, where very few people could see them. Struggling to speak, he said, "I... tried to talk to Linda about it, thinking she'd understand..." He shook his head, then rasped, "After that experience, I didn't talk to anyone again. Ever."

Sabra changed position, sitting next to him, capturing his hand and holding it firmly between her own. "We share something very special," she quavered. "I hope you can trust me enough to tell me, Craig. Whatever it is, it's eating you up alive. I see it in your eyes when the nightmare's got a hold on you. I saw it earlier tonight."

He closed his eyes, tipped back his head and rested it on the headboard, glad of Sabra's steadying touch. "No one knows what happened. Not even the widows and children who were left behind," he whispered, his voice barely audible. "I was flying my second raid of the night. It was windy, very windy, and I was flying 'nap of the earth.' Brent was copilot, and in back, I had two more Recon teams to drop close to the enemy lines. We were responsible for the first assault, before the rest of the forces engaged.

"It was so dark that night, and I've never sweated like I did then. My flight suit was wringing wet. My gloves were so sweaty they were slippery on the controls, and I worried about losing my grip, and sending us crashing into one of those dunes. Cal Talbot was there. He and his men made up one of the Recon teams. We carried a total of ten men...."

Craig opened his eyes and stared up at the ceiling as the scene rolled out as if on film before him. "We were all nervous—except Cal. He came over just before the mission, slapped me on the back and told me how lucky he felt having me as the pilot on this mission. I remember saying I didn't feel lucky that night. I was scared. I'd just come back from the first drop, and the damn wind was so bad it had nearly knocked us into a high sand dune. Luckily, Summers saw it and warned me in time. We'd had three grenades launched at us, too, though we'd managed to avoid them somehow.... Still, my hands were shaking like leaves, and my knees were so weak I sat in my chopper for fifteen minutes before I had the strength to get up and walk out of there.

"Cal thought I was joking. He'd never seen me scared. He pulled a small plastic bag from his pocket. In it was a lock of hair from each of his daughters. He told me he carried it for good luck and gave it to me to hold onto for this trip. I said no, that he should keep it, but he just laughed and stuck it in my left sleeve pocket. He laughed and said that if we crashed, I'd survive.

"I stood next to my bird while they were refueling, just shaking. Cal went back to check his team before boarding, but I had this knot in my gut. Finally I ran away from the lights and the crews and puked my guts out. That's how scared I was."

"With good reason," Sabra said unsteadily. All the fear Craig had worked so hard to control was alive in his eyes as never before. Did he realize how strong he was? How brave he was to try to behave normally in society while carrying these awful memories?

With a shrug, he muttered, "I came back, washed my mouth out with some water from a canteen I borrowed from one of the ground crew and climbed into my bird. Once we had everyone on board, Cal came up, patted my shoulder and slipped a white envelope into my hand. He told me to hold it for him until he got back. There wasn't time to talk, so I jammed the envelope into my uniform.

"The wind was just as bad the second time, and the mission was more dangerous because we had to fly through the Guard lines to drop the teams behind them. I was really worried about SCUD missiles and grenade launchers. Summers kept a sharp watch calling out the elevation of the terrain as we flew along only about ten feet above it at any given time.''

Craig felt sweat popping out on his brow, and shame swept through him as he lifted his hand to wipe the moisture away. Sabra's lips parted, and her eyes grew sad, but her hand remained strong and stabilizing on his. Taking a ragged breath, he forced himself to go on. ''Things got really tense near the drop zone. We'd already had two grenade launchers shoot at us. Luckily Summers saw the flash from the barrels, and I was able to haul the bird up and out of target range. But each time we did that, I knew we were exposing ourselves to enemy radar. It couldn't be helped. I was afraid we'd been spotted, but I had to drop the two teams near an ammo dump they were going to blow up. That action was necessary to create a diversion that would allow a much-larger force to sweep down and catch the Guard off-balance.''

More sweat broke out on Craig's upper lip, and he could feel perspiration trickling from his armpits. His voice was shaking now as the adrenaline began to surge through him, like it always did when he relived the event. Sabra reached over and gently wiped the moisture from his brow and upper lip with her fingers. The empathy in her eyes gave him the strength to continue. ''We were almost to the drop zone when it happened. The wind jostled us badly and threw us off course. I was wrestling with getting us back below radar range and Summers was calling out the elevation.''

Craig shut his eyes tightly, his voice breaking, his breathing becoming erratic. ''Neither of us saw it coming. Neither of us . . . I don't know how many times I've replayed it in my mind. Why didn't we see that third grenade being fired?'' He squeezed Sabra's hand more tightly. ''I remember Summers screaming out, jabbing his finger toward the right, but it was too late. The grenade hit the main rotor, and the bird flipped up, like a wounded thing. Shrapnel and fire showered through the cabin. The Plexiglas shattered and blew in on us. The fire was over my arms as I wrestled with the bird, trying to stop it from sinking tail first.

"We slowly turned over, the rotor screeching and I heard screams from the rear. Brent was slumped forward, hit by something. Probably shrapnel. All I could do was try to control the helo enough so that we might survive the crash. Everything slowed down, as if I were moving in slow motion. Smoke clogged the cabin, and I lost my sense of direction. No matter what I tried to do to control the bird, it wouldn't respond. I figured out later that the cables to the rudders and tail assembly had been severed by the grenade blast.

"We went down. The bird flipped onto its side and crashed on the slope of a very steep dune that felt like concrete. It hit on Summers's side, and I thought the jolt would snap his neck. I heard the metal tearing, and I remember Cal's voice above everything, ordering his men to not panic. I was amazed at his calm—that he was even conscious, much less thinking clearly. He was such an amazing man...."

Wiping his face savagely, Craig squeezed his eyes shut. Every word became a major effort, and his chest rose and fell as he went on, perspiration covering his entire body now. "When the bird came to rest, I managed to cut myself free of the harness, and I pulled Summers out through the nose. The screams of the Recons were awful. It was so dark, and the fire's dancing light hurt more than it helped. I scrambled around, trying to locate the hatch. Since the bird was on her side, one of the escape routes was blocked. I managed to climb up on top, and I tried—God, I tried to get to that other door. It was jammed from the grenade blast, and I couldn't open it. The fire was getting worse, and I could hear the screams of the men inside. They couldn't escape through the cabin because it was already consumed by fire."

Craig opened his eyes and slowly lifted his hands. "I tried to open that door. The fire was so bad. I threw myself against it, I lost count of how many times. The screams—those screams for help... I could hear the men pounding against the inside of the helo. I heard Cal crying out." His hands shook and he let them fall into his lap. "There was an explosion. I felt this blast of heat, and I was thrown through the air." His brow furrowed deeply. "It was the last thing I remembered."

Shaken, Sabra slid her arms around his damp neck and held his broken, dark gaze. "Oh, Craig, how awful...."

"For me? No," he said harshly, "I survived. I was the only one to survive. It was a lot tougher for Summers and Cal, and the other Recons." He managed a tortured grimace. "I was the lucky one."

"Were you captured by the enemy?"

"No. Another helo with an Air Force flight surgeon on board was sent in to pick up survivors. I—I don't remember anything until I woke up at a burn unit behind the lines. My hands—" he picked them up and studied them darkly "—suffered third-degree burns. They were suspended away from my body when I regained consciousness. The left side of my face was pretty much totaled, too. I had a real deep gash on my left cheek. But compared to what those men suffered before they died, it was nothing."

Sabra gently touched his set jaw, feeling the tension in it. "You did what you could."

His hands closed slowly into fists. "It wasn't enough," he rasped harshly. "I should have kept working that hatch. It was starting to give way.... I should have—"

"The lock mechanism had melted from the blast," Sabra interrupted quietly. "Or it jammed, Craig. If you couldn't get it open, no one could have."

He shrugged wearily, the silence deepening. "I remember a woman doctor leaning over me, telling me I'd broken my left ankle in two places and cracked four ribs on my left side. My right arm was fractured. When I told her how I'd gotten Summers out and then tried to open that door, she said it was a miracle I was alive. I shouldn't have been able to do any of it with so many broken bones. Adrenaline, I guess..."

"It was," Sabra whispered, fighting back her tears. "How you could walk on a broken ankle, much less try to force open that door covered with fire is beyond me."

"I'm no hero," he said flatly. "So don't look at me like that. I should have rescued them. I should have gotten to them—"

"No!" Sabra gripped his hands—now knotted, white-knuckled fists in his lap. His skin felt damp and clammy. "No," she rattled, "you did as much as you could do, Craig. What you accomplished was beyond ordinary human strength and courage. I know Cal was your friend. I can't even begin to imagine how you felt, hearing him scream...."

Blindly, Craig reached out, sliding his arms around her, pulling her hard against him. Tears squeezed from beneath his tightly shut eyes. Her arms went around him, strong and steadying. He buried his face in her hair, his heart pounding wildly in his chest.

"Let it go," Sabra whispered, holding him as tightly as she could. "Cry, Craig. Cry for Cal. Cry for Brent. And for Linda and the children...." She slid her trembling hand across his hair and her voice cracked. "I'll hold you, darling. Just let it go, please...."

The huge fist of pressure, followed by the burning sensation that was always there in the nightmare, came swiftly. Sabra's husky voice and firm touch broke down the last barriers within him. She was holding him, and the whole poisonous nightmare spilled up through him. His throat constricted, a huge lump jamming there, and he gasped for breath, pressing his face against her hair, trying to avoid it. Trying to stop it. But it was impossible. Sabra's soothing voice shattered the hold the nightmare had on him. The past warred with the present, the choking odor of oily smoke and burning metal warring with her sweetly feminine scent. A sound like that of an animal being wounded tore from his contorted lips, and he clung to her, as the first strangled sob ripped out of him.

Sabra caressed Craig's damp cheek, feeling the slow, hot tears begin trickling down his face. She pressed her jaw against his brow, allowing him to bury his face against her. A second sob shook him, making his whole body tremble in the wake of the violent release. Tears scalded Sabra's eyes, her heart breaking with the sounds that began to tear from deep within him. Craig had gone through so much. He needed to cry—to release the horror that had lived in him for the past two years. She kept rubbing his shoulders and down his back. With each stroke of her hand another sob broke loose. Why was it so hard for men to cry? Sabra had long ago lost count of the times she'd cried. It was a wonderful, healing release. Didn't men realize that? What in their stoic natures prevented them from being human?

She knew all too well that the military frowned on men crying on the battlefield, believing it showed weakness. Craig's arms were so tight around her that her rib cage hurt, but she didn't care. He was holding on to her as if she were the last person on earth, afraid to let go for fear that she, too, would reject him.

Gradually, over the next fifteen minutes, his harsh sobs diminished. Sabra was able to settle next to him, her body a fortress for him after the fury of his emotional storm. She guessed that with his military background, Craig would be ashamed that he'd cried in her arms. Frustrated, she realized she could do little to prevent those feelings. Now that he'd told her the whole story, she knew what she'd already believed. Craig's only real fault was the depth of his guilt at not being able to rescue the men he'd loved as brothers. Sabra could only guess how awful he must feel to have lived through such a horrifying experience, but her heart broke for him.

"Here," she offered tremulously, handing him the edge of the sheet, "you can use this as a handkerchief."

Craig slowly eased away from Sabra, taking the proffered fabric and wiping his face dry of the perspiration and tears. It hurt to look up and meet Sabra's eyes. What would she think of him now? He'd admitted his cowardice. He'd told her of his inability to help his dearest friends in their worst moment. Would he see the accusation in her lovely gray eyes as he had in Linda's? Anguish cut through him in a new way, because he was vulnerable now as he'd never been before. Allowing the sheet to drop aside, he risked everything, and looked up—into Sabra's luminous eyes.

Instead of accusation, Craig saw her pain for him. Her lips were parted, glistening with spent tears. Her tears. As she reached out and touched his cheek, trying to smile, he released a tightly held breath. "How can you look at me like that?"

"How can I not?" She framed his face with her hands and looked deeply into his reddened eyes. "No one in their right mind would accuse, Craig. You did nothing wrong. My God, you almost died trying to help your friends." She picked up his scarred hands. "Look at this. You burned your hands so badly that you'll carry the scars for the rest of your life. You walked on a leg that shouldn't have supported you. You should never have been able to pull at that release handle with your broken ribs and arms." Her voice cracked. "You're a very brave man in my eyes. I don't know that I'd have had the courage you did. Somewhere in the back of your mind, you must have known that your helicopter could blow up, but you disregarded it and went after your friends." Tears ran down her cheeks, and Sabra ignored them, holding his wounded gaze. "You rescued Summers. That has to be enough. With all your wounds and broken bones, you tried. It's enough, Craig."

Her quiet tear-filled words acted as a balm to Craig's raw emotions. He saw not the least accusation in her eyes. Amazed, he took her hands and held them in his own. Sabra was crying—for him. No one had cried for him, only for those who hadn't made it back. He bowed his head and shut his eyes. "When I got flown to Germany, the old uniform they'd cut off me came with me. I—I asked a nurse to look in the pockets. She found the small plastic bag with the locks of hair. I kept asking her to find the white envelope, but she couldn't. I remember being frantic, knowing how important that letter was. I didn't know what was in it, but I knew I had to find it. I was nearly out of my mind with pain, but the pain of losing that envelope was worse. They had me on drugs, and I remember floating in and out for days.

"Every time I regained consciousness, I asked that nurse for the envelope. I don't know why she didn't tell me to go to hell, because I bugged her incessantly. About the fourth

ay I was in Germany, I woke up and saw a dirty white en-
elope, the edges burned away, lying on my chest. When I
ealized it was Cal's letter, I started yelling until finally a
urse came running into my room—a different nurse. I
egged her to open it and read it to me, because my hands
nd arms were a mess."

Craig took a deep breath and looked at Sabra. "I think
Cal knew he wasn't going t make it. I'll never forget what
e'd written. He'd asked me to take the letter to Linda, to
ive it to her."

"Did you?"

"Yeah, after I got out of the series of hospitals I was in.
didn't make it to Cal's funeral. I couldn't be there for
Linda and her daughters the way I wanted. I was going
hrough so many operations, it wasn't funny, and without
he use of my arms, I couldn't even call. I had a nurse dial
er, and she held the phone to my ear so I could tell her how
orry I was." His mouth flattened. "All Linda could do was
ry. I don't remember a whole lot about the call, anyway,
ecause I was on painkillers at the time."

"You tried, Craig."

"Yes," he admitted softly, "I tried. But I knew Linda was
laming me. I could hear it in her voice."

"How long was that after Cal died?"

"Two weeks."

"Listen," Sabra said hoarsely, "she was in a state of
hock, Craig. For that matter, so were you. You were on
rugs, and I'm sure it skewed your perception."

With a shrug, he said, "Four months later, I finally
lipped out of the hospital and went to see her. I was ex-
ecting the worst. Linda had moved away from Camp Reed,
ack home to Seattle. She and the girls were living with her
arents. I—it was a mess. Her parents looked at me as if I
vas some kind of monster. The oldest girl, Sammy, started
rying when I came into the house. Claire, their youngest,
vho Cal had named after my mother, just lay in Linda's
rms, staring up at me as if I was a stranger. Before—be-
ore we left, Claire had known me. I would go over to their
apartment for dinner, and that little girl treated me like an

uncle or something. She'd hold her arms out to me the m
ment she heard my voice.'' He looked away. ''Maybe it w
my burns. I had a pretty ugly face at the time. I guess
didn't look much like my old self. The kid was probably ju
frightened.''

Sabra laid her hand on his arm, hurting deeply for hin
''Did you give Linda the letter?''

''Yeah, I did. Her parents were there behind her, silent
accusing me for not saving Cal's life. Sammy was crying ar
clinging to her mother's skirt, and Claire was just staring u
at me with those huge green eyes. I felt like a coward. I fe
like apologizing for having lived. I gave Linda the plast
bag back, too. I tried to explain, but her father starte
cursing at me, and I couldn't handle it. I left. I left withou
saying goodbye. I did apologize to Linda, though.''

Swallowing hard, Sabra held his watery gaze. ''Y
shouldn't have apologized for anything, Craig.''

''Maybe... At least I got her the letter. At least Cal ge
to tell his family that he loved them.''

''Did Linda read the letter right away?''

He shook his head. ''No. She just pressed it to her hea
and looked up at me with tears in her eyes.'' He released
breath. ''Hell, Sabra, it was a messy situation all the wa
around. I found out later that the State Department hadn
told them how Cal died. They said it was top secret and the
couldn't divulge the details. About a year after that, Lind
contacted me. Over the phone, I told her exactly what ha
happened. She cried a little and thanked me and hung up.

''Did she thank you for trying to save Cal?''

''No. She was hurting, Sabra.''

Nodding, she smiled slightly and touched his scarre
cheek. ''You've been through so much alone, Craig.''

Ignoring her compassion, he added, ''After I got out c
the military hospital, they wanted me to resume flying. '
went back to get some flight time.'' His mouth flattened. '
couldn't do it, Sabra. I went back to Camp Reed and stoo
on the tarmac, looking at the same type of helicopter I'
flown in Iraq. I got shaky and vomited. I couldn't get in th

bird." He wiped his mouth with the back of his hand. "I knew they thought I was a coward—"

"No!" Sabra bit back the rest of her cry. "No," she told him in a low, off-key voice, "you weren't *ever* a coward, Craig. Not ever."

"The instructor was understanding. Each day, we'd meet at a specific time, and each day I'd get a step closer to that bird. Finally, after a week, I forced myself to sit in the pilot's seat. I started sweating like a dog and wanting to cry. I remember vomiting out the window. I'd never felt so ashamed. So—so cowardly. He'd been over there. He'd flown missions just like mine."

"Only," Sabra rasped, "he hadn't suffered through a crash like you had."

"That's true," Craig said tiredly. He forced a bitter smile. "Well, the upshot of it was I couldn't fly. I froze at the controls. The instructor would get the bird going, ready to fly, but I couldn't lift it off. The muscles in my arms and legs would freeze. I couldn't do it."

"Everyone has a personal wall," Sabra said, holding his tortured gaze. "We all hit it if we've been pushed beyond our emotional boundaries. They shouldn't have forced you back into the cockpit so soon. They should have given you more time."

"Time? After that little incident, they sent me to a shrink. He said I was unfit to fly, which was true. I resigned my commission and got out, Sabra. I wasn't going to embarrass myself like than anymore. Then I went home to New Mexico to heal. I stayed home for six months, got some kind of grip on myself and looked into Perseus. Morgan knew I was an ex-marine pilot, but he never questioned me about why I'd left. I think he knew."

"Morgan is very astute about people," Sabra agreed gently. "He was in a war, too, so he knows."

"Yeah, I think he did know a lot about me, but he never said anything. It takes one to know one, I guess." Craig held up his hands. "Of course, the scars were pretty obvious. I think he put two and two together." With a shake of his head, Craig added, "For some reason, I didn't care if Mor-

gan knew. I trusted him, and I knew he trusted me. When
told him I didn't want any assignments that involved fly
ing, he just said, 'Fine.' That was the end of it. After that,
began to relax more. I got the jobs done for him, and I be
gan to feel like I could do something right. In a way, I thin
Morgan was assessing my stability. He gave me missions tha
would build what was left of my confidence. Over the pas
six months, I really began to mend.''

"Morgan is wonderful with people," she quavered
hurting for both Craig and her boss. "I'm beginning to ur
derstand your initial reaction to this mission now."

He shot her a wry look. "Yeah, well, it sort of took th
wind out of my sails, believe me. Maybe it wouldn't hav
been so bad if Jenny hadn't just been killed."

"You've been reeling from one trauma to another," sh
said, even more aware of the level of stress on him.

Craig met her luminous gaze. "Well, now you know ev
erything, Sabra." Holding up his hands, he said, "I'm n
hero. I've screwed up in ways I never thought possible. I'v
lost lives. I'm a coward behind the stick of a helicopter. I'r
a loser, big-time."

Shocked, Sabra stared at him. It was on the tip of he
tongue to refute his allegations. But she realized Craig sav
himself that way because he was still blaming himself fo
everything that had happened. What war did to men wa
unconscionable in her opinion, making them feel like cow
ards when in reality they were terribly brave under inhu
man circumstances.

Gently, she slid her hand up his arm until it came to res
on his slumped shoulder. She saw the fear in Craig's eye
and understood it now. "The man I see in front of me," sh
said quietly, "is a hero to me. You did the best you could
Craig, and that's all anyone can ask of you—ever. I don'
care if Linda or her parents ever forgive you. I don't care i
you can never sit in the cockpit of a helicopter again." Sh
tightened her hold on his shoulder. "What about the mai
who saved my life last night? You didn't lose it when the
tried to kill us. No, you kept your wits about you. If any
thing, Craig, I was the one who was shaken up. You wer

hinking all the time. You thought of digging the trenches or us to hide in.''

''Maybe I just got lucky.''

''I don't think so.'' Sabra leaned upward and placed her ips against the tight line of his mouth—a mouth that held back so much force of emotions. Gently, she slid her lips gainst his and felt the hard line dissolve beneath her exloration. Time was not on their side. As much as she vanted to love Craig again, she knew it was impossible. She elt him groan, his mouth opening and taking her deeply. miling to herself, she sank against him, allowing him to bsorb her presence. She was the less wounded of the two of hem. Let her kisses help heal him, if only a little bit. As she lid her arms around his shoulders, Sabra didn't fool herelf. She knew PTSD wasn't something that was easily hased away. The healing took place on an individual's time lock. Some men never got over it. She did realize how far Craig had come in such a small amount of time. That spoke f his courage—a courage he no longer admitted he had.

Easing her mouth from his, she smiled into his stormy yes. ''I wish we had all the time in the world right now, Craig.''

He ran his hand along the smooth line of her spine. ''So lo I, but we don't.'' Frowning, he eased away from her and eluctantly pushed the covers aside. ''We need to shower, get Iressed and start thinking about a new plan of attack.''

Sabra watched him stand, then slid off the bed and moved nto his welcoming arms. ''Do you think Jason is there?''

''I don't know, but we're going to find out. First things irst. We need another rental car. Then we're going to hide ut the rest of the day at another motel. We'll start work onight. There's less chance of being detected then.''

''So, you think Garcia spotted us on the hill?''

''It's hard to say. This could be an inside job. Someone in he police department could have tipped Garcia off.''

With a quirk of her lips, Sabra said, ''I hope not.''

''We can't trust anyone right now,'' he said, leaning down nd placing a kiss against her temple. How Sabra could vant him to hold her after what he'd told her was beyond him. He was still reeling from the release of his dammed emotions. Sharing had been less painful than he'd thought but then, Sabra wasn't an ordinary woman. Craig couldn' trust his good fortune at finding someone who wasn't ac cusing him of being a coward.

As he stood there with her in his arms, Craig could n longer convince himself that the unnamed feeling tha swelled so powerfully through his chest was anything bu love—and he was stunned by the force of it. Looking dow into her warm gray eyes, he realized just how much he care for her. His emotions ragged and confused from the event of the past hours, he said nothing. The situation right no was too dangerous for him to contemplate his feelings wit the kind of attention they deserved.

Still, his burgeoning emotions made him hesitate. Bu how could he let Sabra know? Why would she return hi love? He had no right to think he deserved someone a beautiful from the heart outward as she was. Besides, h rationalized, the mission would be jeopardized by furthe emotional involvement with her. If there was ever a time h needed to force away any romantic notions and count on hi realist nature it was now.

Even as he questioned his own motives, Craig decided t set aside his feelings until he and Sabra could have the safet and leisure to explore them properly—if it was meant to be With his past, Sabra probably wouldn't be interested in hin beyond these moments of passion born of the fires of dan ger.

"Come on," he said gruffly, "let's get going."

Chapter Ten

"We need to get a change of clothes, so we'll blend in like tourists," Sabra said as she slipped on her shoes. Craig had showered, though he hadn't been able to shave, and his darkly shadowed jaw made her pulse race. He stood in the bathroom, the door open, pushing his hair into place the best he could with his fingers. His wrinkled, white cotton shirt outlined his magnificent chest—the chest she'd slept on last night, where she'd heard the thud of his brave heart.

Frustration trickled through Sabra. Craig still thought he was a coward. What would it take for him to see himself as she did? Telling him obviously wasn't enough. As she walked toward him, she smiled softly. But when he turned his head and met her gaze, shock bolted through her. The look in his blue eyes was once again coldly efficient. Sabra's world spun out of control, and her smile dissolved. Craig was suddenly unreachable, and she felt stripped. Hurt flowed through her as he moved briskly past her.

Craig scowled. He saw Sabra's vulnerable features register shock, then confusion. Her lips were still pouty from his kisses, and he longed to pick her up and carry her back to bed. He shook his head, forcing his heated thoughts away. "First, we need to get a rental car. We'll leave the equipment here, for now. Then we'll change motels and get some clothes and toiletry items."

"Good idea." Sabra struggled to get a grip on her rioting feelings. Craig had always been up-front with her. He'd warned her he was bad news to any woman—especially her. Why had she let her heart get involved?

"We'll wear our weapons."

She hesitated. "I can't. I don't have a jacket to hide the holster."

Craig grimaced. "Okay." He slipped into his shoulder-holster assembly, picked up his weapon from the carpet and took the bullet out of the chamber. "We're going to have to be careful. I didn't get a look at who was after us."

"We should take back alleys or side streets."

"Right." He pushed the clip back inside the pistol and holstered it. Sabra handed him his jacket, and he shrugged it on. "If we get attacked, we need to split up."

She sat on the bed, frowning. "I wish we had backup."

"We don't. At least not until Killian gets here with the Learjet. We need to call in and find out his arrival time."

Sabra felt his hand brush the top of her head in a brief caress, the gesture surprising her. She quickly looked up at him, but Craig's face was expressionless. Still, she gloried in his small, meaningful touch. Why had he done it? There was so much she wanted to talk about, but none of it was relevant right now.

"Ready?" he demanded.

"Yes." Sabra rose and gathered what was left of her courage. As they approached the door, she whispered unsteadily, "Craig, I'm not sorry about what happened between us. No matter what goes on out there. Okay?"

He placed his hands on her shoulders. "Do you think I'm sorry?"

Sabra shook her head and drowned in his hooded blue eyes. "I—no, but I just wanted to let you know in case..." She couldn't say it. *In case she was killed. Or he was.*

She chewed on her lower lip, unable to hold his burning gaze. "There's something I need to tell you, Craig, before we leave this room." Even if he didn't love her, she knew he respected her. And that was enough.

Craig's heart pounded with dread, but he nodded. "Okay, what is it?" It was impossible to steel himself emotionally for whatever Sabra might say, but he suspected it wasn't going to be anything good. As desperate as he was, he had no guard against her. He smoothed the fabric of her blouse across her shoulders, where he felt the accumulated tension.

"Once," Sabra whispered, looking away, "I loved a man. His name was Captain Joshua David. He was a pilot in the Israeli Air Force. I—I met him when I was with the Mossad. I met him at a party one night for officials. He came over and told me he'd fallen in love with me with one look. I didn't believe him, of course, and to tell you the truth, Josh was a jokester who played tricks on everyone. I didn't know it at the time. I just thought he was one of the crazy, drunk pilots at the party.

"Over the next year, Josh made a point of seeing me. He was very extroverted—always smiling. I wondered how he could be that way with the job he had to do. His life was on the line every time he rode that plane into the sky. We'd lost many pilots to the enemy, and I couldn't figure out how he could laugh and smile so much.

"Josh kept telling me he loved me, but I wouldn't believe him." She compressed her lips and shut her eyes. "Then I was at the office one day, and I heard that one of our pilots had been shot down. We didn't know who it was, if he was dead or captured. My father came to my office and told me it was Josh."

She forced herself to look up at Craig. "I cried like a baby when he told me. Then we had to wait two weeks before we found out that Josh had died."

He saw the tears in her eyes. "What did you learn out of that?" he asked her gently, framing her face with his hands, holding her agonized gaze.

"I never believed him," she said in a strained voice. "I always thought he was joking. I guess—I guess, somewhere along the way, I did fall in love with him, Craig. He was a nice guy. He was loved by everyone. There wasn't a mean bone in his body, and he was so patriotic. Oh, he'd steal kisses from me every once in a while, but he'd joke about that, too. Sometimes he'd send me flowers, but then he'd turn around and say he'd meant to send them to his mother or aunt instead. I—I just couldn't trust myself to trust him, I guess."

Craig took his thumbs and wiped the tears from her cheeks. "Maybe he was afraid to be serious with you. Maybe he was afraid you'd turn him down."

Sniffing, Sabra said brokenly, "I don't know. I don't know to this day. I just carry this awful pain around in my heart. I feel guilty in a way, Craig. I never took him seriously."

"He didn't take you seriously, did he?"

"Well...no, but Josh was like that with everyone."

"You never knew when he was being real or joking."

"Y-yes, I guess that's the bottom line." Sniffing again, Sabra moved over to the bedstand and got a tissue. She wiped her eyes and blew her nose.

Craig studied her in the silence as she turned toward him, her eyes bright with hurt. "How long ago did this happen?"

"Five years ago."

"And you still carry him in your heart. I think you loved him, don't you?"

She sighed and walked up to Craig. "If I did, it went unfulfilled."

"He was probably scared to death to tell you seriously that he loved you," Craig said. "Maybe joking was the only was he dared say it. Those words are a big step for most men. Especially if they're afraid of responsibility."

"The responsibility of loving me?"

"Could have been. I've known some men who were so afraid of fearing their feelings weren't returned, they never said said anything at all to the woman they wanted most."

"I see." Miserably, Sabra sighed. "I just felt gutted by it, Craig. I must have cried half a year away after that."

"Then you loved him." He shook his head. "He was never intimate with you?"

She shook her head. "No . . . just a stolen kiss every now and then, that was all."

His throat tightened. "I'm sorry." And he was. He could see the pain in her ravaged eyes. "My mom always said it was better to love and lose than never love at all. I guess, in a way, you know that better than most of us."

"Over the years, I came to the conclusion that if Josh did love me, he was afraid to get serious. For a while, I was so angry at him. Looking back on it now, though, I can see that I wasn't so stellar in our on-again, off-again relationship, either. One day I thought he loved me, the next, I knew he didn't. I didn't have the guts to confront *him* on it, either, Craig."

Craig walked over to her and dropped a light kiss on her cheek. "How has what happened with Josh affected your relationships since then?" It was an important question to ask. Did Sabra think he didn't have the guts the guts to level with her? *Was* he afraid to tell her how he felt? Hell, he wasn't sure what he felt. Maybe he was like Josh. Still, what was most important now was their safety. The mission came first.

Sabra glanced up at Craig's darkened features, then back down at the floor. "I question every man's intent toward me," she admitted. "I shouldn't think they're Josh David in disguise. The first two years, I was afraid of getting involved with a man again, for fear of reading him the wrong way. When I did have a relationship, I misread it anyway." She waved her hand helplessly. "I was never any good at it, I guess."

"I found out the hard way about talking, Sabra." He saw her lift her chin, saw the wounded look in her eyes. "Not that I have all the answers. I don't." He opened his hands. "Over the years, I've had relationships. The woman I wanted to marry, I screwed up on. At that time I was pretty typical of most guys. I didn't know how to communicate.

How to talk. Michelle eventually left me because I couldn't get to my feelings, or share them.'' He smiled sourly. ''That was before the crash.''

''And since then?''

Craig shrugged and said, ''I've stayed away from women for the most part, because I knew what it would mean to open up. That scared the hell out of me. I was worried I'd punch a woman in the face if she slept with me, or hurt her in a million other ways. I didn't dare talk to anyone about what had happened. I was too ashamed, too raw from it, I guess.''

She gave him a look of awe. ''But you were able to—''

''You're different,'' he rasped. ''For whatever that's worth, Sabra, you're different.'' The need to tell her about the chaos of feelings she aroused in him was nearly overwhelming. Though he wasn't a joker like Josh, Craig could see the lasting damage she'd suffered from the pilot's way of handling the situation.

Craig noticed immediately the hope spring into Sabra's eyes. Her lips parted softly, and all he wanted to do was sweep her into his arms and love the hell out of her—love the questions out of her eyes. He wanted to convince her that he wasn't pulling a trick on her as Josh had. But was he? Craig was sure the Israeli pilot had loved Sabra. The man had no doubt also been afraid of commitment, or he'd have met Sabra as an equal and told her the truth of his feelings.

''Let's get this show on the road,'' Craig said abruptly. ''We've got a lot to do in preparation for tonight. We're a good team. We know how to work with each other.'' He saw Sabra's face reflect the hurt of his sudden brusqueness. ''Let's use what we have to keep us alive and try to find that little boy,'' he reminded her a little more gently.

Sabra felt a cramp beginning in her right lower leg, so she slowly moved from her position near Craig. It was around 2:00 a.m., and they lay undetected on the steep hillside near Garcia's estate, surrounded by thick vegetation. Wearing the night goggles they'd luckily carried in the camera bag, she could see the comings and goings of the guards near the empty helicopter pad. She and Craig had been timing the guards' movements and watching for Jason since nightfall.

Haleakala loomed far above them. Everything appeared yellow-green through the goggles. Sabra moved slowly, not making a sound. She saw Craig glance at her, a question in his eyes. Holding up her hand in a sign that she was all right, she moved to a kneeling position. To her left, Sabra saw fog forming higher on the slopes of the inactive volcano. Slowly, the white mist thickened and began to move silently down toward Kula.

They were surrounded by the darkened shapes of eucalyptus trees. Earlier, they'd rented another car, found an out-of-the-way motel and changed. The stretchy black nylon was perfect cover in the darkness, but it wasn't very warm, and the early morning chill made her teeth chatter.

Luckily, they had been able to contact Perseus in the late afternoon, report in and find out that the Learjet was grounded for repairs in Los Angeles. One of the engines had sucked up a flying bird as it came in for a landing at the Orange County Airport, and Killian was stuck with the plane on the mainland for at least another twenty-four hours.

Sabra knew she couldn't talk to Craig. Garcia might have sensitive equipment placed along the fence to detect human voices as much as a mile away. They were within half a mile of his estate, having come around the mountainous side this time, under cover of darkness. Thus far, no one seemed aware of their presence, but that didn't mean much.

She stretched her right leg out and, with her fingers, deeply massaged the cramping calf. Out of the darkness, she heard the *whap, whap, whap* of a helicopter's blades. Turning slowly, she looked up into the night sky. Where? Yes, she saw a darkened shape coming from offshore, its red and green running lights highly visible through the night goggles.

Sabra felt Craig's hand come to rest on her shoulder and squeeze, to let her know he heard the aircraft, too. Garcia's helicopter wasn't on the landing pad at his estate. Could this be his aircraft coming in? Rising slowly to her knees, she watched, her heart picking up in beat.

The whapping of the blades grew stronger and louder upon approach, and Sabra realized it *was* Garcia's aircraft as it swung widely above the estate before hovering and then slowly descending to the concrete landing pad below. She hunkered down, watching. Lights suddenly flooded the landing area. Jerking off the night goggles, she grabbed for the binoculars and pressed them to her eyes. In the wash of bright light, Sabra saw the passenger side as the aircraft landed. Her pulse bounded. It was Garcia! As the helicopter stopped, the blades whirling lazily, a guard ran around to open his door.

Garcia climbed out. She held her breath. Someone else was there. Sabra nearly stood up. Her hands bit into the binoculars as she saw Garcia hold out his hand to a smaller person. Jason? As the boy grasped the man's hand, she saw Jason's face for the first time. Her heart thudded hard in her chest, and she became aware of Craig's heavier breathing next to her. He saw him, too.

Sabra's mouth went dry as she watched Jason climb unsteadily out of the helicopter. Garcia picked him up, laughing, and turned and walked into the estate, a guard following them. The door shut.

Sabra lowered the binoculars. Her eyes met Craig's. She saw fear in them, and anxiety. His skin glistened with sweat. It was only then that she realized the sound of the helicopter had triggered his nightmarish memories.

Reaching out, she gripped his hand hard in her own. Sabra could say nothing, so she slid her arm around his shoulders and pressed him against her for a moment, to let him know she cared. There was very little else she could do. She felt his hand tighten around hers, and as she eased back, she read the anguish and turmoil in his eyes. What was the cost to him to sit this close to the helicopter? It was a great sacrifice, Sabra realized belatedly, some of her joy at discovering Jason diminishing.

She saw Craig wrestle with his inner demons. He rubbed the sweat off his face with the back of his gloved hand, his profile hard and resigned. Hurting for him, Sabra stowed the binoculars back in the canvas bag hidden beneath the leaves in front of them. She looked up to see the fog moving swiftly now, covering the lower slopes of the volcano, like a cottony white blanket.

Soon the fog had drifted down to hide them, too. It was damp and wet, and Sabra shivered. The leaves of the surrounding vegetation became purled with moisture. Soon the eucalyptus leaves above them began a steady *drip, drip, drip* as water ran off their surfaces.

Craig made a sign for her to follow him as soon as the outdoor lights around the helicopter had been switched off. The pilot had gone inside, and the landing area was deserted. It was nearly three in the morning. Easing to his feet, crouching behind the foliage, he began to move stealthily toward the estate.

His heart was pounding with fear, and he wrestled wildly with the nightmare of emotions that the aircraft had triggered. But he had to know if Garcia had any kind of detectors—lasers or otherwise—around the fence. The only way to know was to test the defenses. It was risky, and his heart was thudding like a sledgehammer in his chest. Worse, he worried for Sabra's safety. If Garcia had invisible lasers or sound detectors on the fence, they could set of a silent alarm inside the huge estate. In moments, armed guards could arrive, firing in their direction.

His mouth grew dry as he moved soundlessly through the greenery. The fog was an excellent cover and, better yet, might well disclose the light from any laser alarms. At least it was warm moving around. The fog became so dense that he could barely see five feet ahead of him, and he constantly had to refer to the compass strapped to his left wrist, heading toward the no-longer-visible estate.

Craig knelt and gestured for Sabra to come up. Sensing her approach, he glanced over at her. Night goggles were useless in fog, and his hung around his neck, as hers did. He saw the sheen of perspiration on his brow, saw the intensity in her narrowed eyes as she settled close to him. He held up his hand, showing five fingers. They were within five feet of the fence. She nodded, her lips compressing with tension.

Slowly, he got to his feet. He could detect no laser activity as he finally got close enough to see an outline of the wrought-iron fence. With excruciating care, he began to run his gloved hand slowly up the expanse of the first iron rod. It was slippery with moisture, cold to his touch. He made a painstaking search for any wires or other equipment that might be attached to the fence. Finding nothing on the first rod, he gestured to Sabra to test the next one. If they so much as stepped on a branch and it cracked, they could be found out. Despite the chill, sweat trickled down the sides of his face, soaking into the black fabric.

Each wrought-iron rod had to be checked. The fog thickened, eerily muffling all sounds. The minutes dragged by as they continued around the fence and helicopter-landing area. There was a gate at one end of the concrete landing pad, and Craig carefully searched it for wires, but discovered none. Could it be that Garcia had no perimeter defenses? He found that hard to believe. Perhaps the drug dealer felt smugly safe here on the island, Craig thought as he continued to slowly run his fingers up each wrought-iron rod.

Finally, they came to the edge of the fenced-in area. The estate sat on the edge of a cliff, and the fence stopped at the four-thousand-foot drop. Craig turned around and faced Sabra. The darkness was so complete in the thick fog that they could no longer see each other: they were limited to communicating with brief touches of their bodies as they moved back the way they had come.

Gripping Sabra's hand, Craig tugged at it once to let her know she was to follow him. He placed her hand on the back of his belt, silently asking her to hold on, so she wouldn't get disoriented in the fog. As he crouched down and carefully made his way back up the slope toward where their canvas bag was hidden, he prayed they hadn't been detected. Using the compass they were finally able to make their way back to their original spot.

It was 4:00 a.m. The fog was thicker, if that was possible. And they had at least another hour's walk ahead of them. Craig placed his night goggles back in the bag and hefted it quietly across his shoulder. Sabra maintained her hold on his belt as he began the trek down the slope. As they moved farther away from the estate and possible detection, she began to relax a little.

By the time they reached their car, hidden down a dirt road and shielded from the highway leading to Kula, Sabra was rubbing her arms in an effort to get warm. They changed clothes there, and goose bumps sprang up on her skin as she shed the damp nylon in favor of a dark blue sweatshirt and sweat pants. Neither of them spoke as they hurriedly changed, tossed their gear into the trunk and climbed into the car.

They were at least five miles away from Kula before they spoke. Sabra was holding her hands up to the heater, trying to warm them. Craig drove, his mouth set.

"Are you okay?" she asked.

"Yes and no."

"Jason is with them. I'm so glad we found him." She glanced at him. "I could tell the helicopter brought back bad memories for you."

His mouth tightened. "Yeah, it did. But more important, Jason looked okay, and for that, I'm grateful."

Sabra released a long breath. "Me, too." She studied him. "Terry used to hit the deck every time a car backfired, no matter where he was. He said it was an automatic reflex action."

Craig nodded. His stomach was still twisted in painful knots. Nothing was as frightening as the sound of a helicopter, having it land so close to him. The rush of images from the crash had nearly overwhelmed him. "I thought I was going to scream in terror back there," he admitted roughly. "I was so damned scared my knees were shaking."

Sabra gave him a compassionate look. "You have so much courage, Craig. My heart goes out to you. I wish I could help you—"

"You do." His eyes cut to her quickly, then back to th
road. The fog was thinning, and he could see fifteen o
twenty feet ahead on the highway. Sabra was a friend–
someone he could trust with his life. Having her nearby gav
him something to hold on to.

Heartened, Sabra smiled unsteadily. What she felt fo
Craig was good and strong. If only he felt the same way! Bu
he'd been without a woman for a long time—that was wha
he saw in her. She couldn't dare hope for anything more.

"Sometimes people can be good for each other." Crai
shook his head. "Damned if I know what I give you i
trade, Sabra. I'm a jumpy, thirty-year-old ex-marine wh
has insomnia and will hit anyone who touches him whe
he's asleep."

Sabra heard the derision in his voice and ached for him
"You've always been honest with me, with no apologies,"
she whispered, a catch in her voice. "You don't joke, yo
don't make light of serious things. I'd rather share you
honesty than have you hide from me."

His heart filled with pain. "Yeah, well, there's no get
ting around my problems. They're all pretty obvious."

Sabra said nothing. She knew they would go to anothe
public phone, and she'd make the call to Perseus. Her hear
swelled with joy at being able to share the good news tha
they'd located Jason. The feeling was quickly dampened b
reality. How could they rescue him? Could they? As soon a
they made the call, got something to eat and showered, the
would have to get back out to the estate and watch.

She knew Laura would be ecstatic over the news abou
Jason. Sabra hoped Jake and Wolf could make her frien
understand that just finding her son didn't mean all tha
much. The worst part was ahead of them. They couldn'
trust the police. They could trust no one but themselves. /
ragged breath eased from Sabra's lips, and she reached ou
and squeezed Craig's hand. It was a strong, steady hand
covered with scars that would always remind him of his pas

Covertly, Sabra stole a look at him as he drove cau
tiously through the fog. Dawn was just touching the hori

zon somewhere to the east of the island, the fog like a gloomy blanket.

"Craig?"

"What?"

"Do you have any dreams?"

He gave her a wry look. "Plenty of nightmares."

Sabra glanced back apologetically. "No, I mean dreams of the future—of what you want your life to be like."

"Me? I live hour to hour. Day to day. I'm afraid to look at the future because of the past that sits on my shoulders in the present." He saw her eyebrows dip. "What are you getting at?"

"Oh, I just wondered."

"Do you have dreams?" he countered.

"Yes." Tentatively, Sabra nodded. "Well, I used to."

"Until Josh died?" he asked out of sudden intuition.

"Yes," she admitted.

"What did you hope for before then?"

"I'd always dreamed of marrying a man who would love me for the way I was, not for what he wanted me to be. I'm afraid I'm not much of a cook or housekeeper. My mother went crazy with me in the kitchen. I burned more stuff than I care to think about. I ended up wrecking several of her pots and pans in the process. I hated to dust. I hated to do dishes."

"What would you rather do?" He studied her shadowed face, now set with unhappiness.

"I loved to play soccer. I liked being outdoors. At night I always had my window open, even in the dead of winter, because I loved the fresh air. I guess that's why I like Perseus so much—most of my assignments are outdoors."

Craig tried to tell himself that as her friend, he wanted to share other, private parts of himself with Sabra. Or *was* it friendship? Damn this mission. There was no time to sort through his feelings. What the hell, he wanted to share with her. "You sound a little like a mustang my brother Joe got from one of his Navajo friends for his fifteenth birthday," he ventured.

"Oh?"

"His friend Tom Yellow Horse gave him a mustang no one could tame—a pinto mare, I think. She'd been on the rodeo circuit and she'd bucked off everyone. She hated saddles and hated being snubbed to a post. She'd lash out with her legs if Joe tried to get near her."

Sabra studied his grim features. "What happened to her?"

"Joe eventually realized that the mare wanted her freedom. She didn't like humans. So he let her go."

"He did?"

Craig nodded. "He got me and Dan up early one morning, kicked us out of bed and made us help him. That mare would charge you if you got in the corral with her, so he wanted our help. I remember opening the gate for Joe and watching his face when she galloped off to her freedom. He cried."

"Your brother sounds like a guy with a heart."

"He is," Craig murmured. He glanced at her then frowned. "You're like that mustang, because you don't want to be saddled with house chores or indoor duties."

"One of my stellar eccentricities . . ." she whispered, her voice trailing off. How she ached to see that tenderness return to his eyes, but it was gone—forever. All Craig had needed was her body, she reminded herself—her ability to love him that one, beautiful time. Sabra wanted to cry, but choked the tears down deep inside herself.

Chapter Eleven

Sabra waited, gritting her teeth as she knelt on the ground beneath the thick foliage. They were less than fifty yards from Garcia's estate. For the fourth night in a row, they had crept close to the wrought-iron fence near the helo-landing pad. For the past three nights, at exactly 0300, Garcia had arrived by helicopter with Jason in tow. He always left again shortly after 1800.

Sabra had no idea why, since they couldn't contact the police or any federal agency to help them track the helicopter's route. One thing was evident, however: Jason was never out of Garcia's sight or far from his side. Tonight, she and Craig had decided to rush forward shortly after the helicopter landed and take Jason away from Garcia.

Not liking the plan, but having no other, Sabra crouched on the ground, fear eating at her. She hated operations like this one, for there was nothing clean or simple about it. What if, instead of one guard meeting the helicopter this morning, three or four appeared, armed with submachine

guns? As it stood, even if only one guard came out, they ha
to render him, the pilot and Garcia unconscious.

Instead of bullets, they carried pistols loaded with
powerful tranquilizing agent that Killian had provided then
with. Almost as soon as it pierced the skin, a victim fell un
conscious. Sabra agreed with the decision. They didn't wan
an all-out war with Ramirez or Garcia—they only wante
the boy back. Sending the message that they weren't goin
to kill unless absolutely necessary might help Ramirez de
cide to spare Morgan's life—if he was alive.

Still their choice left them uncomfortably in the line o
fire. Sabra had no doubt that the guard had real bullets i
his submachine gun, and she was sure the pilot and Garcia
were also armed—and more than willing to shoot to kil
Adjusting the bulky armored vest she wore beneath her ny
lon suit, Sabra knew it was the only thing standing betwee
her and sudden death. She was glad Craig was wearing one
too. He knew as well as she did that Garcia didn't hir
slouches who couldn't shoot straight.

Her mouth grew dry as she glanced down at her watch,
dark piece of cloth shielding the luminous dials. It was 0255
Her heart pulsed strongly in reaction. They would sneal
close, wait until just after the helo landed, then leap up o
the edge of the concrete pad, open the wrought-iron gat
and fire. If Jason was accidentally hit, he would survive th
dart tranquilizer—another reason to use them rather tha
bullets.

She raised her eyelashes and squarely met Craig's dark
narrowed gaze. Anxiety was clearly registered in his eyes
Tension hung around them, and Sabra's thoughts turned t
their recent time together. What they shared was like thi
mission—surprising and unstable. Precious moments of in
tense friendship, communication and awareness were bro
ken by awkward silences, sudden coldness and confusion
The snatches of sleep they'd gotten over the past few day
were always in each other's arms, but they were too tired t
make love, sleeping only two or three hours at a time. Eac
day they'd moved to another motel to avoid detection, an
each day they'd hidden in another area to keep tabs o

Garcia's movements. The situation was too crazy for anything to be properly resolved. Sabra had been forced to put their relationship on the back burner until the mission was completed.

The only real hope she felt over their situation was the fact that the Perseus jet was finally on the Maui airport tarmac, and Killian was shadowing them from a safe distance. He'd landed two days ago, and they'd met near dusk in a remote motel on the south side of the mountainous island, crosschecking all their information. He'd provided them with tranquilizing darts and other gear for the mission. Perseus had put out feelers, trying to discover if there was a leak in the local police department, but it had to be done carefully. In the meantime, Killian had contacted the FBI for help.

Again Sabra ran the plan through her mind as they lay quietly beneath Garcia's silent estate. They would snatch Jason and make a run for it down the slope to where their camouflaged car waited on a dirt road off the highway, four miles away. Then they would speed down the highway to the airport, another twenty miles away, near the center of the island. They would meet Killian and the FBI at the Learjet, which would be ready to take off, with Dr. Ann Parsons, an emergency-trauma-trained physician, as well as a psychologist, standing by. Sabra prayed that Dr. Parsons's help wouldn't be needed. Of the utmost importance in every action was Jason's safety.

Trying to moisten her dry lips, Sabra closed her eyes, continuing to review the plan. They each wore headsets, with microphones close to their lips, should they need to talk. Killian had brought a special radio, set at a frequency that wouldn't likely be detected by anyone on the island. And the FBI agents involved were from D.C., not local island agents.

So far, no one knew where the leak was, and everyone was suspect until it could be found. But the two agents with Killian had worked with him a number of times before he retired from active duty with Perseus. Sabra knew Killian's reputation for caution and trusted his choices with her life.

She tried to relax, but it was impossible. Her emotions swung wildly between worry over Craig and worry for Jason. She knew the guard would open fire. He had to be taken out first—and that was her job. Craig would take care of Garcia and the pilot. She had to disable the guard and watch to make sure no others came out the rear door at the end of the building nearest the pad. But what if Craig was wounded? What if she was? If either of them was hurt, they were to be left behind. Get the boy and run. Saving Jason was paramount.

A fierce tidal wave of fear threatened to suffocate Sabra as she ran various scenarios through her overactive imagination. If Craig was shot, she knew in her heart she couldn't leave him behind. But if she didn't run with Jason in tow, all of them would be captured. So much depended upon their swift initial assault—and on luck. She glanced over at Craig's set profile as he watched the estate. How unlike Josh he was. Craig made no apologies for his problems. Miraculously, during the times they had slept in each other's arms, the nightmare had not stalked him. Craig was amazed and grateful, but had warned her it wasn't gone.

Sabra knew it, but she also knew that Craig trusted her as he had no one else since that ugly crash. In trust, there was friendship, and she accepted that. Not that he'd ever said a word to suggest anything more. No, he was very careful about how he phrased things to her, even in their brief moments of passion. Sometimes the look in his eyes belied the distance he'd been treating her with. Nor could Craig stop that endearing half smile, filled with vulnerability, that inevitably pulled at his mouth when she made him laugh. As wounded as he was, there was so much to love about him. Sabra knew he was ashamed of his fears and reactions. And she wondered if he could possibly love her.

Every night when he heard Garcia's helicopter, Craig broke out in a heavy sweat and his hands shook. He couldn't control either action. Sabra hurt for him, but there was no way she could help him. All she could do was hold him for those precious few hours afterward, and let him know through her actions that she loved him with a fierceness that defied description.

Moving carefully, Sabra turned to study the night sky. The fog was beginning to form in earnest between four and six thousand feet on the volcano, as it had every night. If she didn't know better, she'd think Garcia had ordered it, using the fog as a cover for his early morning returns to his estate—to hide from the prying eyes of the law, perhaps. The fog was coming in sooner than usual tonight, and she could see fingers of it reaching the estate, muting black shadows to gray. Would the helicopter come soon? Would it still land, with the fog already approaching?

Worriedly, Sabra glanced at Craig. His face had been blackened, a black knit cap drawn tightly over his skull, with the headset beneath it, the mike almost touching the hard line of his mouth. Sabra's flak vest chafed beneath her suit. Shivering as the fog stole across them, she began to chew nervously on her lip. If it settled too soon, the pilot might divert the flight to the airport. That would mean putting off the operation to another night, waiting for another chance.

The *whap, whap, whap* of helicopter blades sent a shiver down Craig's back. He felt every hair on the back of his neck rise in response. Cutting a glance to Sabra, he saw that she, too, was aware of the incoming flight. It was 3:05 a.m.; the aircraft was five minutes behind schedule. Earlier this evening, they'd seen Jason board with Garcia. Would he be there now? Gripping the night goggles, Craig settled them over his eyes. Normally, the helo made a low pass directly over them on its way to the landing pad, where it would stop at about one hundred feet, hover, then slowly descend to the waiting concrete. His chance to verify if Jason was on board would be on the pass.

Anxiously, he studied the thickening fog. It was coming in too soon, and a light haze covered the area. Would the pilot assess the situation and leave without landing? The conditions were iffy for a helicopter. As a pilot, Craig had hated fog. Helicopters weren't properly equipped for such weather. Military ones were now, but civilian or commercial helicopters ones such as this didn't have the advanced

instrumentation to fly safely through thick fog. Looking up
he saw the lights twinkling beneath the belly of the ap
proaching craft. Soon. Very soon.

He was sweating heavily, exacerbating his concern over
Sabra. She could be killed in the coming firefight. They had
no lethal weapons on their side, and Garcia would be sure
to use some against them. Craig's only consolation was the
armored vests they wore over their vital organs. Still, a shot
to the head would kill them instantly.

Was Jason on board the aircraft? Craig's hands felt
clammy and damp with tortured anxiety. Positioning himself, he held the night goggles steady against his eyes. The
whapping of the blades grew more powerful—and more
emotionally shattering.

His stomach knotted so painfully he felt like groaning as
he swung his gaze skyward. The helicopter was coming in
for a landing despite the worsening weather! Good. The fog
could work for them, if they were lucky. Right now it was
drifting in—thin here, thick there, offering more cover than
they'd anticipated. But could they take out the three men
before a bullet was fired? One shot could alert the entire
armed compound. Craig's heart was pounding hard in his
chest. Particles of the nightmare crash blipped before his
eyes. Sweat ran down his face. Cursing to himself, he forced
the images aside. The belly of the helicopter roared overhead, the vibration pulverizing him. Yes! He'd gotten a brief
glimpse of Jason. The child was on board!

Dropping the goggles, he leapt to his feet and made one
sharp gesture to Sabra, confirming Jason's presence. The
whapping sound thickened as the blades hit the dense fog at
the estate. The lights were switched on at the helipad, as always. Craig drew his tranquilizer pistol and crouched,
snapping a look to his right. Sabra had her gun drawn, too
Her face was taut, her eyes slitted in intense concentration.
He couldn't see the bird, could only hear it laboring in the
thick moisture. Helicopters didn't do well in heavy moisture or high humidity. As Craig moved swiftly through the
foliage toward the iron gate, he knew the pilot had his hands
full right now. *Let it make him less alert,* he prayed silently.

Plant fronds slapped at his body as he lunged up the slippery, damp slope. The fog was thicker, but the vibration of the helicopter shattered through him, shaking his confidence. Blips of the crash again blinded him momentarily. Angrily, Craig forced through the scene. Sabra passed him and moved swiftly toward the gate. It was her job to get the guard who would appear shortly at the door. Craig would leap up on the fence, fire at Garcia and then at the pilot. They would be rapid shots. He'd have to be accurate when Garcia opened the door to climb out. Timing was everything. One missed shot and they could be killed. One mistake and Jason could die, too.

But, as he'd hoped, the fog had become their friend. It was so thick that the lights around the landing pad took on a hazy appearance. He marveled at the pilot's skill. Craig could hear the aircraft descending slowly, carefully. The mist whipped and swirled violently around them, foliage dancing as the whirling blades of the helo disturbed the area. Wind buffeted him as he crouched beneath the fence, waiting.

Sabra disappeared into the fog as she headed for the gate, and his throat constricted with fear. He couldn't see her at all! Would she be able to spot the guard in time? Looking around, Craig could see the fog moving in bands, torn by the helicopter's blades. Straining his eyes, he could make out the white underbelly of the aircraft. Twenty more feet and it would make contact with the pad. His mouth went dry and his heart rate tripled. His fingers nearly cramped around the pistol as he held it ready.

Where was Sabra? They had communications, but they didn't dare break the silence. One of Garcia's sensitive pieces of equipment might pick up their voices, and their cover would be blown. His heart ached in his chest. Why in hell hadn't he told her earlier that he loved her? What if he died? What if she was hurt? Captured? The bitterness in his mouth swept through him. What a fool he'd been. He'd never loved a woman as much as he loved Sabra. Now it was too late.

In the dim, scattered light, Craig saw Garcia sitting griml
on the passenger side of the helo. Right now the guar
should be coming out to open the door for him. No on
came. Had Sabra gotten to him? Craig gripped the bottor
of the wrought-iron fence, ready to aim the pistol. He sa
Garcia's strained features, saw the perspiration on his thick
mustached upper lip. The helicopter landed. Anger was i
Garcia's eyes as he twisted around, waiting for the door t
be opened. The pilot looked harried, stressed by the dange
of the landing.

Come on. Open the door! Craig compressed his lips a
Garcia jerked the latch and swung the door—wide open
Craig raised his pistol and fired once. The dart sank deepl
into the druglord's neck. He slumped, tumbling heavily ou
of the helicopter.

Craig saw the pilot's eyes widen. The man leaned down
Damn! He had a gun! Craig saw Jason, his eyes puffy wit
sleep, looking around in confusion. Leaping upward, hi
muscles straining, Craig took aim as the door swung on
way and then another. There! The dart slammed into th
pilot's chest. The man let out a little cry, then slumped for
ward in his harness, the gun dropping from his hands to th
deck of the aircraft.

As Craig scaled the fence, he heard a sharp retort of
high-powered handgun. It sounded like a .350 Magnum
Damn! *Sabra?* He reached into the helicopter for Jason. Th
child gave a cry and threw up his hands to protect himsel
The blades of the helicopter were still turning at full speed
the pilot hadn't shut the engine down! It took everythin
Craig had to climb into the aircraft, wrap his hand aroun
Jason's arm and haul him out of it.

Two more shots were fired. He whirled around, the bo
under his arm. Jason gave a shriek and started fighting him
Out of the fog, Craig saw Sabra running toward him.

"I've got him!" he rasped. Just as he turned to go ove
the fence, he heard a series of shots ring out. In horrifyin
seconds, he saw Sabra fly forward. Her body crumpled. Th
pistol flew out of her hand. He held back a scream as h
watched her strike the ground. Part of the nylon uniform o

her back had ripped away. Had the armor protected her? He turned, dragging Jason with him, heading toward her.

More shots flew through the air. Craig was halfway to Sabra when he saw her rise to her hands and knees. Voices carried above the sound of the whirling blades. Sabra motioned violently for Craig to go back. The fog thinned just enough for him to see three men running from around the front of the estate. To his left, on the slope, he saw two more guards coming toward them. They were trapped!

Jason shrilled and hit at him. Craig tightened his grip around the boy and gestured violently to Sabra, who was now on her feet, running toward them. There was no choice. None at all. Glaring at the helicopter, he ran toward it. The only way out of this situation was to fly the bird out of the estate. More bullets whined around them. One bit into the concrete, shards flying upward, stinging his lower legs.

"Get to the chopper!" he gasped to Sabra.

"Go!" she cried. "Go!"

He tossed Jason into the helicopter. "Don't move," he roared at the frightened boy. He unsnapped the harness on the unconscious pilot. There! Craig jerked the man out of the cockpit and leapt into the seat. Slamming the door shut, he quickly assessed the controls. His hands shook badly. He felt like crying. Anxiously, he looked around. Sabra jerked the passenger door open, her mouth contorted with pain. He saw no blood on her. The armor vest had protected her. He grappled with the control surfaces, his fingers curving around them. He twisted the cyclic, and the blades whirled faster. The machine shook around them. Bullets began pinging against the helicopter. The fog was their only defense. The aircraft shuddered. They had to lift off now or become sitting targets for the guards rushing in to capture them. *Now! Now or never!*

Craig's mouth flattened as he pulled back on the control. He hadn't flown in nearly two years, yet, it seemed like yesterday. The helicopter strained to break the hold of gravity, the blades shaking and pounding above them. Bullets struck the Plexiglas. He heard Jason cry out and saw Sabra lunge to cover him with her body. The Plexiglas of the

nose shattered, the material exploding inward, and Craig
jerked his head to one side, feeling the hot sting of fragments striking him. The bird was lifting off, but the bullets
were striking it with deadly accuracy.

In moments, the fog closed in below them. Craig used the
rudders beneath his feet and pulled the aircraft in a steep
bank. How close were they to the trees? He had no idea.
Gasping, he tried to ride it out by feel alone. There was absolutely no terrain radar on board the helicopter. It was
dark all around them. Which way was up? Down? His eyes
strained on the gyroscope and flicked back and forth between it and the altimeter.

"It's all right, all right," Sabra gasped, easing away from
Jason. "It's Auntie S, Jason. Look. Look, it's me, honey."
She tried to wipe away some of the frightening greasepaint
that must make her seem like a monster to Jason. She saw
the child's face go from terror to relief. Instantly, he lunged
toward her.

"Auntie S!" he shrieked.

Sabra gulped unsteadily and pulled Jason into her arms.
They were safe. Safe! She glanced over at Craig. His face
was frozen. The wind whipped into the helicopter, buffet-
ing and icy cold. Blood trickled down the side of his face.
She felt a huge, bruised area pounding unremittingly in the
middle of her back where she'd taken the the hit from the
well-aimed bullet. The armored vest had saved her life.

She felt the aircraft moving unsteadily. Anxiously, she
looked at Craig again. He was wrestling with the controls.
Could he fly it? Was he panicking? What was going on?
Afraid for them all, she held Jason to her tightly.

"We're in trouble!" Craig rasped, working the controls.
"The oil pressure is going down!"

Sabra could smell something hot and oily invading the
cabin. She began to hear a high-pitched screech above them.
They were still in the fog. Where the hell were they? How far
from the estate? "What can I do?"

"Strap in!" he roared, wrestling with the sluggish controls. "We aren't going to go far. I'll try for altitude. If the

engine quits, we'll have to make a crash landing. Get on the radio. Call the airport for help.''

Sabra quickly hauled the harness over herself, keeping Jason in her arms. Fumbling because her hands were shaking so badly, she got the radio from her uniform belt and began making a Mayday call to the Maui airport. Where the hell were they? The fog was thinning now. The helicopter was bucking and groaning, the shriek becoming louder. Sabra kept shouting into the radio, using the Perseus call sign for help. She knew Killian and the FBI would be monitoring them. If only they could get to the airport or somewhere near it!

The fog thinned even more. The aircraft lunged and lagged, the whine of the rotor above them coming and going. The smell of hot oil stung her nostrils. She flung a glance at Craig.

"Where are we?"

"About ten miles west of the airport. Tell them I'm following the highway in."

It was a good choice, Sabra thought, as she shouted the information over the racket in the cabin. The fog was completely gone now, and she realized they were roughly a thousand feet above the island, limping along. Jason burrowed his head into her chest, and she held him tightly against her. Her throat ached with tension as she divided her attention between him and Craig. Craig was managing the aircraft. Each time the helicopter dropped a little, she watched him struggle with the controls. The physical effort it took was tremendous, and she saw how pale and taut he'd become.

"Can we make it?" she shouted.

His gaze shot to the oil pressure. They were only five miles from the airport. If only they could get there! If only he could set the bird down before the engine quit. The smell of burning metal struck his flared nostrils. His hands tightened on the controls. "We aren't gonna make it. Prepare to crash!"

The order roared through Sabra. She bit back a scream as she smelled the hot odor of melting metal. Without the precious oil as a lubricant, the shriek and grinding of engine parts continued. The helicopter was ceasing its forward motion. She heard Craig curse.

"It's no good! I've got to shut the engine down or it's gonna explode!"

She saw him reach for the control that would switch the engine down. Cold, icy wind whipped into the cabin. She was frightened as never before. The moment the engine was shut down, the helicopter plummeted downward. Jason screamed in terror, his small arms wrapped around her. Sabra shut her eyes, buried her head against the boy and held him as tightly as she could. She heard Craig gasp.

To his left, Craig could see the lights of the airport. They were less than three miles away! Everywhere else it was dark. Murderously dark. The helicopter was dropping like a rock beneath him. All of his training came back to him in a rush. He pushed the nose down, aiming it toward the island. He heard Sabra give a cry, but ignored it. He had to aim the nose down in order to pick up enough speed to haul the aircraft up at the last minute, to flare it so the swinging blades would catch the last pocket of air. If he didn't do that, they would crash and burn. There was almost three-quarters of a tank of fuel still on board and no time to dump it. If he couldn't bring the wildly swinging, bucking aircraft in for a crash landing, they would all die in the resulting explosion or burn to death afterward.

Below, he saw the highway and a few stabbing lights of cars. Wrestling with the aircraft, he shoved hard right on the rudder and tried to get the bird to move to the west of the highway. He couldn't see any lights of homes. Maybe it was a sugar cane or pineapple field. Craig prayed that wherever he was heading, there were no people below.

He had no way of judging anything except through instinct honed by years of experience. The helicopter was picking up speed, the blades still turning sluggishly. It was a matter of intuition to know when to lift the nose, hopefully at the last possible moment. Because he'd shut down the engine, Craig had no instruments to tell him how close he was to the ground. All he had now was his ability to judge where the night sky met the darkened horizon. The smell of hot metal was still strong and stung his nostrils. The engine could burst into flames at any moment.

Something told him to haul back on the nose. He heeded the voice inside his head. Gripping the controls hard, he pulled back, pitting sheer, brute strength against the gravity-driven force of the aircraft plummeting out of the sky. As he reared back hard against the seat, every muscle in his body screamed in sudden protest. Hot pain raced up his arms as he held the controls in place. *Come on, come on! Come up! Dammit, come up!* His lips pulled away from his clenched teeth. His eyes widened.

At the last moment, he saw the ground racing up at them. It was a sugar-cane field! Had he pulled up too late? Were they going to nose into the earth? Die in the explosion as the fuel sprayed around them like a fiery rain? Horrible thoughts paralyzed him as he called on every last ounce of his strength. It couldn't happen again! Blips of the fire after the crash in the Iraqui desert struck him. Savagely, he shook his head, his eyes on the ground coming up fast below them.

He heard Jason crying. He heard Sabra gasp. The nose came up. The flailing blades caught the last of the air. Bracing himself, Craig held the controls steady. The helicopter groaned and shrieked. The blades whooshed thickly overhead. The plummet subsided. The bird steadied about fifty feet from the ground. At the last possible moment, Craig guided the bird downward, playing the rudders with his booted feet. He felt the tail strike the field first, the jolt vibrating through the cabin. Because he wasn't strapped in, he was thrown forward. The aircraft bobbled. He jerked back on the controls, hearing the tail drag more deeply into the ground.

The aircraft groaned and slammed onto a left skid. Craig felt himself being torn out of the seat, and he threw up his arm to protect his head. The aircraft plowed into the field, metal tearing and scraping. He heard the blades striking, breaking. A person could be cut in half by one of those blades. The aircraft rolled over and over. Craig found him-

self lying against the instrument panel. Sobbing for breath
he realized they'd stopped tumbling.

"Sabra!" His voice was scratchy with terror. He blinked
the sweat out of his eyes. She was hanging upside down, he
saw, trapped in the harness. Jason was still in her arms, alive
and unhurt.

"Get me out of this," she gasped.

Craig scrambled toward her, feeling like he was moving
in slow motion. He experienced pain in his left arm, but ignored it as he pushed himself upward on unsteady feet. In
one motion, he took the knife strapped to his left leg and
began to saw through the harnesses to free her.

"We've got to get out of here," he rasped. "I smell fuel
leaking. This bird could go at any moment."

"I know, I know," Sabra sobbed, allowing Jason to crawl
out of the broken window. The last strap was sawn through
and she fell unceremoniously to the floor of the aircraft.

"Get out. Get out!"

Sabra felt Craig's hand biting into her arm, shoving her
through the broken nose of the helicopter. She could smell
the nauseating odor of fuel around them, as well as the hot
metal of the rotor assembly. Craig was right: the aircraft
could explode at any moment.

She fell out onto the damp soil, on her hands and knees.
Jason sat there, his eyes wide with terror, looking up at the
broken helicopter.

"Craig?" She stumbled to her feet and twisted around.
Where was he?

"Get Jason. Get the hell out of here!" Craig shouted. His
foot was trapped in some wreckage. *Damn!* He leaned down
and jerked on a piece of metal that had been twisted in the
crash. He was breathing in sobbing gasps. Yanking at the
metal that held him, he cursed. Glancing up, he could see
Sabra pick up Jason and start flailing through the eight-
foot-tall sugar cane.

"Son of a bitch!" He used all his strength on the metal.
There! He was free! In one motion, Craig dived out of the
broken nose. He hit the ground hard, rolling to reduce the
impact.

Suddenly, he heard a *whoosh*. He was less than six feet from the aircraft when he got to his feet. His eyes widened. Fire had started on the rotor assembly. Damn! Scrambling, he dug the toes of his boots into the damp soil. He had to get away. Any second now the bird would explode.

Craig had made it barely twenty feet from the helicopter when the explosion occurred. A powerful shock wave hit him first, scorching his exposed skin. The next thing he knew, he was flying though the air, knocked at least twenty feet more by the blast. The whistling and shrieking of metal torn loose in the explosion screamed about him. He slammed to the ground, throwing his arms over his head, rolling end over end.

Hot, burning sensation struck him in the legs and arm. Shrapnel. He knew the stinging bite well. Dazedly, Craig rolled over and sat up. The flaring fire from the burning aircraft made it seem like daylight for several hundred feet in every direction. The thick stalks of sugar cane, with their sharp, cutting edges, had been laid out horizontally, flattened like so many toothpicks in the wake of a hurricane.

Above the roar of the fire, he heard a child scream. Jason! Shaken, Craig shoved himself to his feet. He wobbled unsteadily, suddenly dizzied. Where were they? Anxiously, he searched the hellish landscape of dancing firelight and shadows. Stumbling around the end of the wreck, he saw Jason standing about seventy-five feet from the aircraft. His eyes narrowed. Sabra! He opened his mouth to scream, but nothing came out. She lay unmoving at the boy's feet.

Oh, God, no! He dug his feet into the slippery cane stalks, running brokenly, as fast as he could. Jason's small face was dirtied, streaked with tears as he stood helplessly beside Sabra's body. As Craig approached, the boy covered his face.

Craig fell to his knees near Sabra's head. She lay on her belly, her face buried in the flattened sugar cane. One arm was outstretched, the other tucked beneath her body. Gasping for breath, he called her name.

"Sabra? Sabra...." His hands trembled as he rapidly skimmed her body, searching for wounds. Had the blast knocked her unconscious? Slowly, he turned her over on her

back, her head and shoulders resting against his knees. A
cold, violent fear gripped him. In the dancing firelight, he
could see a dark trail down the side of her neck.

Reaching down, Craig's fingertips touched the black
surface. It was warm. Sabra's blood. Wildly, he searched her
hair and the back of her skull. A piece of shrapnel lay buried in the rear of her neck. Leaning down, sobbing, Craig
could see by the glow of the fire that the metal had partially
severed an artery. *Oh, God, no! No!* Sabra was bleeding to
death beneath his hands! She couldn't die! His mind whirled
with options—and near-paralyzing terror.

Jason had come up to him, sobbing wildly, calling Sabra's name. Jerking a look up, Craig realized dazedly that
the lights of cars were coming their way, bouncing over the
piles of cane stalks. Were they friend or foe? It could be
Garcia's men having followed the noisy, limping helicopter.
Sobbing for breath, applying pressure to Sabra's neck, Craig
knelt in the field, feeling her lifeblood leaking through his
aching fingers. Sabra's face was startlingly pale in the flickering light. Her lips were parted, as if in a scream she'd
never released. Her body was limp and slack against his.
Tears stung his eyes as he continued to place pressure on the
wound.

The headlights halted, trained squarely on them. Was it
Garcia? Oh, God, he'd kill them all right now. There would
be no mercy. With his free arm, Craig dragged the boy behind him, trying to shield him with his body. They had no
weapons. No way to defend themselves. Tears splattered
down his drawn face. Sabra was dying. With each thud of
her heart, he could feel the pulse beneath his fingers weak-
ening—from a beat, to a feeble flutter.

Craig's heart clenched in grief, and he watched helplessly
as four men appeared from the two cars. The headlights
were blinding him. He couldn't see. Jason stopped crying
and clung to him, hiding behind him.

Then, in the harsh glare of the lights, Craig recognized
Killian's taut features. He let out a cry for help. Instantly
Killian came on the run, followed by the others. To Craig's
relief, he saw Dr. Parsons awkwardly flailing toward them

her physician's bag in hand. As Killian ran up to him, Craig's voice cracked with alarm.

"Sabra's dying! She's bleeding to death. Oh, God, help her! Help her!"

Chapter Twelve

Craig sat numbly in a plastic chair on the surgery floor of the Maui Hospital. The ache in his heart wouldn't stop, the pain encompassing more and more of his chest. He rubbed his smarting eyes tiredly, with dirty, bloodstained hands.

"Talbot?"

He heard Killian's gruff, low voice. Gradually, he became aware of the other man's presence and the fact that he was holding a paper cup of coffee toward him. Woodenly, he reached for the cup, his hand shaking badly.

"You need to go down to emergency and get looked at," Killian said, slowly easing into a crouched position in front of him. "There's nothing you can do up here to help Sabra. Dr. Parsons is working with the best surgeon this hospital has. If Sabra has a chance, it's here and now."

Sliding both hands around the small cup, Craig felt the warmth of it begin to permeate the iciness inside him. How long had it been since they'd arrived at the hospital? Shutting his eyes, he bowed his head, feeling the last of the adrenaline giving way to utter exhaustion. Tears leaked out of his eyes, small beads clinging to his lashes. Working his mouth against a sob, he stiffly rose to his feet. Unable to meet Killian's gaze, Craig opened his eyes only after he'd turned away. Walking on sore feet and aching legs, he forced himself over to the window. He carefully set the cup down on the windowsill before his shaking hands splashed the burning contents all over him. Not that it mattered. The only thing that mattered was Sabra.

He felt Killian approach and glanced at him out of the corner of his eyes. The merc stood next to him, his mouth thinned, a scowl on his brow.

"She could die...." Craig forced out the statement in a low, shaken voice.

"Yes."

Killian wouldn't lie about anything, especially not something this serious. This heartbreaking. Craig tried to shore up his roiling emotions. "How's the kid?"

"Jason?"

"Yeah."

"They took him to the children's wing. The doctor on duty said he was fine. No wounds. At least, not physical ones."

Craig heard the derision in Killian's tone. "Yeah, he was pretty shaken up."

"It's none of my business, but I think you ought to get looked at and then go visit Jason. He's asking for you."

Turning, Craig said, "Me?"

"Yeah. Why?"

"He doesn't know me from Adam. He knew Sabra."

"Maybe so, but the kid knows you helped save his life. I think he's reaching out." Killian looked at the bank of phones on the wall. "Laura's on her way. I just got off the phone with her and Jake. She's taking the first commercial flight available out of D.C. Shah Randolph, Jake's wife, is escorting her." Killian looked at his watch. "It's 0500 now. She'll to arrive in Maui at 1500 this afternoon. I'll go pick them up and bring them down here, but until then Jason's alone."

Craig stood tiredly and tried to swallow his unshed tears.
"Sabra's still in surgery—"

"Dr. Parsons knows you'll be in the hospital some
where, if she gets done sooner than you think." Killian
placed his hand on Craig's slumped shoulder. "Get medi
cal treatment, get a shower and then go see Jason. The kid
needs you. He needs to be held."

Brokenly, Craig nodded. Even now, he couldn't be self
ish. The boy had gone through a hell few people would eve
encounter in their lives. To have endured it at such a young
age had probably traumatized Jason forever. Rubbing his
brow, he nodded. "Okay, I'll go down. Will you—"

Killian nodded darkly. "I'll stay up here. When Dr. Par
sons comes out of surgery, I'll tell her where you've gone."

The lump in Craig's throat refused to go away, no matter
how many times he swallowed. Belatedly, he looked down
at his hands. They were cut all over from the flying Plexi
glas. Dimly, he was aware that he'd probably have to have
shrapnel taken out of his legs, too. The pain of a doctor
digging the metal out of his body would be easy to take
in comparison to the mere thought of losing Sabra. She
couldn't die. She just couldn't. He loved her. And God for
give him, he'd never told her that.

As he wearily turned toward the elevators, Craig re
played the awful trip by ambulance to the hospital. If Dr
Parsons hadn't been there, Sabra undoubtedly would have
died en route. And all Craig had been able to do was sit
there, watching dumbly as Parsons worked to stabilize Sa
bra's life. Bits and pieces of the crash in the desert had
overlaid Sabra's ghostly features as tears leaked uncontrol
lably from Craig's eyes. He had wished over and over that
it had been him hit by that unlucky metal fragment. If
anyone deserved to live, it was Sabra. He was worthless
in comparison, a man controlled by a haunting past he
couldn't overcome, while she was so strong and beautiful
and confident. Life hadn't tortured her as it had him. She
had hopes and dreams. Craig wished with every bone in his
body that he could trade places with Sabra on that gurney.

All that time, Jason had been in his arms, clinging to him, his head buried against Craig's chest. Craig divided his attention between them, keeping his hand on the boy's dirty hair to protect him from seeing the blood, from seeing someone he loved like that. No child deserved such trauma. Craig had rocked Jason back and forth, numbly whispering that it would be all right, that Sabra was going to be all right. The boy had sobbed wildly, almost hysterical in the aftermath. They were lies, Craig thought bitterly as he repeated the soothing words. But he felt helpless and didn't want Jason to be any more upset than he already was. It had been the longest forty minutes of Craig's life.

Now in the elevator, he tried to pull himself together. Only then did he become aware of how badly he stunk, as the odor of fear and the metallic scent of blood registered in his sensitive nostrils. As he left the elevator and headed for the emergency room, Craig saw nurses and patients staring at him as if he were some kind of avenging ghost come to haunt them. He was covered with mud from the field, bloodied by glass and shrapnel. He must look like hell. Or the walking dead.

One of the nurses in ER gave him another cup of hot, black coffee to drink. He sat on a gurney, stripped down to his shorts while a doctor examined him. Later, he lay on the gurney, fighting waves of pain as the doctor pulled more than thirty pieces of glass from his face, neck and shoulder, and two pieces of twisted metal from his lower legs. But the pain of the extraction remained small in comparison to his worry for Sabra. He lay there afterward as his wounds were being swabbed and dressed, wondering how she was doing. How much blood had she lost? Had he put enough pressure on that torn artery to save her life? Had he not?

The agony of waiting shredded Craig. Finally, a nurse showed him to a shower and brought in a surgeon's smock and pants for him to wear in lieu of his filthy, bloody clothes. Craig stood under the warming flow of water, hoping it would ease the pain in his chest. All his injuries were minor, and a shower was permissible. Awkwardly he ran the bar of soap through his hair, then stood beneath the spray again, tears streaming freely down his cheek. Sabra couldn't be torn from him! She just couldn't. He gasped for breath, the water stinging his eyes as he leaned weakly against the stall, his fists clenched against the wall at that terrible possibility.

She had loved someone who hadn't had the guts to tell her he loved her—whatever his reasons. Craig had thought it too soon to tell her. But why hadn't he? Oh, God, why hadn't he? If Sabra had known, it might have helped her fight harder to live. He bowed his head, water running in rivulets across his frozen features as his chest shook with a great sob. In here, no one would hear him cry. It was the only safe place to weep for a loss he was sure was coming. Even with tightly shut eyes, he could see Sabra's warm gray eyes dancing with love for him, and suddenly Craig knew, deep in his injured soul, that she did love him. Sabra wasn't the kind of woman to rush into anything; that's why she'd withheld her real feelings from him.

Why did everything have to happen so suddenly? He'd become so jaded, so hardened against life since the crash. The idea of falling in love with someone as beautiful and warm as Sabra had never entered his sordid reality. Not until she'd crashed into his life, tearing that sense of hopelessness away from him, breathing new life into him, making him reach out and hope once more—and realize the depth of the personal, lonely hell he'd fallen into. Bitterly, Craig opened his eyes and slowly eased away from the wall. Would he ever be able to tell Sabra how much she'd given him? She'd literally handed him back his life. When he'd slept in her arms, he'd felt peace for the first time in years. Her presence strengthened him and allowed him to amass his own strength for healing himself.

Such was the miracle of Sabra, he realized, turning off the faucets and standing, dripping, in the stall. Life hadn't exactly been kind to her, either, yet she'd moved ahead despite it. Craig opened the door and reached for the thick terry-cloth towel. Damn his practical realism. He'd been so good at being logical, he'd almost missed the most important person in his life—Sabra. He rubbed the towel against his face, uncaring if some of the small cuts started to bleed again. Water dripped off his hair, and he went through the motions of drying it, feeling overwhelming numbness coupled with exhaustion.

Jason. He had to see Jason. After donning the green cotton clothes, Craig went in search of a nurse who could direct him to the boy. With every step he took it felt like twenty extra pounds of weight were bearing down on his legs and feet. He couldn't recall ever feeling this low. But then, he'd never before had the woman he loved lying on a surgery table, her life in jeopardy.

Nurse Bonnie Blaire, a pert, young, red-haired woman, led him to Jason's private room.

"The doctor has given him a mild sedative because he was hysterical, Mr. Talbot." She smiled sadly as she halted at the door. "If you want the truth, I think the little boy just needs to be held...."

Craig nodded wearily. "Okay, I'll see what I can do." Who didn't need to be held right now? Hell, he ached to have Sabra's arms slide around him. He'd crush her so tightly against him that the air would rush from her lungs. Well, that wasn't possible, but maybe he could help the boy.

The nurse quietly closed the door behind him, and Craig tiptoed forward. Jason looked awfully small in the large bed. Someone had given him a toy—a well-loved teddy bear. Absently, Craig remembered that Jason's favorite blanket and toy were still in their car at Kula.

He lay on his side, his face pressed into the stuffed bear. The numbness left Craig's heart as he walked closer. Jason's eyes were shut, and the tracks of tears he'd cried had dried across his flushed cheek. Craig reached over and gently mussed his hair.

The boy gave a small whimper. Craig kept stroking his head and watched the effect it had on him. The small hands, once clasping the teddy bear in tight fists, gradually began to loosen. The blanket that covered him was thin, and Craig felt him trembling.

Easing down the guardrail, Craig sat on the edge of the bed, facing Jason. A long time ago his mother had rubbed his shoulders and back when he was sick, so he did it now for the boy. Craig knew he couldn't take the place of Sabra, Laura or Morgan, but at least he could try to give Jason some solace. Little by little, he felt him begin to relax. The child looked so innocent lying there, and he himself felt so beat-up and battered by life. Jason had his whole life in front of him. Sabra might have hers taken from her. And Craig would be left alone.

Pain shattered his heart, and without thinking, he eased himself up on the bed and gently bundled the small boy into his arms, teddy bear and all. Maybe he couldn't hold Sabra, and he knew no one was going to hold him, but he could make Jason feel safe—and loved. Jason moaned a little and buried his head on his chest, his small hand stretching outward, then relaxed completely against him.

Craig's mouth curved slightly as he felt the child entrust himself to him. The feeling was warming. Almost euphoric. He slid his arm across Jason's small back, his own eyelids closing. Craig could feel Jason's tiny heartbeat against him. The shallow rise and fall of the boy's chest told him he was now asleep. A ragged sigh escaped Craig's lips as he felt his muscles, one by one, begin to release the tension they'd held so long. Then he fell into an exhausted sleep, holding a little boy and praying for Sabra's life.

"Craig?"

He felt fingers squeezing his shoulder tentatively. Sleep pulled at him, and he fought to come awake. The voice was unfamiliar. *Who?* He forced his eyes open and realized groggily that Jason was curled tightly in his arms, still asleep. Blinking to clear his vision, he looked up toward the voice.

Dr. Parsons smiled wearily. "Killian told me to be careful how I woke you."

Instantly, Craig came awake. He eased Jason onto the bed, still keeping one hand on the boy's shoulder. "Sabra?" His voice was hoarse with sleep. His heart pounded hard in his chest, fear gutting through him.

Ann tightened her grip on his shoulder. "I think she's going to make it. Right now, she's critical, but she's in recovery."

Relief avalanched through Craig. He was dizzied by the news. Dr. Parsons still wore her green surgery gown, the cap over her hair, the mask hanging around her neck. Searching her smiling eyes, he rasped, "She's alive?"

"Very much so. We had to give her a blood transfusion. Nearly two pints." Ann lost her smile. "She went into cardiac arrest on the table due to blood loss, but we brought her back, thank God." She patted his shoulder. "She's doing much better."

Cardiac arrest. Stunned, Craig felt tears flood into his eyes. He'd nearly lost Sabra. Somehow, he had known that; such was the invisible line of communication he had with her. Wiping his mouth with the back of his hand, he fought against the tears. "When can I see her?"

"Now, if you want. She won't know you're there, though. It will be an hour or two for the anesthesia to wear off. You can't stay more than five minutes an hour until we upgrade her from from intensive care."

Carefully, Craig divested himself of the sleeping boy. Easing himself off the bed, he made sure that the teddy bear took his place as much as possible. Tucking the blanket over Jason's shoulders, he said, "Will someone be with Jason? He's really shook up over all this."

"I'll make sure a nurse comes in and sits with him," Ann said gently.

"What time is it?"

"It's 7:00 a.m."

He'd slept two hours. It wasn't much, but it was enough. Craig's heart soared with joy as he turned to the physician. "Thank you for saving her," he rasped, and he reached out, gripping her long, lean hand. If Craig didn't know better, he'd have guessed Ann Parsons was a painter, not a surgeon. But he supposed both were artists in their own way. One painted beautiful things, the other used the artistry of her hands to save a life. In this case, Sabra's life.

"I'll be over shortly, Craig."

He nodded and quickly left the room, heading down the hall toward the bank of elevators. Feelings raged unchecked through him as he waited impatiently for the elevator to take him to the recovery floor. The depressing numbness that had sunk its claws into him had miraculously disappeared. The weight that inhabited his legs was gone, too. What was left of his exhaustion was torn from him as he hurried down the hall to the ICU nurse's station.

Sabra was going to live! The thought kept playing through him like a wonderful chord of music. Craig barely felt the tile floor beneath his feet, was scarcely aware of anything beyond an inner joy that made him feel as if he were walking on air. A nurse spotted him coming and must have known who he was, because she met him and walked him to the recovery room.

"She's not conscious yet, Mr. Talbot, but Dr. Parsons said for you to stay with her, talk to her and hold her hand. She won't respond, but that doesn't matter. I'll come for you in five minutes."

Craig stepped inside the room. Sabra was the only patient there, IVs in both arms, the white sheet emphasizing her pale, slack features. Swallowing hard, he moved to the side of her gurney. Her thick, black hair had been gathered up in a white towel, and he saw the dressing that now hid the ugly, gaping wound the shrapnel had made in her neck. Her lips were colorless, her lashes lying softly against her taut skin.

Gently, ever so gently, Craig leaned over the bed and placed his mouth against her slack lips. He didn't care that she didn't know he was there. He wanted to kiss her, to welcome her back to life—to him—if she would have him when this was all over. Life had never seemed so tentative as now, as he felt the coolness of her lips beneath his own. Her breathing was so shallow that at first he was alarmed, thinking she wasn't breathing at all. He eased his mouth from hers and watched her chest for a long, fearful moment. Only when he saw the minute rise and fall of the white sheet draped across her did he release a ragged breath of his own.

Lightly, he grazed her smooth, flawless brow with a fingertip, lost in the soft texture of her skin. Even now, Sabra was beautiful—untouched. Yet the woman had the heart of a lion, there was no doubt. She had faced death with him—and won. Slipping his fingers over hers, he felt how chilled she was and grew worried again. Was she warm enough? How badly Craig wanted to take her in his arms, hold her and warm her as he had Jason.

"Five minutes," the nurse murmured from the entrance, giving him an apologetic smile.

Craig nodded. He leaned down, his lips close to Sabra's ear. "Sweetheart, this is Craig. I want you to know I love you. I should have said it earlier." He closed his eyes, choking back a wealth of feelings. "Listen, I just want you to get well, okay? Dr. Parsons says you're going to make it. You've lost a lot of blood, but you're going to be fine. I love you, Sabra. Don't ever forget that. No matter what happens, no matter what life throws at us, just know I'll always love you...."

Sabra heard voices, heard a little boy's high-pitched, excited tone. Then she felt the touch of a small hand on her arm—a warm little hand. Another voice. A woman's, soft and strained. She fought to come awake, but her lashes felt like weights against her cheeks. And then she heard a very familiar voice, along with a touch that could never be mistaken. It was Craig. She felt his strong fingers wrap around her left hand. On her right hand, she felt the boy's touch. The voices melded together in confusion. She stopped struggling, feeling so very weak. The voices ebbed away, and she felt as if she were floating once again within a warm cloud of light.

The touch of Craig's hand brought her back to consciousness, drew her out of that floating cloud of light. She felt his fingers stroking her arm gently, with reverence. This time she recognized the other voices—Jason's and Laura's. Fragments of scenes blipped in front of her closed eyes—of being hit with a bullet and flying five feet forward. Dully, Sabra felt the bruising pain in her back where the vest had

stopped the bullet from penetrating her body. She should b
dead, she thought.

Then she remembered the helicopter crashing, remem
bered jerking Jason into her arms and running as hard an
fast as she could through the cane field, away from th
smoking aircraft. The explosion... Sabra's brows knit at th
memory. She recalled the heat rolling across her, recalle
pressing Jason hard against her chest to protect him fror
flying debris. And then a white-hot sensation had slamme
into her neck, making her drop him. It was the last thin
Sabra recalled: falling in slow motion to the muddy, we
ground and hearing Jason screaming her name.

"I think she's coming awake."

Sabra heard Laura's tremulous voice and felt her hand o
her shoulder. Her whole focus swung to Craig's touch
which never left her hand.

"I think so, too," he murmured.

Craig's voice was low and off-key. Sabra felt the warmt
of his mouth press briefly against her brow. She absorbe
his unexpected kiss, feeling a joy and lightness flow throug
her. How she loved him!

Where was she? Was he all right? And Jason? Thos
anxious questions forced her to barely open her eyes. Th
first person she saw was Craig, looking down at her, worr
in his dark, exhausted gaze. She was alarmed at the blood
scabs on the right side of his face, the redness in his eyes
as if he'd been crying, and the tortured line of his mouth
Opening her lips, she tried to speak, but only a whisper c
sound came forth.

"Ssh," Craig said, squeezing her hand gently, "don't tr
to talk, sweetheart. We're all safe. You're going to make it.
He tried to smile and failed, drowning in her shadowy gra
eyes.

"Thank God," Laura whispered, leaning over an
touching her shoulder, "you're going to be fine."

Sabra divided her limited attention between them, as the
stood on either side of her bed. Laura looked gray with fa
tigue, her eyes red rimmed, filled with tears. Only Jason'

bubbly smile encouraged her. The boy leaned over and placed a very wet kiss on her cheek.

"Get well, Auntie S! Mommy says you get to come home with us. We get to fly in Daddy's airplane!"

Sabra's mouth pulled into a slight smile, and she held Jason's sparkling, shiny gaze. Of all of them, he looked the least damaged by what had happened. She found it hard to believe that he could spring back so quickly from the kidnapping. Perhaps that was a testament to his youth—his small, innocent view of the world. Craig's fingers interlaced with her own, and she slowly moved her head to meet his blue gaze. The warmth in his eyes, the unabashed welcome for her alone, made her try to smile again. Weakness spread through her, and though she wanted to speak, it was impossible.

"Honey," Laura said to her son, "I think Auntie S wants to sleep now...."

"Ahh, Mommy, I want to tell her what happened!"

"Not now, honey. Come on, let's leave Craig to stay with Auntie S. Come on...."

Craig watched Laura pick up her son and leave the room. He brought a chair over to Sabra's bedside and sat down. Stillness fell over the room, and only her soft, shallow breathing could be heard. At least the beeps and sighs of the multitude of ICU instruments and monitors were gone. In twenty-four hours, Sabra had gone from critical to serious. No one had breathed a greater sigh of relief than Craig. Gently, he slid her hand between his again and held it. Her flesh was still cool to the touch.

When Sabra's lashes moved, he realized she hadn't fallen back asleep. Clearing his throat, he rasped, "Can you hear me, Sabra?"

She squeezed his hand weakly. Did Craig realize how wonderful it was to be touched by him? To hear his roughened voice once again? Did he know how much she'd feared for his life? Tears stung her eyes, and she felt them bead and slip down the sides of her face. She felt Craig release her hand. Then his trembling fingers eased the tears from her cheeks.

"It's okay," he said unsteadily. "Everyone is okay, Sabra. You're the one we were worried about." He hesitated. "Worry wasn't even close, sweetheart. God, I thought you were going to die out there in the cane field. I was so scared. So damned scared, Sabra."

What little strength she had she used to open her eyes again. She saw the tortured look in Craig's gaze, felt the terrible pain in his voice and in his hand as he barely touched her arm once more. She wanted to ask questions, but the weakness claimed her, and all she could do was surrender to that white cloud of light. As she drifted away, she could hear Craig speaking to her, but the words became garbled and distant. Right now, she needed to sleep.

Craig sat for a long time just watching Sabra sleep. Had she heard him? He'd quietly told her he loved her, but he wasn't sure if she'd understood. Dr. Parsons had warned him that the first twenty-four hours, Sabra would sleep a great deal, mostly due to the shock and trauma of the surgery, as well as getting rid of the anesthesia in her system.

He studied her fingers in the silence, looking at the wedding ring on her left hand. It was a fake one, of course, for the mission. She'd never taken it off even though their cover had been blown after the first day. Was that a fluke? Had she worn it for other reasons? His wistful side, which was working overtime lately, said that she wore it because she loved him, wanted him for her husband someday.

With a soft snort, Craig eased out of the chair and placed Sabra's limp hand across her blanketed form. The day was coming to a close, the sunlight streaming through the venetian blinds, creating bars on the opposite wall. The door opened and he looked up. Dr. Parsons gestured for him to come into the hall.

Outside, Craig noted that she was back in her blouse and slacks. He wondered briefly why Ann, who was certainly attractive, had never married. He knew little of her, knew little of the reasons why she'd gone to work for Perseus. Maybe Morgan had known her before he'd formed the company.

"I just got a call from Jake," Ann said, walking with him down the long hall, "and he wants all of us to come back as soon as possible. I told him Sabra needed another twenty-four hours before she could be moved."

"I don't think it's safe to stay here," he agreed, his gaze constantly roving up and down the hall. When Killian wasn't keeping guard on Sabra's room, he was. They took turns every twelve hours to ensure that Garcia wouldn't get to her and finish the job. Nowhere was safe.

"Jake is worried about that, too," Ann continued in a low voice. She clasped her hands behind her back as she walked. "The FBI has apparently found a leak in the Maui police department." She traded a frown with him. "Sam Chung is a mole for Garcia."

Groaning, Craig halted and thrust his hands onto his hips. "We stepped right into the middle of it, didn't we?"

"Yes, you did. Jake said to tell you that you did a good job. He's as relieved as we are that Sabra's going to recover. Right now, the Honolulu police are investigating Chung. They placed a wire tap on his phone and monitored several calls to Garcia's estate. It's a good thing you never went back to the Westin. Jake thinks they were waiting for you."

Grimacing, Craig nodded. "We just kept moving around, Ann. A different room every night, under different names. It worked, thank God."

She smiled absently and halted in the middle of the hall. "Listen, I know you've got a lot on your shoulders right now...."

"What do you mean?"

With an embarrassed smile, Ann said, "With Sabra, I mean. You do care for her, don't you? At the crash site I saw the look on your face, heard the tone of your voice...."

"Yes," Craig rasped heavily, "there's something there, Ann. But I don't want it all over the place. I haven't even had time to talk to Sabra. I don't need gossip floating around."

Touching his arm, she said, "If Killian suspects anything, he's keeping it to himself. It's just that I saw the look in your eyes..."

Crossing his arms, he leaned against the wall and studied her. "What are you leading up to?"

"Sabra is going to need some care when we get her back to the mainland. I thought...well, since you do care for her, that perhaps she could stay at your apartment for a couple of weeks. That artery in her neck was partly severed. We've sewn it back together, and all should go well, but she has to really take it easy. If she should fall, or make some kind of quick, jerking motion, she could rip it open again and—"

"I understand," he rasped. What would Sabra say to such a plan? he wondered. "What if she doesn't want me to play nursemaid?"

"Then she'll have to stay in the hospital for the next week, and have a full-time nurse for the week after that."

"I see. Well, let me ask her, okay? I don't take anything for granted anymore."

She nodded thoughtfully. "Just let me know. I'll have to call an ambulance once we land back in Washington. Listen, I've got to go check on Laura now. She's got me worried."

Laura was looking extremely thin and nervous, Craig agreed silently. "She looks like she's ready to break."

"I know," Ann whispered, frowning. "I hate to prescribe more tranquilizers for her, but I don't know how long she can go on this way. She's lost ten pounds so far, and she's eating next to nothing. She doesn't sleep, and when she does nap, she gets nightmares about the rape."

He placed a hand on her shoulder. "Take it from someone who knows about nightmares. Just let her talk. It helps a lot."

Gratefully, Ann reached out and touched his arm. "Thanks, Craig. I hope Sabra knows what she has."

Stymied by that last comment, Craig watched the physician hurry down the hall toward the elevators. With a sigh he turned and went back to Sabra's room. It was his turn to watch her. Not that he minded. He really didn't want to be anywhere else, anyway. He hoped Sabra felt similarly. A part of him waited in anxious frustration for when she'd be completely conscious so that they could talk. Would Sabra want to stay at his apartment and allow him to help her through her next two weeks of recovery? *He'd* never wanted anything more. But what did Sabra want?

Chapter Thirteen

"You look a hundred percent better this morning," Craig exclaimed, greeting Sabra with a smile. He'd just gotten up after sleeping deeply for six hours, and Killian had given up his post outside her hospital door in exchange for a hot cup of coffee.

Sabra gazed up at Craig as he approached her hospital bed. It was 8:00 a.m., and the nurse had awakened her to give her some medication. He had recently showered and shaved and was dressed in a bright purple-and-white Hawaiian print shirt, stuffed haphazardly into a pair of tan chinos. She hungrily absorbed the sight. "I like your new fashion," she teased weakly, her voice rough from disuse.

Craig stopped and looked down at his shirt. "Oh, this—yeah," he murmured, touching it with his hand, "I was in a hurry to get some clean clothes, so I bought the first thing this Hawaiian lady thought I'd look good in, at a shop just outside the hospital." He grinned, a little embarrassed. "Think purple's my color?"

"It looks good on you." She wanted to say he looked good in everything—and nothing.

When Craig saw the corners of her mouth lift slightly, his heart took a powerful leap in his chest. Halting at the edge of the bed, he placed his cup of coffee on the nightstand.

"That looks good, too," she noted hopefully.

"What? The coffee?"

"Yes."

He grinned a little, drowning in her clear, gray eyes, in the warmth spinning in their depths. This morning Sabra wasn't so pale. She was completely conscious, and inwardly, he heaved a huge sigh of relief. Resting his hands on the bar along the bed, he said, "So you're getting hungry?"

"Starved," Sabra admitted wryly.

"When did you wake up?"

"The nurse got me up to take some medication about half an hour ago."

Craig couldn't help himself. Reaching out, he gently stroked her hair, which needed to be combed. He watched as her lips parted softly at his touch. To hell with it. Leaning over, he captured her mouth with his own. Never had she felt so good to him, her lips pliant beneath his, giving as well as taking—a far cry from two days ago, when she'd lain cool and nearly lifeless. Gently, he moved his lips against hers, tasting her, giving back to her, breathing into her his urgent desire for her not only to live, but to gather strength from him. They were wet and warm beneath his, and he felt her weakly lift her hand to place it on his shoulder. Though he longed to deepen the exploration, Craig cautioned himself. A fire of aching need grew in his lower body. The urgency to wrap Sabra around him and love her slowly and thoroughly, nearly caused him to lose control.

As Craig eased his mouth from hers, he opened his eyes and stared down into her lustrous gray ones. The words *I love you,* were almost torn from him, but he bit them back for now. Giving her a slight smile, he rasped, "Welcome back, sweetheart. I was so scared I was going to lose you...."

Shaken, Sabra felt Craig wrap his hand around hers. "The nurse told me I almost died," she quavered, absorbing his nearness and warmth. The burning look in his eyes was unmistakable, and Sabra knew the feeling she had flowing through her was love. Real love. Swallowing against a dry throat, she added, "I don't remember much, Craig...."

With a grimace, he straightened up and continued to hold her cool hand in his. "Maybe it's just as well. I'm sure it will all come back to you soon enough."

"Jason?"

"He's fine. Laura's here, too. They visited you yesterday, but you were still coming in and out of consciousness."

"I remember voices." She smiled weakly. "I remember your voice and your touch, though."

"That's a good sign," Craig said, heartened. Gathering what was left of his courage, he said, "Today Dr. Parsons wants to fly all of us home, including you. She says you can travel. There's only one slight problem."

"What?" Sabra saw the darkening in his eyes and heard reservation in his voice.

"She says you need two weeks of rest and close watching. With that artery mending, you can't be doing the normal things you'd do at home by yourself."

Wrinkling her nose, Sabra muttered, "I won't stay in a hospital, Craig."

Giving her a hopeful look, he placed his hand on top of hers. "Would you settle for my place? For me helping you out when you need help?"

Stunned, Sabra stared up at him. She saw the hope in his eyes and saw him trying to steel himself for her rejection. The idea shocked her only from the standpoint that she'd never in her wildest dreams have expected such an offer. "Well," she stammered, "can—can you stand me under foot for two weeks?"

Heartened, Craig rasped, "Sweetheart, I want you around for a lot longer than two weeks. I don't want to push you into what I want, though. This is your call."

If only they weren't here, in a busy hospital. Sabra's smile was tremulous with emotion. "If you'll have me, I'll come home with you...."

On the way home in the jet, Sabra dozed. The gurney was in the rear of the plane, in a special area where it could be locked into the bulkhead, much like a seat. Dr. Parsons had come back to check the IV drip, had arranged her blankets to make sure she was comfortable, then had gone forward to be with Laura, Jason, Killian and Craig. Somewhere below was the Pacific Ocean, but Sabra couldn't see much from her makeshift bed. The vibration of the jet surrounded her, and this time it was a lulling sensation.

She watched through half-closed eyes as Jason huddled in Laura's arms. He seemed the least affected by the trauma they'd survived, but Sabra worried for the child, who seldom left his mother's side. More than once she'd heard Jason ask where his daddy was and seen Laura wrestle with an appropriate answer that gave some of the truth, but not enough to shake the boy up.

One of the two pilots came back, making his way through the narrow cabin. Sabra liked him. He was a hard-looking ex-Air Force fighter pilot by the name of Sloan MacKinley. The coffeepot was near her bed, and he nodded in her direction as he stopped and poured two cups of coffee.

"You want any, Sabra?"

She smiled a little. "No, thanks...."

He turned and studied her, both cups of coffee in hand. "You look a little lonely back here. Maybe I ought to get someone to keep you company?"

"That's okay...." Sabra was amazed that MacKinley, who had a rough-hewn face, possessed such sensitivity. But why should it surprise her that some men had this sort of intuitive knowing? Craig possessed it, though at the moment, he was exhausted and sleeping in his seat. She didn't blame him for not realizing how lonely she felt. Looking up into MacKinley's narrowed green eyes, she saw care radiating from them. He was a relatively new employee with Perseus, and she knew little about the man. But then, Sabra realized that those who joined Morgan's organization usually had a lot to hide, one way or another.

"We'll be landing in San Francisco in a couple of hours," MacKinley said, sipping his coffee. "Then we'll refuel and head for D.C. I imagine you'll be glad to get home."

"More than you'll ever know."

"Yeah, hospitals suck, as far as I'm concerned." He managed to lift one corner of his thin mouth. "Gotta get back up to the cockpit. Richmond doesn't do well without his IV of coffee every hour."

It hurt to laugh, but Sabra did anyway. MacKinley's wry sense of humor was typical of military pilots. He was a lean man, reminding her of a hungry wolf on the prowl. She saw a lot of Josh in him, with his teasing, and the same basic build. On the way up the aisle, balancing the cups of coffee, the pilot slowed his pace and look intently at Dr. Parsons. He hesitated, evidently thought better of stopping, then moved on by her. Sabra wondered if Ann was even aware of the pilot's interest in her. She was quietly working some needlepoint in her lap, apparently oblivious.

Sabra's attention was diverted when she saw Craig get up and walk back toward her. He'd slept soundly since the plane had taken off, and she was glad to see him. Instantly her heart started pounding slowly with joy. Did he know how happy he made her feel? Sabra ached for the time and place to share that with him. She saw the light in his eyes shadows no longer plaguing them. Holding out her hand she felt her fingers touch and clasp his. A sizzling heat tingled upward through her arm.

"Mac giving you a hard time back here?" he asked leaning against the side of the gurney, studying her in the gloom.

"Yes and no. He's like all the pilots I know."

"Mmm." Craig pressed a small kiss to the back of her hand. "You had an odd look on your face. Does he remind you of Josh?"

Sabra's lips parted. "Are you a mind reader?"

"I wish," he said. "Just something in your eyes, was a Maybe a look of loss."

With a sigh, Sabra nodded. "When I woke up in the hospital, I started to realize a lot of things, Craig."

He ran his fingers lightly across the back of her hand. "Like what, sweetheart?"

She held his worried gaze. Craig had had so much taken from him over the years, yet he was able to reach out and make her feel better. Every time he called her sweetheart, she wanted to cry. She tightened her grip on his hand, her voice low with feeling. "That a certain man in my life has taught me I can let the past go once and for all."

Craig stared down at her, shaken. He saw tears gathering in her eyes. She was so beautiful lying there her hair dark against the pristine white of the pillowcase. Despite her injury, Craig felt as though Sabra hadn't been wounded emotionally as he had been in the Iraqui crash, that her inner resiliency had somehow seen her through. He couldn't explain why; it was just something he sensed. And for her, he was glad of that. "Josh loved you," he said in a low voice, "but from what you've told me, he didn't have the courage to act on it."

"But I didn't know that," Sabra said wearily. "I realize now that I had fallen in love with him. I wanted to give myself to him, but that wasn't enough."

"Listen," Craig growled, "any man worth his salt would go to his grave knowing he had everything if you offered yourself to him." His mouth turned downward. "Josh was a guy who lived on the edge, Sabra. His way of life didn't include marriage."

She nodded, absorbing the intensity of his words. The burning anger in his eyes told her how much he was upset for her, for what she'd lost. In reality, she'd never had it to lose. "I guess I'm more of an idealist than I gave myself credit for," she murmured reflectively. "Josh crashed into my life and made me look at other possibilities."

"Such as what?"

"Such as marriage. Having children. I was so busy trying to be the son my father never had that I think I lost sight of a lot of other things that were important to me. They got pushed aside, Craig."

"Josh made you aware of your femininity."

"Yes."

He ran his fingers along her smooth, high cheekbone, her skin soft and warm beneath his touch. "After the crash in Desert Storm, I got real clear on a lot of things," he told her grimly. "I guess all the adventure of what I was doing for a living burned up in that crash. Living in a hospital for nearly a year afterward, going through the hell of one operation after another, I had a lot of time to think. It's funny in a way, Sabra, but before the crash, I had a certain detachment from everything. When you fly, it's easy to drop a load of bombs, or pull a trigger that will send a missile a couple of miles away to blow an aircraft out of the sky." He shrugged. "The enemy shows up as a colored blip on your radar screen, not as a human being who has a wife, children and parents. It's almost like a video game."

"That's pretty removed," Sabra admitted quietly, seeing the torture return to his eyes.

"Yeah, well, the crash took care of that." He managed a twisted smile and studied her. "What has this last mission taken away from you?" he asked solemnly.

The depth of his insight forever surprised her. Sabra realized again how Josh's joking about everything had badly skewed her reality about men in general. Craig was not only thoughtful, but perceptive. She licked her cracked lower lip and whispered, "I'm afraid now."

Tightening his hand around hers, he nodded. "I know what you mean. Life isn't some promise hanging out there in front of you anymore, is it?"

She shook her head, feeling the fear within her. "You were right, Craig."

"About what?"

"Remember you told me that because I'd never had a close call with death, I didn't know real fear?"

He nodded and held her troubled gaze. "Reality is a son of a bitch, isn't it?" He saw the same look in her eyes that he saw in his own every morning when he shaved in front of the bathroom mirror. It hurt Craig to realize that fact, and he wanted, somehow, to give Sabra back her previous belief that life would always be good, always be there. Sadly, he knew that once that veneer had been ripped away, it could never be put back in place.

"Isn't it?" Sabra agreed. She settled his hand against her stomach, her hands over his. "I was so intent on protecting Jason," she whispered unsteadily. "I don't even remember being afraid for myself as I was running away from that helicopter. I was only afraid that I wouldn't be able to protect him. This crazy thought was screaming in my head as I ran. I didn't want someone telling Laura her son had died because I couldn't do my job. The poor kid," she murmured. "I crushed him so tightly against me he's lucky he didn't have cracked ribs."

Craig moved a strand of hair away from her wrinkled brow. "You didn't think of yourself. That's normal, Sabra."

Blinking away the tears, she held his sad gaze. "You're the real hero in all of this, Craig. I know how much courage it took for you to get into that helicopter in the first place."

His mouth contorted. "Wasn't much choice, was there?"

"There are always choices," Sabra said brokenly, "and you took the bravest. That helicopter was our only escape. If you hadn't flown us out, Perseus would have an even bigger mess on their hands right now."

He shrugged and nervously rubbed the top of her hand with his fingers. "I didn't like the alternatives. I guess I traded one fear for another," he said, trying to joke about it. "I wasn't even aware I could have a greater fear than flying a helicopter, but when the chips were down, I didn't want anything to happen to you or Jason."

"I couldn't believe your skill with that aircraft," she said softly, holding his shy gaze. "I know enough about flying to realize that every aircraft is different, and if you don't have experience flying it, it's twice as hard."

"Don't give me more credit than I deserve, Sabra. Helicopters are basically the same. Maybe the control panel is set up a little different, maybe a toggle switch here or there is changed, but they all have a cyclic and a collective."

Sabra refused to be detoured by his deadpan explanation. "You deserve a medal for your heroism, Craig. I know you'll never get one. I know that no one, except maybe me, knows the true extent of your courage." Her voice grew soft with tears. "I never realized what real courage was until I met you, until you showed me. In my eyes, you're the most courageous human being I'll ever meet."

Craig felt heat move into his face, and he avoided her sparkling eyes, which told him she honestly felt he was a hero. The knowledge was at the same time euphoric and frightening. He hoped Sabra didn't put him on a pedestal, because sure as hell, he'd fall off it sooner or later and end up disappointing her. He didn't want that to happen, but he didn't know how to give voice to his concern.

"Well," he said gruffly, "I'll just be glad when we get stateside. I don't know about you, but home sounds pretty good right now." Good and safe and filled with promise.

"You give my place a new look," Craig said, making sure Sabra was comfortable on the sofa. They'd arrived over an hour ago, with Killian helping to bring over some of Sabra's clothes and toiletries from her condominium in Fairfax, Virginia, not too far away.

Sabra smiled tiredly. "I feel safe here," she murmured. The side of her neck was aching, but she didn't want to take a pain pill. They made her groggy, and her mouth always got dry. She had already taken a long, relaxing bath and was dressed in her white silk nightgown and white chenille robe. Craig stood, hands in his pockets, looking a little nervous. Well, so was she, she had to admit. It was early evening, the light of dusk filtering through the front drapes of his west facing apartment. Snow was falling lightly outside, covering the lawn and bare trees with white. It was a far cry from Hawaii.

Craig moved to the sofa. *Safe* wasn't a word he'd use in regards to Sabra. She wasn't safe from him, but he didn't think she realized that, and it was just as well. Her face was ashen again, and he attributed it to the long, draining flight. "What you need right now is a nap," he told her.

"I think I do." Sabra moved carefully, placing her stocking feet up on the couch and stretching out. The apartment was warm, and she closed her eyes. "Wake me in a hour or so?"

Craig crouched next to her and rested his hand on her shoulder. "You sleep all you want, sweetheart. You're still healing." He remained at her side until she fell into a deep sleep. Getting up on creaky knees, his body now feeling the full brunt of the crash, he went into the kitchen to fix himself a cup of coffee. Luckily for him, he had some frozen dinners. He was hungry, though his stomach was jumpy. Rubbing that region, he hunted through the freezer, found a turkey dinner and pulled it out.

Sabra's words never left his heart; he was a hero in her eyes. With a snort, he opened the package and tossed the cardboard container into the trash. Eleven men had died with him at the controls, leaving their wives widows and their children fatherless. They hadn't called him a hero. Resting the palms of his hands against the kitchen counter, he dropped his head and stood a moment, feeling the emotions twisting within him. How could Sabra see him as a hero? And was she seeing him through honest, realistic eyes, or some kind of warped idealism?

The apartment was quiet. Too quiet. He left the frozen dinner on the counter and went back to the living room to check on Sabra. She appeared to be sleeping soundly on the couch. He felt restless. He wanted to pace. He wanted to laugh and cry at the same time. Where the hell were all these crazy emotions coming from? He'd never felt like this before. Sabra touched him like an ethereal rainbow with her luminous eyes, her soft mouth and her low voice laced with such vibrant feelings.

Forcing himself to leave the living room, Craig told himself he was just overreacting to the past few days. Funny thing, though; the virulence of his nightmares had ebbed considerably. Was it because he'd climbed back into the cockpit? Or been through another crash and survived this time, with his passengers alive? Shaking his head, Craig moved the frozen dinner into the microwave and decided

that life was crazy at its worst and at its finest. All he needed
was Sabra. Did she need him as much?

Snow was falling thickly outside Craig's large picture
window. Sabra watched the flakes twirling lazily downward from the gray sky, which embraced the Virginia landscape. Absently, she heard Craig in the kitchen, putting
things away after lunch. She felt tension in her shoulders
and moved them slowly first one way, then the other. The
strain between her and Craig was evident. She called herself a coward because she wanted to speak of her love for
him, but was unsure how he'd receive such news. So she bit
back the words.

Hearing him enter the living room, Sabra slowly turned
toward him. How handsome he looked in a dark blue, long-
sleeved chamois shirt and well-worn jeans. She saw the
worry in his gaze and the tightness at the corners of his
mouth. He'd been so nervous since she'd come to his apartment. Why?

"Do you have a few minutes?" she asked, gesturing toward the overstuffed sofa next to her.

"Sure...." Craig wiped his damp hands on his jeans and
tried not to stare at Sabra. She looked beautiful and exqui-
sitely fragile in a pale pink angora sweater with a cowl collar. The dark pink skirt she wore brushed the tops of her
feet, which were covered incongruously with fluffy white
slippers. The pink emphasized how wan she still looked
though she was bouncing back surprisingly strongly from
her brush with death.

He eased himself down next to her. Craig had only allowed himself brief touches—an arm around her shoulder
from time to time, a grazing touch of his hand on hers—in
the three days she'd been at his house. What he really
wanted was to take her to his bed and hold her forever after
making hot, melting love with her as they had in Hawaii.
Had that all been a pipe dream? Something that had arisen
out of the strain of the mission? His throat constricted at the
thought. Easing his hand along the back of the couch behind her, he turned and devoted his full attention to her.

"I'm afraid," Sabra said with a slight laugh, "that I'm scared to death, Craig." She rubbed her hands slowly together in her lap. Stealing a glance at his dark, frowning features, she saw his eyes lighten with surprise. "Well... maybe I'm being dramatic. I don't know..."

"We're both experts on fear," Craig agreed slowly, allowing his hand to slide forward and caress her back. Her hair was shining and lustrous, curling around her shoulders and framing her face. "If you want the truth," he said, clearing his throat, "I've been wanting to sit down and talk to you like this, too."

Sabra saw amusement in his eyes. "You have?"

"Yeah." He touched her hair briefly and forced himself to meet her unsure gaze. "I've got all these crazy thoughts and feelings running around in me. I'm not sure if I should talk to you about them or not. Sometimes I think it's me. Sometimes—hell, I don't know. Being around you, I feel like I'm walking on air, sweetheart. But then I get scared. So scared, my stomach knots up. Stupid, huh?"

She shook her head slowly. "Your stomach—my heart."

"Oh?"

"Every time you look at me, Craig, my heart pounds. I..." Sabra raised her hands in exasperation. "It's never done that to me before. Ever."

"You don't give me knots in the stomach," he offered lamely. "It's fear doing it." He took a deep breath and held her clear, intelligent eyes. "Fear of losing something I don't have a right to have, I guess."

Sabra sat very still, gauging the pain in his voice along with the hope burning in the depths of his eyes. "What are you afraid of losing?"

He looked around the apartment. He was such a coward. Finally, he looked at her. "You," he said, his voice rough with emotion. There. It was out. Fear moved raggedly through him as he saw the look on Sabra's face. Her lips parted, and he groaned inwardly. How badly Craig wanted to kiss her. "I had this crazy notion," he muttered nervously, "about us. I never believed anyone could fall in love with someone with just one look. It's crazy. Dumb." He pulled away and rested his elbows on his thighs, clasping his hands between them. "I guess life is pretty crazy. I ought to know." He laughed sharply, talking more to himself than her. "I saw you, and I felt my world crumble around my feet, Sabra. I was angry at being pulled for the mission, angry that you were going to be the leader and just angry at the world in general, I guess. But it wasn't you I was angry at. It was me." He hung his head and released a sigh.

Raising his head, Craig looked over at her. "I kept fighting how I felt toward you. I didn't think I deserved someone as fine and good as you. I thought once I told you how much of a coward I'd been, how many lives I'd lost, you'd drop me." His mouth flattened. "You didn't, though."

"Why would I?" she asked softly.

"Because," he said harshly, "I'm not whole, Sabra. Part of me is run by that damn PTSD. I'm still afraid of flying. Every time I think that I climbed back in a helo, I break out in a sweat and get the same fear in my gut all over again." Craig shook his head. "Nothing's changed, not really." He rubbed his hand together, feeling the dampness between them. "I have these moments of hope. Can you believe it? Hope. Me, of all people, feeling that emotion after everything that's happened. You gave it back to me, you know."

Leaning forward, Sabra reached out and settled her fingers against his arm. She felt the tension in his muscles and saw it clearly in his stormy, ravaged-looking eyes. "Craig, I love you." Her voice trembled dangerously as she said the words. Fear shot through her. What would he say? Would he tell her she was crazy? Swallowing hard, Sabra tightened her fingers on his arm. "I woke up in that hospital realizing I'd loved you from the first moment I laid eyes on you." She managed a soft, embarrassed laugh. "Just like my parents, I suppose. Just one look." Taking a deep breath, she watched as he slowly straightened and turned toward her. His face mirrored shock. His lips had parted, as if to deny her halting words. Would he laugh at her? Think she was a world-class fool?.

"You—love me?"

She nodded and smiled a little. "How could I not?"

Craig sat very still, absorbing her words, her tear-filled eyes. Was he hearing things? He searched her face intently. "I'm no prize," he rasped. "I'm a loser—"

"No!" Sabra gripped his hand. "You've never been a loser, Craig. Yes, you've been hurt badly—more than most—but you're not a loser. If you think that, how do you explain climbing back in the same aircraft that nearly killed you before? Surely you knew the risks you took when we climbed on board with you. If you were such a loser, how did you manage to get that helicopter down in one piece, and us with it?" Her voice broke with feeling. "Do you think I love you because I only see your heart, your courage? I see what the war's done to you, Craig. I accept that, too. I accept all of you, scars and all." Her voice faltered. "I—I just hope you can accept me, the way I am. Josh once called me a piece of work, and I don't know to this day whether he meant it as a compliment or an insult. He—he was just that way. You never knew where you stood with him."

Whispering her name, Craig gently slid his arm around Sabra's shoulders and brought her to him. Releasing a ragged sigh as she surrendered to him, settled her head against him, he pressed a kiss into her hair. How brave she was to admit her love. He soared on an inner euphoria at knowing she loved him despite all his problems.

"I love you," he told her gruffly. "I've loved you from the beginning. I was just too thickheaded to realize it at first. I may be slow," he said, his mouth curving ruefully, "but what I feel for you is real. It's not a game, Sabra. I want you to know that." He saw the tears gleaming in her eyes as she lifted her face just enough to meet his gaze. "I'm no prize. But you are." He squeezed her shoulders, wondering how to make her realize just how precious she was to him. "Josh wouldn't have found a pearl in front of his nose, in my opinion. He was afraid of you, maybe because of your career in the Mossad. I don't know. It doesn't matter anymore."

"No," she whispered tremulously, "it doesn't." Reaching up, she slid her fingers along his cheek. "I'm so glad to know you love me, too."

He caught her hand and pressed a long, slow kiss to her palm. "Didn't you hear me tell you in the hospital? You woke up, looked at Laura and Jason and then over at me. They left shortly afterward, sweetheart, and as you were closing your eyes, I leaned over and told you I loved you." He shrugged. "I wasn't sure if you heard me."

"No... I didn't hear you say it." She smiled bravely and blinked back her tears. "It all happened so fast, Craig. I wasn't expecting to fall in love. I returned to Perseus so shaken up over Terry's heart attack. I was a mess emotionally."

"We both were," he said, feeling the fear in his gut dissolving for good.

"We have the time," Sabra whispered. "I never thought we would. We could have died in that mission. It was one of the worst I've ever experienced."

He rubbed her shoulder gently, soothing her. "It was rough," he agreed, resting his brow against her hair. Sighing, he felt Sabra's arm stretch across his chest. "This is all I want," he said huskily against her ear. "I want you. I want to build on what we have, Sabra. We got lucky. We survived. I thought we were going to die, too. I don't know how many times I almost turned to you during that mission and told you I loved you. But I was afraid if I did, you'd laugh or turn me down."

"I'm afraid—" she laughed softly "—we're very much alike. Do you know how many times I wanted to admit my love to you? I was afraid, too."

"Fear has a hell of a hold on us, doesn't it?"

Sabra closed her eyes. "We had the courage to walk with our fear, Craig. We didn't let it stop us from telling each other in the end. That," she said, rubbing her palm against his well-sprung chest, "is what counts."

Joy flowed through Craig. "I never thought," he rasped hoarsely, "that I'd ever find someone who'd love me. I really didn't. After that crash, I just gave up living. I had n hope left. I had nightmares for my companions—until you walked into my life.'' He kissed her brow. ''I want to spend the rest of my life telling you how many ways you've helped me, how much hope I have because of you.''

Sabra snuggled closer, a contentment like none she'd ever experienced stealing through her. Craig's arms were strong and supportive around her. As much as she wanted to love him, it was impossible right now because of her neck injury. In another week, she promised him silently, she would love him until he realized how very special a man he was—despite the horror of his past.

''I've watched my parents in their marriage,'' she told him in a hushed voice, absorbing the strength of his chest beneath her hand. ''I'm sure we'll fight—''

''Constructive discussions,'' he amended. ''My parents have a long marriage like yours do, and the one thing I never forgot was that they never fought personally—they stuck to the topic that needed discussing.''

She smiled up at him. ''Don't you think we have a chance, considering all we've weathered so far? We didn't exactly meet under good circumstances.''

Tunneling his fingers through her hair, feeling the silky thickness of it, Craig said, ''We have the time, Sabra. And we won't waste a moment of it.''

She closed her eyes, feeling his fingers gently massaging her scalp. Her skin prickled pleasantly. Did Craig realize how unique he was among men? He was a toucher, a holder, and that's what she needed most—someone who valued such things as she did.

''I worry about my nightmares,'' Craig admitted after a few moments of silence. He eased his hand from her hair and touched her flushed cheek. ''I haven't slept with a woman since the crash for fear of hurting her.''

''You've slept with me four nights in a row under some pretty dangerous circumstances,'' she told him, holding his uncertain gaze, ''and never once did you have a nightmare.''

''I think that was a fluke,'' he admitted, frowning. ''The last thing I want is to hurt you, Sabra. The last thing...'' He couldn't stand the idea of lashing out and striking her lovely face, possibly breaking her nose or jaw. The thought sent a wave of nausea through him.

Closing her eyes, she sighed and rested against his strong body. "Let's take our lives one day at a time, darling...."

He nodded and said nothing. Just holding Sabra made some of his fear go away. Right now, he knew that Perseus was working hard to locate Morgan. He might be dead. The thought made him wince internally. What he should be doing was helping Jake, Wolf and Killian. They needed all the help they could muster to keep the company going while widening the search for Morgan.

Having Sabra in his arms, he thought about Laura and the awful pain she was carrying twenty-four hours a day. She had no one to hold her. Especially at night, in bed, when the darkness brought out the fears. In another week, he would go back and help Perseus in any way he could. Would Sabra go back to her apartment then? Or would she stay with him? A part of him wanted to hurry the process and keep her with him. That was the part that feared losing her, he admitted to himself. Loving a woman meant allowing her her freedom, too.

His mind ranged back over the past, to his parents. Although his father had been a rancher most of his life, then bought the trading post on the reservation after fracturing his back, he'd never made a servant out of his wife. If anything, his parents had been a hardworking team who pulled together. Craig wanted that same thing for him and Sabra. She was free to choose whether she continued to work for Perseus, just as he was.

Craig had so many questions for her, but he squelched them as he felt her falling asleep in his arms. She was still exhausted from the mission and the surgery. He smiled faintly as he eased his hand slowly up and down her limp arm sprawled across his chest. Right now all he wanted to do was love her, give in to the sweet, haunting, unfilled need that flowed through him. But that had to wait. Love w more than sex, much more. Making love with Sabra was another way to show her how he felt about her, and he ached to bring them together even more since they'd admitted their love for each other.

Chapter Fourteen

"I've got good news and bad news," Craig told Sabra as he entered the apartment. The cold wind rushed in the open door and a number of snowflakes swirled in with him. Shutting it, he turned around. Sabra was on the couch, reading the newspaper. It was only 1:00 p.m., and he saw the surprise on her features. Pulling off his dark blue knit muffler, he dropped it on the desk next to the door.

"What do you mean?" She set the paper aside and rose. Her heart tripled in beat as she realized Craig was not only home early, but unannounced. A week ago, at her urging, he'd begun going to work with Killian at the Pentagon to try to help track down Morgan's whereabouts. Usually, he got home late in the evening after spending a good twelve hours on duty. She had persuaded him she was well enough to make her own meals. Besides, he wasn't happy cooped up in a small apartment with little to do.

Shrugging out of his coat, Craig hung it on the peg above the desk. He made sure the dead bolt was slid into place on the door, then turned to meet Sabra. She wore a cream colored sweater that emphasized her olive complexion and dark, ebony hair. He could still see little telltale signs of her recent trauma, but only a small dressing covered the spot where her stitches had recently been taken out by Dr. Parsons. Yes, she looked healthy again.

Opening his arms, Craig groaned as Sabra walked into them and pressed herself against him. It was something he looked forward to each night, hungrily absorbing wherever her body touched his, molding against him. This time she reached up and placed an eager hungry kiss on his mouth. Stunned by her unexpected response, he monitored his returning pressure.

"Craig, I'm well now," she whispered fiercely against his lips.

He pulled away just enough to look down into her dark gray eyes, which smouldered with desire. How many times had he seen that look in her eyes? Every night. It had been hell sleeping apart—him on the couch, she in his bed. Craig didn't want to risk hurting her in the night, and he'd coaxed her into agreeing to sleep separately until Dr. Parsons said she was her old self again. That had happened yesterday afternoon. Hotly aware of her breasts and hips pressing against him, provocatively this time, he gripped her shoulders and gently eased her away from him.

"It's a good thing," he said gruffly. "Listen, we've got to get out of here."

Sabra's mouth fell open. "What?"

"We picked up a dispatch between Garcia and Ramirez less than an hour ago," he explained swiftly. "That's why I'm home early. The good news is we've located Morgan we think—in Peru, at Ramirez's jungle estate." His hands tightened briefly on her shoulders. "The bad news is Ramirez has ordered hits on every Perseus employee they can find."

Gasping, Sabra pulled out of his grip. "You're joking."

"I wish I were," he said tiredly. Gazing around the apartment, he said, "I want you to pack a bag with just necessities. We're going undercover until this thing blows over."

"What about Laura and her children?"

"Jake already has them in hiding. Killian is making sure Susannah is with them. Shah, Jake's new wife, will be with her, too. Right now, Laura isn't too stable. She knows we've found Morgan."

"And he's alive?"

Craig shrugged and walked back to the bedroom with her, his hand pressed against the small of her back. "We're not sure. From what Killian said, and Wolf double-checked it, Ramirez is the kind of bastard to keep Morgan alive as long as possible. We're sure he's been tortured extensively, but to what end, we don't know. Wolf was in his prison for almost a month, and Ramirez tortured him daily. If he lost consciousness, the bastard had a doctor there to bring him back with drugs so he could torture him some more. He's a real pro at that kind of sick stuff."

Hurriedly, Sabra took her small suitcase from the closet and placed it on the bed. She shivered just thinking about Wolf—and Morgan—being injured by Ramirez. "Are any of the teams back from a mission yet?"

Craig threw a canvas bag on the bed, went to the dresser and pulled open a drawer. Right now, haste was essential. "We have one possibility," he said, throwing underwear into the bag. "Culver Lachlan, who always works solo, just came in from an undercover assignment in Ireland."

"You can't send him into that rat's nest alone," Sabra protested, quickly putting some lingerie and sweaters into the suitcase. She glanced up at Craig's set features. He was tense and worried. So was she. Ramirez always made good on his orders, though this would be the first time he'd made such an open attack against an American company.

"Jake's working on another angle. There's a Peruvian agent by the name of Pilar Martinez who he's trying to contact. A long time ago, Pilar and Culver worked together on a Peruvian undercover assignment, but something happened, and they split up. At the time, Culver was a CIA agent and she was an undercover government agent in Lima. They worked on a huge cocaine bust for three months. But that was eight years ago. Jake knows Pilar pretty well. She was partly responsible for getting Wolf and Killian away from Ramirez. She's worked on a lot of cocaine busts over the years, and she knows the jungles like the back of her hand. Her family is Indian, and they live near where Ramirez hides out. She's the perfect choice for the assignment—if he can find her in time, and if she'll work with Culver again." He frowned. "There are a lot of ifs to this."

"Frankly," Sabra murmured, shutting the suitcase, "I don't think two people on their own could rescue Morgan. Ramirez has five or six estates throughout South America, I know. The one in Peru is deep in the jungle and mountains. Jake can't be thinking of sending them in alone."

"No," Craig said, zipping the canvas bag closed and hoisting it over his left shoulder. "I think he's trying to get the Peruvian government to work with us. But that's iffy, too. Come on, let's get out of here."

Hurriedly, Sabra picked up her suitcase, but Craig caught her hand and shook his head.

"I'm well. Remember?" she protested.

"I don't care. You're only one day well, sweetheart. I'll carry the bag."

"Craig, stop treating me like I'm some fragile, breakable doll."

He grinned tightly and followed her out of the bedroom. "Am I?"

"Yes!" Sabra retorted with pretend exasperation, throwing a look over her shoulder at him. "And it's driving me crazy!"

"I'm crazy for you." Now was not the time to discuss much of anything, except leaving the residence. "Get my jacket? Let's go down the basement stairs. I've got the car parked inside the garage, and the door is shut and locked." He didn't want to take any chances. He'd nearly lost Sabra two weeks ago, and he was damned if she was going to be placed in jeopardy again so soon.

Sabra gave a helpless laugh, shook her head and shared an amused look with him. She opened the door that led down the stairs to the garage below. "You're hopeless, Talbot."

"Hopelessly in love with you, Ms. Jacobs."

She colored prettily beneath his warming gaze as he approached. "Where are we going?"

"The DV at Andrews Air Force Base."

"DV?"

"Yeah, it stands for distinguished visitor's housing." He halted and smiled. "The best accommodations on the base for us. Usually only generals and congressional people stay there. It will have everything—a stocked bar, video, television, all kinds of choice food. You'll want for nothing."

"Nothing," Sabra muttered, following him down the steps. All she wanted was him.

"It's a good place to hide. The Air Police are aware of the threat and have been alerted at the gates to Andrews." Craig put the suitcases in the trunk and shut the lid. "Get in," he told her. How fast could Ramirez put hit men onto them? The orders were exactly one hour old. Craig worried because he lived the farthest away from Perseus. Time was precious.

Backing out into the icy street, made more slippery from the foot of snow a recent storm had dumped on the Eastern Seaboard, Craig narrowed his attention to driving without sliding on the unsalted pavement and watching for any cars that might be tailing them. The early afternoon sky was leaden, and not many vehicles had ventured out on the slick streets lined with bare-branched maple and walnut trees.

Sabra swiveled her attention between Craig and their surroundings. She, too, watched for cars that might be carrying a hit man or group of thugs. The snow made everything look white and clean. Trying to relax, she realized that for nearly two weeks she'd been in a safe cocoon in Craig's home. Now their lives were threatened again.

"I don't know how Laura can take all this danger and intrigue," she murmured, watching the traffic. "I think I'd have had a nervous breakdown by now."

"She's a lot stronger than she looks," Craig said, guiding the car onto the interstate that would take them to Andrews Air Force Base. He breathed a little easier, because this roadway had recently been plowed and salted. "Besides, she's got Shah and Susannah looking after the kids, which takes some pressure off her."

"I'd like to help her...."

Craig shot her a quick glance. "You're supposed to focus on getting well."

"I *am* well."

Craig grimaced. "Let's discuss this when we get to Andrews."

"You've got a deal."

It was nearly midnight when Sabra took a bath, then pulled on a pale green, silk nightgown that brushed her ankles. The DV house was everything Craig had promised and more. Tension had been strong since they'd arrived, however. Sabra didn't put as much faith in the Air Police as Craig apparently did. Three different times, Wolf had called them. First to report that they had intercepted a cryptic message at CIA headquarters and found out Morgan was indeed alive. Sabra had burst into tears over that news. She loved Morgan more like a brother than a boss, and she cried for Laura, too, who had to be feeling at least some relief.

Wolf's second call was sinister. The Customs Department had already intercepted three known Columbian hit men at Miami International Airport. The men had been carrying photos of Perseus employees—among them, Sabra's.

The third call had come less than half an hour ago. It had been Killian, phoning to tell them he would need their help to coordinate the huge plan to rescue Morgan. Sabra had been overjoyed at the idea of getting back into the type of work she was best at. Craig hadn't looked too happy, because he was to go to the Pentagon with Wolf, while she would be working with CIA officials monitoring satcoms from South America, trying to pick up more information on Morgan.

Opening the door, she moved soundlessly down the hall toward the other bedrooms. The house, impressive looking inside and out, was single story with a basement. The furniture throughout was Queen Anne, and Sabra loved the warm cherry wood that adorned the place. It was only a house, though, she admitted—without Craig's presence, it would have seemed hollow and empty.

She heard a noise on her left and hesitated at the half-open door that led to the master bedroom. Pushing it wider, she saw that Craig had showered in the adjoining bathroom. He wore nothing but blue-and-white-striped pajama bottoms, which hung dangerously low around his narrow hips. A soft smile touched her mouth as she watched him unpack his clothes and put them into the drawers. His hair was dark and shining—still wet. The play of muscles on his back was beautiful, and Sabra leaned against the door, appreciating him in silence.

As if sensing her presence, Craig turned.

"What do you think you're doing?" she asked, walking toward him. Sabra had deliberately left her robe behind. The V-cut gown barely hid the swell of her breasts, and she wanted him to take notice of her. Judging from the narrowing of his eyes as he straightened and faced her, her plan was working.

"I was unpacking," Craig said, distracted. The silk gown shimmered in the room's low lighting, and Sabra moved like a graceful ballerina, each sway of her body flowing into the next movement. Her thick hair had been brushed until it shone, draping around her proud shoulders. The look in her eyes was unmistakable—a smoldering glow for him alone. Groaning inwardly, Craig tried to put a check on his desire. It was impossible.

"Why are you unpacking your stuff in here?" she asked, reaching out, sliding her arms around his shoulders.

"This is the bedroom I chose," he said. Sabra's touch was electrifying. He slipped his arms around her waist and drew her against him, seeing her lips part provocatively. She tilted her chin upward just enough so that he could kiss her if he wanted to. He wanted that and more.

"I thought," Sabra murmured, leaning forward and moving her lips against the line of his mouth, "we agreed to sleep together from tonight on?"

It was hell trying to think coherently beneath her gentle assault. He felt the soft, sliding movement of the silk between them, the warmth of her loving body pressing against him, of her lips teasing his. Gripping her shoulders, he eased her away.

"I think we said we'd discuss it," he rasped. An ache filled him and a hot, burning sensation flowed through his lower body. He inhaled her fragrance, wondering if she'd used gardenia soap on her peach-soft flesh.

The corners of her mouth lifted slightly. "Craig, there's no discussion on this. We're sleeping together. That's what I want. It's what you want."

Worriedly, he rasped, "I'm afraid for you—"

"I'm not," Sabra whispered, nibbling at his lower lip, feeling him harden against her belly. She tightened her arms around his neck, closed her eyes and moved her lips across his.

Groaning, Craig gripped her to him. The roundness of her breasts pressed against his chest; the slickness of her lips molded to his and, with the heat of her supple body, conspired against him.

"Love me..." Sabra whispered against his questing mouth. "Love me, please...." She felt him tense for a split second, then, to her delight and surprise, he lifted her off her feet and into his arms. His stormy blue eyes were hungry—for her. She sighed and rested her head against his. "Take me to *our* room."

Hesitantly, Craig glanced around the master bedroom and then down at her sultry, half-closed eyes. "So much for our discussion," he rasped thickly, a hint of a smile on his mouth.

"I love you," Sabra said, running her fingers through his recently washed hair. *"I need you...."*

The words fell across him like fire. He walked down the hall to their bedroom, a smaller room with a queen-size bed in it. As he entered, Craig saw that Sabra had lit some candles on the dresser, their light reflecting in the mirror behind them. With his foot, he gently shut the door.

"You're a woman with a purpose," he teased as he laid her on the pink silk coverlet of the bed, where the soft light glimmered on her features.

"And you don't mind?"

Craig stretched out next to her, reveling in the feminine strength of her body. "No...not really. I guess I'm not used to it, that's all." He smiled a little. "But I'll get used to it."

She sighed and reached up, framing his face between her hands. "With you," she murmured, "I had to use my sharpest tactics and strategy skills to get you to realize I'm well."

Running his hand up her long thigh, the silk warm and sleek beneath his fingertips, he shrugged. "I guess my mind knows it...."

"Your heart doesn't."

"No." He leaned over, sliding his arm beneath her neck and gently cradling her against him. "I feel like a man who got his only wish in the world. Now that I have it, I'm afraid of losing it."

"I understand," Sabra whispered, stretching up and claiming his set mouth. "Let's make tonight a new start for both of us, darling." She felt Craig's hands tightening around her, felt his hand move upward to cup her breast beneath the silk. Heat purled through her, and her voice dropped to a husky whisper. "We love each other. That's all that matters. I don't want to spend one more night without your arms around me, Craig. Please...."

Her plea tore at him as nothing else could. In that moment, with Sabra in his arms, her lips resting teasingly against his mouth, he realized the depth of her commitment to him. "It won't be easy," he warned gruffly, easing her onto her back.

"What won't be easy?" She trailed her hand downward across his flat, hard belly, tracing the line of his pajama bottoms across his hips. She saw his eyes go thundercloud dark, felt his hand stop caressing the side of her breast.

Craig couldn't think any longer, nor could he talk. Sabra's body was like a branding iron, moving ceaselessly against him like the rhythm of an ocean tide. Her fingers eased the fabric away from his hips, and he stiffened as she slid her fingers downward to caress him. Gripping her shoulder, he groaned. Whatever worry, whatever concerns about her injury he'd had, melted beneath her exquisite exploration. All he could do was tense beside her, lost in a storm of electric sensation, drowning in the desire to make her his.

Candlelight suffused the room, flowing across her shoulders and face, revealing her inner and outer beauty. He eased his hand beneath the silk nightgown, drawing it upward, pulling it off her so that she lay naked before him. How vulnerable she looked—with such trust in her eyes as she met and fearlessly held his gaze. Her flesh was hot and demanding. Her lips parted, silently begging him to continue his exploration. At the same time, he felt the cloth he wore being pulled away, and he pushed the pajamas aside. Gazing at her intensely, as if she were his quarry, Craig entangled her legs with his own. Sliding his hand beneath her hip, he eased her on top of him. He saw surprise and then pleasure in her shadowed eyes, which now burned with longing. Trembling with need, he tried to hold himself in check as he positioned her above him. This way, he wouldn't accidentally put too much pressure on her recently healed neck wound. This way he could watch her every fleeting expression, like a greedy man too long without sustenance, too long without love.

As she settled over him, he groaned. The moistness met his hardness, and he gripped her hips, pulling her down upon him even more. He heard a soft gasp escape her, felt her hands grip his arms in instant reaction. Her thighs tightened against him, and he smiled to himself, savoring the melting fire of making her one with him. There was such power in claiming her, in easing into her depths and feeling her heat as she moved with abandoned pleasure.

Like the ceaseless ocean tide, he felt her rocking against him, in perfect rhythm. Whatever worry he'd had was burned away in the molten flames of their joining. The slickness of her body met and matched his and he thrust more deeply into her, hearing her soft cry of joy. Moments glided into one another, like hot wax pooling at the base of a candle flame. Closing his eyes, his teeth clenched with the effort of holding back, Craig brought Sabra into a fast, frantic union with him. Each sliding movement, each explosion heat from the friction between them heightened the pleasure.

He felt her fingers tense and release rapidly against his arms, and he gripped her hips more firmly, thrusting hard and deep into her. The intense explosion within her translated to him, and he felt her stiffen and throw back her head, her hair flying out across her shoulders and back. In those fiery moments, with Sabra a part of him, Craig had never felt stronger as a man, or more in control of his destiny. He moved again, prolonging the pleasure of her climax, and watched as a rosy flush swept up her glistening body. Only then did he release the hold on his own desires. Only then did he give her the gift of himself.

Sabra moaned softly as she collapsed against Craig, her head next to his on the pillow. His breath intermingled with her own, and she closed her eyes and slid her arm across his damp chest. "I love you so much," she said tremulously.

Craig slipped his hand across her back, slick and warm from their lovemaking. "Sweetheart, I'm the luckiest bastard on this planet." He kissed her cheek and saw her lashes flutter open. His smile was male. "I've got you. That's all I'll ever need . . . ever want." He slid his fingers across her flushed cheek and held her drowsy gaze. "Come on," he rasped, "let's go to sleep. I want to hold you in my arms all night and wake up tomorrow morning to find you beside me."

Sabra smiled weakly as he readjusted her at his side. The sensation of fire still burned brightly within her, and she felt deliciously consumed by it. How wonderful a lover Craig was. Did he know that? Had any woman ever shared that knowledge with him? As she eased beneath the covers, then snuggled against him, she promised to tell him that tomorrow morning, over breakfast.

The candles would burn out on their own, and Craig was content to have the low light dancing in soft, muted shadows on their bedroom walls. Sabra was damp against him, and he pulled the covers up to her shoulders, his arm around her to keep her close. As he shut his eyes and settled down with her at his side, his mind refused to work any longer. Exhaustion pulled at him. Before he plunged into a deep, healing sleep with the woman he loved at his side, Craig realized that no matter what lay ahead of them, they could triumph together. Sabra gave him hope—for himself, for a future he once had thought would never be his. Her love for him was as strong and unerring as she was. Silently, Craig promised her that no matter how dark it got for him in the future, no matter how he had to wrestle with his past to heal, he would do so—not only for himself, but for her. She'd had the courage to reach out and tell him of her love. He could do no less for her.

As he felt her soft breath against his chest, Craig sighed, feeling the last of the tension flowing out of him. Somehow, he knew that tonight there would be no nightmares. They were as safe as possible under the circumstances.

In the weeks ahead, Craig knew, there would be continued danger and tension, until they were able to rescue Morgan. If it could be done, and if he could be brought home safely, then Ramirez would probably cease his hunt for them. For now, their future was clouded with danger, and each day was going to be a miracle. No matter what happened, Craig knew life was worth living again as long as they had each other. He would love Sabra forever.

* * * * *